ANN BEATTIE'S

LOVE ALWAYS

"Flatly a brilliant concoction. . . . Like Jane Austen, Beattie rides the surface of her characters' lives with an amazing agility. . . . She's funnier now than ever."

—BEVERLY LOWRY
THE DALLAS MORNING NEWS

"Through Beattie's agency we are brought within sufficient sympathetic distance that our empathy is engaged. And that is how most good writing begins to achieve the level of literature."

—RICHARD FORD
ESQUIRE

"This shrewd and entertaining novel is finally about getting a handle on adulthood. Beattie's sense of timing doesn't fail her—she makes you care for her characters at just the right moment, and care a lot."

—GLAMOUR

"Ann Beattie has filed yet another anthropologist's report on a certain part of America, warts and all. Every bit of it is good entertainment—especially the warts."

—ANN TYLER
THE DETROIT NEWS

"She stunningly captures the horror and beauty of life."

—THE CLEVELAND PLAIN DEALER

"Her considerable intelligence, sharp eye, and arch humor rips into media madness and the so-called glamour professions."

—VANITY FAIR

Also by Ann Beattie

Distortions
Chilly Scenes of Winter
Secrets and Surprises
Falling in Place
The Burning House

Love Always

A Novel by

Ann Beattie

Vintage Contemporaries

Vintage Books
A Division of Random House
New York

Published in the United States by Random House, Inc., New York, and
simultaneously in Canada by Random House of Canada Limited, Toronto.
Originally published by Random House, Inc., New York, in 1985.

Grateful acknowledgment is made to Macmillan Publishing Company, Inc., and A. P. Watt Ltd., for permission to reprint an excerpt from "The Second Coming" by William Butler Yeats. From *The Poems of W. B. Yeats*, edited by Richard J. Finneran: Copyright 1924 by Macmillan Publishing Company, Inc., renewed 1952 by Bertha Georgie Yeats; and from *The Collected Poems of W. B. Yeats*, Macmillan London Ltd. Reprinted with permission of Macmillan Publishing Company, Inc., and A. P. Watt Ltd. as agent for Michael B. Yeats and Macmillan London Ltd.

Library of Congress Cataloging-in-Publication Data

Beattie, Ann.
Love always.

Reprint. Originally published: New York: Random House, 1985.
(Vintage contemporaries)
I. Title.
PS3552.E177L.6 1986 813′.54 85-40866
ISBN 9780394744186 (pbk.)

Manufactured in the United States of America

146502721

For John Baer Train

Love Always

1

THE music was appropriate, although Hildon thought this particular version of the song was a downer: Barbra Streisand, singing "Happy Days." His wife, Maureen, was listening to it to rev herself up for the party. The magazine Hildon had started two summers ago, *Country Daze*, had become the hit of *tout* New York, and today was the day of the annual party. Maureen was the hostess, and as she moved around the backyard, placing conch shells on the tables, she smiled to herself. It was a perfect Vermont day—the last day of June—and she was about to stage another perfect party.

The only thing that galled her was that she had to invite Lucy Spenser. Not only was she sure that Lucy and Hildon were lovers, but she knew that Hildon had only married her when he despaired of Lucy's ever leaving Les Whitehall. Hildon, of course, denied the affair. "She's my oldest friend," he had said to her. "Why don't you try to understand the notion of friendship?"

Maureen liked to give parties with motifs, and although Hildon's staff did not deserve such pleasure, she decided on clever parties so that she, at least, would be amused. This time Maureen wore a sarong tied tightly above her hipbone. She served shrimp and lobster. Instead of a tablecloth, she draped an old tennis net over the long metal table. The paper napkins were patterned with little goldfish, swimming with happy smiles. She set out blue plastic bottles of sea salt and put on a record of the sounds of the ocean. The wine was Entre-Deux-Mers. Before everyone showed up, Maureen stretched out on the grass to survey the backyard. She smiled with contentment: Maureen the mermaid. Her hair was in a braid, clipped with a barrette in the shape of a blue starfish.

Matt Smith, the new publisher—the magazine had just been sold, and at a handsome profit—was the first to show up. He was a few minutes early. Hildon was still inside, showering. She poured Matt a glass of wine and paid a lot of attention to him. He was the new boss. As she poured, Maureen beamed her best summer smile.

"Take a sip. Do you like it?" she said.

"I tell you, Maureen, to me, wine is crushed grapes. What I like best is that you don't have to spit out the seeds."

She laughed, pretending that he meant this as an amusing remark.

"What's so funny?" he said.

"Come on, Matt," she said, running her finger around the edge of the wineglass. "You aren't discriminating?"

"I discriminate enough to know who means most to me. *I* mean most to me. I always did say that a man has to know how to play his cards in this world, and sometimes he'd better realize that the best game is solitaire."

Nigel, the photographer, had arrived, and Hildon was talking to him in front of the kitchen door. Hildon accentuated his handsomeness by appearing to be very casual. The shorts he wore were permanently yellowed from swimming in the crater lake. The cotton shirt was custom-made and cost $75. As Maureen watched, Lucy pulled into the driveway and hopped out of the car. She had on turquoise shorts, white running shoes, and a white halter top. It was perfect. Everything Lucy wore and did was perfect. Even Lucy's lover's departure had been perfect: dramatic, unexpected, the quintessential abandonment. The column Lucy wrote was also perfect; it was exactly the right endeavor for the society girl who wanted to stay sour. Hildon and Lucy greeted each other by touching their hands to the other's biceps. Lucy had a way of looking around, taking it all in very quickly, as if hidden cameras were photographing her, every firefly a potential flashbulb. She saw Maureen and lit up with a flawlessly false smile. If Maureen had been Lucy's orthodontist, she would have been proud.

Lucy scampered across the grass, doing one of the many things that drove Maureen crazy. Two, actually, as soon as she spoke. Running like a faerie, on tiptoes, was bad enough, thirty years out of ballet class, but her polite dismissal of Maureen was even harder to take.

"Are you giving another one of your perfect parties?" Lucy called. Everyone but Lucy had the good sense not to ask rhetorical questions unless they were directed to dogs or babies.

"Of course I am," Maureen said.

Lucy shimmered. She acted a little like that woman, whatever her name was, whom the Great Gatsby had been in love with.

"Look at how beautiful everything is," Lucy said.

Maureen swept her eyes over the party. She had fallen into Lucy's trap—she had let Lucy point out to her what was beautiful, even though she had spent the day creating it.

A boy from the high school had come to videotape the party. Maureen had had her doubts about that, but Hildon had made her feel downright paranoid. "No one will even notice," he had said. "They'll just continue to party. The kid needs to practice taping a crowd. It's not going to interfere with anything." How did Hildon meet all these people who wanted something from him? She found it hard to believe that he spent as much time working as he said he did; he must have encouraged these people—suggested that he had a lot to give, that he was very loose. No one would think that Hildon, so casual he seemed not to have the power necessary to grasp his gin and tonic, had that very morning called the shirtmaker in New Haven to rant and rave about the imperfection of the collars.

Lucy moved off, to faerie skip to Nigel. He held his arms open to receive her. Nigel had the ability to turn any conversation into an interrogation. Like an analyst, Nigel, when asked what he thought about something, would either ask why you asked the question or what you yourself thought. It was possible that Nigel never thought anything. He was talking to some woman Maureen had not met. The woman seemed a little drunk. She was trying to remember the punch line of a joke about a nun who stole a jet plane and the penguin who waved her in for a landing. When she couldn't remember how the joke ended, Nigel put his arm around Lucy and began to tell a joke about an Indian chief. He did a very extravagant imitation of the chief, puffing up his chest and changing his voice to an impossibly low register whenever he spoke in the chief's voice. "Oh, I've got it, I've got it," the woman said, clasping her hands. Nigel and Lucy smiled at her. "It's that . . . it isn't the nun who's in the jet plane, but the penguin, and . . ." Nigel exhaled. He waited a few beats, politely, then puffed up and continued his own joke, as if the woman had not spoken.

"You know," Noonan said, clapping his hand around Maureen's shoulder and taking her by surprise, so that she jumped, "the last party I came to, when you didn't offer me the leftovers the way you usually do, I stole half a wheel of cheddar that was on one of the tables. I put it under my jacket and took it home. Did you know that?"

"I had no idea," Maureen said.

"I grated it and made soup," he said. "You know—that excited me, taking that big piece of cheese. I could have bought it in a store and it wouldn't have meant anything to me, but all the time I was grating it, I felt so excited I couldn't stop grinning. If anybody'd seen me, they'd have thought I was a crazy person. And you know what? When I was a schoolboy, I used to steal things from the drugstore near my house, and it gave me the same lift."

Nigel was trying to write down the woman's telephone number, but she couldn't remember the last two digits. She put her shoulder bag on the ground and began to rummage through it. "I know I have it in here," she said. "Just give me a minute, and I'm sure I can find it." She dumped the contents onto the grass. Maureen saw three brushes and several wallets. There was also either a jump rope or a piece of clothesline. Nigel bent and began to examine the contents of the bag, fascinated: a flashlight, a notebook, a large-beaked blue plastic duck.

The record of the sounds of the sea had ended, and Maureen went onto the porch and turned it over. She lowered the needle back onto the edge of the record. She sat in one of the wicker rockers and stretched her legs: they were long and golden, recently waxed. The Korean woman who waxed her legs, patting on the warm wax with a little wooden paddle, spoke no English, except to say, in unison with Maureen, "ouch." Noonan joined her on the back porch. "I also look through people's medicine cabinets," he said, "although I guess that's common. I like to know about people's secret pains."

The student with the videotape machine walked onto the back porch, camera grinding away. Maureen and Noonan both looked as if they had been caught at something. It infuriated Maureen: this was what Hildon thought was no intrusion? She put her hand up in front of her face. Carrying the camera on his shoulder, without comment, the boy crouched slightly and moved into the house. He was like a soldier in slow motion, creeping through enemy territory.

"Tomorrow I'm going to give Hildon the big news, but I'll give it to you first," Noonan said. "I got another job. I'm going to be working for a paper in San Francisco. It excites me," he said. "It excites me to talk about a lot of things, but I've always exercised restraint. I'm a very uptight person. I'm not going to be that way once I get to San Francisco. I want to be truthful from here on out. I told you about the cheese. I'll tell you what's in your medicine cabinet, too: Dalmane, patent medicine, Valium, and Tylenol with codeine."

"Noonan," she said, "I'll tell you something. The people you work with wouldn't be surprised to hear you saying these things. 'Murky' is the word they often use. They think you're murky." Waves lapped at the shore.

"I was surprised that Hildon took Valium," Noonan said.

"He was having periodontal work done."

"You're protecting your husband. I like that. That's a good thing about heterosexuals—that they stick together. Fags move on like flies when they smell meat."

"That's pretty awful, Noonan. Do you feel that bad about yourself?"

"Yes," he said. "It excites me to talk about it. It excites me to be honest."

Another car pulled into the driveway. It was Cameron Petrus, one of Matt's reporters. Cameron had come here from

Boston, after having a heart attack at thirty. He had recently taken up javelin throwing. Ever since his wife left him, he had been giving Lucy Spenser the eye. Cameron had on gray jeans that made his legs look like tree trunks. The bright green fishnet shirt he wore made him look even more like a tree. She said hello to him when she went out to the backyard.

The food had been disappearing fast. The whole crowd really liked to eat and drink. They were laughing and bobbing in and out of groups; in their bright summer colors they reminded her of voracious, exotic birds. At the edge of the lawn, Lucy Spenser and the girl who had been too drunk to remember her phone number had linked arms and were doing a chorus line kick for the camera. Suddenly the boy began to turn, slowly, as if a pedestal rotated beneath him. He panned the crowd. Maureen found herself stiffening, trying to appear picture perfect. She would probably be the one who looked like a fool, not Lucy, who had kicked off her shoes and who was now talking to another couple, her mop of hair thrown forward, doubled up so that her forehead almost touched her legs. The girl she had been kicking her legs with was talking to Nigel again. Hildon went over and joined their group, pouring wine into Nigel's glass. The boy continued videotaping. He turned the camera on her, and Maureen raised her hand again.

"This is the best party I've been to all summer," Cameron Petrus said.

"Summer's hardly started, Cameron."

"Your party certainly is the official beginning of summer, to my mind," Cameron said. "What an evening. Look at those clouds off on the horizon. Simply wonderful."

Cameron was so boring that it almost drove her mad. Apparently he had only two modes: the violently aggressive way he acted when he interviewed people and the mindlessly polite way he was now, ready to sink in the quicksand of his own small talk.

"You're looking very lovely tonight," Cameron said.

"Thank you," she said.

"I had some of those spiced shrimp a minute ago. Did you make them yourself?"

"Yes," she said.

"You really do know how to give a party," he said.

"Thank you," she said.

"Say," he said, "I hear it's going to be good weather on the Fourth."

"I'm glad," she said.

"It's a relief," he said.

Noonan joined them. One large shrimp was curved over the edge of his wine glass. He dunked it in the wine and ate it.

"May I join the conversation?" he said.

"Cameron was just saying that it's supposed to be good weather on the Fourth," Maureen said.

Across the lawn, Matt Smith choked while he was laughing. A woman Maureen had never seen before patted him on the back.

"You know where he got all his money?" Cameron Petrus said. "His great-great-grandfather or some ancestor of the great-great-grandfather invented the jump rope."

"The jump rope?" Noonan said.

"Wooden handles," Cameron Petrus said, spreading his arms as if he were about to conduct an orchestra. He twirled his arms and jumped on his toes.

Hildon was walking the length of the large table, lighting citronella candles. Two of the writers were stretched out on the lawn, arm wrestling. The woman standing with Matt Smith dropped her glass and jumped back as the wine splashed. Maureen looked around. A year before, the party had been in a big canvas tent. She had worn a toga. She had served pita bread and hummus. It had rained on the Fourth of July. Two days later she had been on the phone, ordering a set of glasses from the Horchow collection, when she suddenly felt blood soaking her pants, and miscarried, without having known she was pregnant.

2

THE day after the party, the heat came on so suddenly that the Green Mountains almost disappeared in the haze. Lucy Spenser sat in the grass, on her side lawn, feeling a little sorry for herself. This had been the time, five years ago, that Les Whitehall had gotten a job teaching in Vermont once they had moved here. He had been gone for a year, though the mailbox on the road across from the house was still marked Spenser/Whitehall. It had caught her eye as she returned from her morning walk, and suddenly she had felt the heat, the flies seemed to buzz louder and to be more persistent, and the air seemed as dense as icing.

Since Les had taken off, she hadn't figured out how to get her life going again. It was not that the two of them had had specific plans that had been interrupted, but that when he left she realized that she had lived so long without thinking of the future that now it was difficult to imagine what she should do. There was really no routine to her life except that once a week Hildon drove to her house to pick up the column. It still amazed her that her oldest friend had started a magazine on the $50,000 profit he had made selling land, and that it had become so successful that it had just been bought by a corporation.

Hildon was quite up front about telling his friends that the magazine's success was proof positive that the entire country was coked-out. Hundreds of readers wrote in every month—readers who had caught the slightest, trendiest in-jokes. Unsolicited manuscripts rolled in that were either works of such quality that Swift must have rolled over in his grave or suitable evidence of mass psychosis. Thousands of people had filled out a request form, in the last issue, to have the psychmobile come to their houses. This was one of Hildon's new concepts; it was modeled on the idea of the bookmobile, but instead of books to check out, there was a staff of psychologists to evaluate people's mental condition and see whether they should be checked in.

But Lucy's column was the biggest success, and it had been from the first. She was, as Cindi Coeur, a Latter-Day Miss Lonelyhearts, and the picture that accompanied her column showed her with hair romantically disheveled, eyes wide (presumably with wisdom), and a smile that, coupled with hair and eyes, might have suggested après l'amour, tristesse. The beatific smile was actually après $125 a gram.

These days, Lucy did the column straight—if you could call making up the questions and writing the answers on pieces of pink stationery she had her mother send her from John Wanamaker in Philadelphia and using a fountain pen with lavender ink doing it straight. Lately, Lucy had been thinking that maybe it was time to stop. Just because Jagger was still popping up like a jack-in-the-box, did she really want to be Cindi Coeur at forty? Still, Lucy herself admitted to a morbid fascination with being facile.

Dear Cindi Coeur,

When my husband makes love to me he always has a lot of money under the pillow. I mean, before we get into bed he empties out his wallet, and in the middle of lovemaking, he plunges his hands into the money. His money is always all wrinkled. I think that clerks in stores will see the money and maybe know what is going on. What can I say to my husband to make him stop? Do you think that he likes money more than he likes me?

Sad in the Sack

Dear Sad,

Your husband is sexually excited by money. This is called a "fetish." You have not given me enough information. First, I need to know the ages and educational backgrounds of some of the clerks in order to tell you whether they will know what your husband is up to. You do suggest that your husband has quite a bit of money if there is so much that he can plunge his hands into it. What denomination is this currency? If your husband has as much money as it seems, I want to suggest two things: (1) that you put up with whatever he does and (2) that you not consult your clergyman, as he will expect increased donations.

The phone rang in the kitchen and Lucy got up to answer it. It was her sister, Jane, calling from California. Jane's calls were always a sidestep from whatever she was doing. She would call someone, clamp the phone between shoulder and ear, then become so involved in painting her nails or doing leg stretches that when the phone was answered, it caught her off-guard.

"Oh. Hello," Jane said.

"Hi," Lucy said.

"I set my alarm," Jane said. "I wanted to be sure to catch you. It's seven o'clock here." She sounded offended, as if Lucy had arranged for it to be early morning on the West Coast.

"What's up?" Lucy said.

What was usually up was something involving Jane's daughter, Nicole.

"Nicole's blue," Jane said. "Piggy was trying to set up a spot for her on *Saturday Night Live*, and it fell through. Then you know that gorilla that she liked so much—the one they put in a sailor suit, that she stood next to on the deck of the QE2 for *Vogue*? He just died of pneumonia. I sent a contribution to the San Diego Zoo."

For the last two years, Nicole Nelson had appeared on *Passionate Intensity* as Stephanie Sykes, an abused child from a broken family, a teenage alcoholic who was being rehabilitated by a woman internist and her husband, Gerald, a wimpy would-be novelist who felt misunderstood not only by his wife but by the world. The woman internist, who secretly subjected herself to experimental surgery to correct sterility, then found out that she could conceive. She faced the dilemma of whether to divorce her husband, who was at last working on his novel, to have a child with her true love, another doctor at the hospital, thereby disrupting the family routine she had established that had put young Stephanie on the road to recovery, or to settle for what she now realized was probably the correct thing: a childless marriage. This was also complicated by the fact that her husband's sister, a volunteer worker at the hospital who had always envied her sister-in-law and who had had a brief affair with the same doctor, was now considering blackmail, wanting to force her sister-in-law into the dull routine of motherhood with the wrong man, so that she could make the handsome doctor who would be left behind fall in love with her again. The further complication was that when his wife's wealthy benefactor died, the wimpy husband had buckled down long enough to put his wife through the last two years of medical school. The day of her graduation, he had had a mental breakdown and, when he was recovering, a brief affair with a woman who worked in the lab. Then he had at last gotten an advance for his book, *Barren*, a fictionalized account of his and his wife's failure to have children. What no one but the doctor/lover knew was that Stephanie Sykes was pregnant and begging the doctor to abort her. What even the doctor did not realize was that his lover's husband's ex-lover, the woman who worked in the lab, had found out that Stephanie was pregnant. She was anti-abortion, and if the doctor performed the surgery, she was going to go to the wimpy novelist and let him know what a farce his happy family life was, in hopes of getting him herself.

"Nicole needs a vacation. I want to send her to you," Jane said.

"She'd be bored to death," Lucy said. "You know what happens here? In the late afternoon the cows walk into the field."

"Boredom might be good for her," Jane said. "Don't people develop their imaginations if they're bored?"

Why argue? Lucy thought. If Jane had made up her mind, the visit from Nicole was a *fait accompli*. Only seconds elapsed before Jane's ideas materialized. Their mother likened Jane's mind to a dollop of pancake batter dropped on a hot griddle.

"Both of you come, and we'll go to Philadelphia and visit Mother," Lucy said.

"I'm going to tell you something that you can never tell another soul," Jane said. "I've gained eight pounds since you last saw me. I'm on a macrobiotic regime. I have to stay close to the seaweed store. I'll come visit when I've finished ingesting half of the ocean."

"Does Nicole want to come?" Lucy said.

"She loves you," Jane said. "She had such a good time the last time she visited. She still talks about Heath Bar Crunch ice cream and Hildon's motorcycle."

"He sold it," Lucy said.

He had sold his motorcycle because he wanted a pickup instead, but so far he hadn't found one with the right ambience.

"Come on," Jane said. "Martyr yourself."

Lucy laughed. She spent no more time than other people thinking about being a do-gooder. Like the rest of the world, she was preoccupied and imperfect: she had had an abortion, crushed a few rabbits under tires as she rolled down country roads, turned the page of the magazine when her eye met the eyes of the orphan she could save if she made out a check and sent it before the winds of fate blew the urchin's last grain of rice away.

Take Nicole for the summer? To Lucy, she was still a baby—the poor baby whose father had died before he ever saw her, two months after he and Jane married, off the southernmost point of the United States, in Key West, after drinking ten piña coladas with friends. After Nicole had been born, Jane had gotten engaged again, to an actor. They broke it off when Jane had a miscarriage, but before they did, he arranged for Nicole to meet his agent. Just after her first birthday, Nicole had done a toy ad, hugging a Baby Do-Right doll against her cheek, and the rest was history. From the first, she had not just been personable in front of the camera. Other children had rashes and insect bites, but Nicole's skin was unblemished; she always looked windswept rather than rumpled. She was the perfect California girl long before her mother took her there. Her bedtime lullaby, suitably enough, was harmonized by the Beach Boys, who also played at her kindergarten graduation. She tap danced on the *Tonight* show, sharing the limelight with Charles Bronson and a macaw. The first time Nicole visited her grandmother in Philadelphia, Grammy could not believe that the child had never learned a prayer. Instead of rattling off "Now I Lay Me Down to Sleep" when she was put to bed, Nicole waited patiently to be questioned. At night her mother always asked, "How do you feel about everything?" When Grammy took Nicole to see a Shirley Temple movie, Nicole's whispered comment was, "What's wrong with that girl?"

Lucy had not seen much of Nicole the last few years, so this phone call came as a surprise, but if she needed anything besides Jane's request to persuade her, she had only to remember that Nicole was her only niece: beautiful, intelligent, talented, and famous—the gleam of her deceased daddy's eye that now gleamed in Hollywood. She was also a fourteen-year-old girl who was difficult. But really—how could anyone know how much of Nicole's difficult behavior was the result of fame and how much was just a given with any girl that age? It was perfectly possible, Lucy thought, that like a rabbit drawn into danger by the beam of a headlight, Nicole had been lured away from the relative normalcy of places like Vermont and stunned by exploding flashbulbs. Looking at stars—real stars in the sky—might be just what Nicole needed. As Lucy and Jane discussed Nicole's visit, tiny birds began swooping through the air. Vermont really was paradise in a way—Les had been right about that. It was more beautiful than any invented backdrop, a sky against which Lassie could be painted, noble and romantic, with wind-fluffed fur. White pansies blew like handkerchiefs held in the air. An image came to Lucy's mind of ladies waving goodbye to soldiers as the train pulled out. Just as quickly, she thought that this scene had already passed into myth; handkerchiefs were an anachronism, and the next war would blow the Earth away. Nobody was going anywhere by train. The inevitability she felt about this made her sad. Of course she wanted to spend time with her niece.

By the time she and Jane hung up, Lucy felt energized. As she waited for Hildon, she picked up her clipboard, uncapped the fountain pen, and invented the week's column.

Dear Cindi Coeur,

My brother and I are in big trouble and we don't know what to do. Our parents have grounded us because the cops found us acting suspiciously in a garage that's under a restaurant complex where our parents often eat. What we were doing was playing "Deep Throat," but neither of us thought we could tell anybody. The cops questioned us, and we said we were playing hide-and-seek. See, my brother stands behind a pillar, and I go around the garage until he makes a noise or I catch on where he is, and then I go over with a real serious look on my face and he whispers something to me. Then he closes his eyes and I go off and do the same thing. When we get bored, we make strange telephone calls from the pay phone in the garage, but nobody knows about that. My brother is sick of being grounded and thinks that we should just confess, but I think we should wait it out, or maybe there is another way. Do you have any advice?

Tina the Throat

Dear Tina,

Often I receive letters and worry that, in reading between the lines, I am understanding more than the people realize they are revealing. I would be avoiding the real issue if I did not tell you that Freud would be even more interested in the game you and your brother play than either the cops or your parents. You did not choose to play "Deep Throat" as opposed to Monopoly without a reason, and the reason is that it is a game highly charged with sexual undertones. I am not entirely sure that even the original players, Woodward and Bernstein, realized this. Stop for a moment and think of the pillars as penises, and you will begin to understand what I mean. But what a thing is and what we can make it appear to be is very important. Why not tell your parents about the game, but call it "Woodward and Bernstein" instead of saying that you were playing "Deep Throat?" You can suggest, by carrying a notebook when you speak to them, that you are interested in a career as a journalist.

3

As he pulled into the driveway, Hildon consulted his watch. It had been a Christmas present from Lucy: a watch that would tell him, even as he fell into the ocean, what time it was in Cairo. He sat for a few seconds before getting out of the car. Behind him a tractor rattled by on the dirt road, and he felt a tremor in his ribs as it passed. He was slightly hung-over from the party, and he needed a hit of Cindi Coeur to cheer him up. Some butterflies flickered up from the dust and beat their wings. He watched them fly away, to an area where rhododendron bushes had recently been planted.

Lucy was in the kitchen, sitting on the counter, having her daily lunch: a diet chocolate ice cream cone. What might be mistaken for sprinkles was actually a Diet Trim capsule she had broken into a bowl through which she rubbed the ice cream.

"Mon coeur," Hildon said, kissing his fingertips and flicking them away from his lips.

The door had been open. He had told her a million times to lock it, just in case some lunatic came by, but of course she did not lock it, and today he had no intention of saying anything.

He opened the refrigerator. Perrier on the top shelf, bottles arranged neatly. He considered removing them and setting them up on the floor like bowling pins, which he could knock down with the pomegranate. There was mold inside the applesauce jar. There was chutney. A plate piled high with snow peas. As usual there was nothing to eat.

"What's this?" Hildon said, thumbing a newspaper on the kitchen counter.

"Research," Lucy said. "Jane called today. She's sending Nicole for a visit."

In preparation for this, Lucy had gone out an hour before to buy the tabloids so that she could read the Hollywood gossip. She had found a picture of Ed Harp and Nicole, both in indecent bikinis, at the beach. Nicole with Philippe (Jane had told her in a recent phone call that he was a Greek midget they were trying to pass off as a ten-year-old French boy). Nicole leaving Ma Maison, after dinner à deux with Gillie—another superstar who worked hard to make his affectations antic: he went everywhere, including Ma Maison, with his two Samoyeds. The color reproduction was bad in the photo: Nicole's face, Day-Glo pink, seemed to be sliding off sideways into Gillie's mottled pink and yellow jaw. It was rumored, in another paper, that Nicole had her eye on Brandt Buchanan. That picture showed Nicole riding on the shoulders of a boy who wore a shirt, the main purpose of which was to display unbuttoned buttons. Farrah was still with Ryan—no word on his son, whose teeth he had knocked out. There was a diet that guaranteed you would lose ten pounds a month, snacking on beans. Many women, all of them on TV shows that Lucy had never heard of, were said to be infanticipating. The boyfriends and husbands looked gay. Michael Jackson had added another llama to his menagerie. Alana's life *was* livable without Rod. Another diet featured the eating of squash blossoms.

Lucy handed Hildon the week's column.

Dear Cindi Coeur,

I understand that small children often exaggerate without thinking of it as a lie. My question is about my son, who has been complaining that his best friend has better lunches than he has. He says that instead of bringing tuna fish sandwiches to school, the boy has a whole tuna. I told him that this was not possible, because a real tuna fish would weigh hundreds of pounds. Nevertheless, my son refuses to eat tuna sandwiches anymore, and I feel that tuna sandwiches are better for him than the protein found in the only other sandwich he will eat—pork chop. I am also worried about his telling lies. He refuses to admit that he has made up the story about the tuna. I have questioned him in detail about how this would be possible, and he just continues the lie. He says the boy does not bring the sandwiches in a lunch box, but in a box the size of a bed. Should I discipline him, or just pack tuna sandwiches and insist that he face reality and eat them?

A Worried Mom

Dear Worried,

It seems to me that you have quite a few options. You could refuse to replace the tuna sandwiches with sandwiches made of pork chops, and substitute something such as quiche, which will get soggy and appeal to no child. You could also get a pig and put it in a cage, telling your son that this way he would have something to rival his friend's tuna fish, and that it is his problem to get it to school. You might also consider the possibility that the other boy is being forced to eat sardine sandwiches and is trying to compensate for his own embarrassment by insisting that they are tuna fish. You may want to ask yourself what your son is missing at home that makes him have such a strong empathetic reaction with the other boy. You might also consider the possibility that one or both boys needs glasses.

The phone rang, and Lucy answered it. From her end of the conversation Hildon could tell that she was talking to the kid at the nursery—the kid he had met with her the week before who had now developed a crush on her and who had stolen what looked like quite a lot of rhododendron bushes and planted them in her backyard. Lucy always elicited strong reactions from people. They loved her or hated her—their intensity was the one constant. Hildon, of course, couldn't understand people's negative impressions; he and Lucy had been friends and lovers since their college days.

Hildon wandered into the living room, not wanting to hear any more of the conversation. He had never been insulted that Lucy hadn't wanted to marry him until he met the person she did want to settle down with—Les Whitehall. Les had even more preppie refinement than Hildon, but no sense of humor about it. Hildon thought he bore as much resemblance to a real man as Play-Doh did to a rock. Instead of being a real shit kicker, he was an intellectual shit kicker: he gave lazy paraphrases of philosophers' thoughts, pretended to think ironically of his own existence, and chose the easiest audience a coward could find—college kids.

"No!" Lucy said. "I would *not* think it was funny if you planted willow trees to weep in your behalf in my yard!"

"Come in here, Lucy," Hildon said. "You're acting like a jackass."

"That was my father," Lucy said into the telephone. "He's very outspoken. He gets away with everything because he's six five. Daddy thought the bushes were beautiful, by the way. Let me put him on to thank you."

Lucy came to the doorway and smiled at Hildon. Such a tease. Putting him on the spot. He decided to turn the tables on her. He walked past her and picked up the telephone. "Shtup my daughter and your ass'll fly farther than Johnny Unitas' football," he said. He slammed the phone down.

Lucy looked shocked. Then she laughed. Lucy with the long swing of auburn hair, the long, matchstick legs and arms, the perfect white teeth. His heart really was racing; he had taken such a risk. He went into the living room and sank down into the sofa. She nestled against his side, laughing hard. "It makes me wish I did have an irrational father," she said. "That macho shit really does have its appeal. That was pretty good, Hildy."

"That kid's no more than nineteen," he said, suddenly feeling as stuffy as a real father. "You ought to hang out with people your own age."

"I don't hang out with him—I met him when I went to buy a rosebush."

"The flirting was pretty heavy, Lucy. Pretending that you were debating between a rosebush and a box of petunias. Lucy the dizzy dame." Hildon crossed his eyes and tapped his knuckles on his forehead.

"Hildon—are you serious? You're serious. You really believe what you're saying. What bothers you—that it worked?"

"Yes," he said.

"Hildy—are you *serious*? I'm taking you seriously. Please smile."

"We were having a nice time, and suddenly you just turned your attention on that silly kid and started coming on to him like I wasn't there."

"You're serious, aren't you? Since when are you so easily offended?"

"You've always been able to hurt me when you wanted to."

"Hildon—you're out of your mind. We're having a serious discussion. Why are we doing that? Did something bad happen to you before you came over?"

"Tell the truth," Hildon said. "Don't be cute for a minute. All I want is for you to admit you were flirting. Yes, I'm overreacting. It's your right to flirt. But you have to be serious for one second and admit that I'm right."

"Is there some reason why you want to get into a fight with me?" Lucy said.

"I never won a fight with you in my life, so I'd be crazy to want that, wouldn't I? You're taking the easy way out by pretending that every disagreement is a fight, and therefore you don't have to lower yourself to take part in it. Just say that you were flirting, and I'll shut up about my personal code of ethics that says a thirty-five-year-old woman shouldn't turn on a teenager."

"He's not a teenager."

"You're changing the subject."

"What *is* the subject, Hildon? That you want to make a big production out of some silly person's crush on me?"

"You kid around with those people. You take them seriously and you've dismissed me."

"We talk on the phone almost every day."

"I edit the magazine you write for."

"It has nothing to do with that. I could mail the pieces in."

"Go ahead," Hildon said. "Keep talking. Convince yourself, and then it'll be all over."

"Hildon," she said, putting her hands on his shoulders. "Are you all right? Are you going to keep this up?"

"Are you?" he said. "All you have to do to stop me is admit that I was right and that you were flirting."

"Hildon," she said, closing her eyes, "Close your eyes and we'll both be quiet for a minute, and when we open our eyes we'll pretend this didn't happen."

"I don't want you to pretend anymore," he said.

Her mouth showed a flicker of annoyance; she squeezed her eyes shut. She did not open them. She had her hands on his shoulders. In a few seconds he kissed her hand. She squeezed her eyes shut tighter and did not react. He looked at the hand he had kissed. Thank God she had not married Les Whitehall. He closed his eyes and opened them again. Her eyes were squeezed shut. The lines in her forehead and fanning above her nose made him realize that someday Lucy would be old. He would be old. He would be old without ever having won a fight, but he would still have Lucy. He put his cheek on her hand and closed his eyes. He kept them closed for much longer than a minute. He felt her breath on his hair, and a slight breeze coming through the window. When he opened his eyes she was looking at him. Her face was almost expressionless—that look that had first lured him to her side when they were twenty years old. The look was a mask: because she was pretty and she had been looked at, appraised, so often, she wasn't going to let anybody have anything easily besides their own false assumptions. She was so pretty that many people made the mistake of thinking she had to be dumb. Her immobile face reinforced that effect. It seemed almost intimate when she smiled, and a real turn-on when she laughed. She smiled at him. It was over. Another moment when he might have lost her had passed.

She got up and went into the kitchen. "Do you want a drink?" she said. He had shook her up a little. He was sorry he had done it. He looked at the rug and tried to compose his thoughts. She came to the kitchen doorway and looked at him. Now she did look upset. She walked back to the living room and sat beside him.

"Did you do that to scare me?" she said.

"I just went out of control," he said.

She leaned back against the sofa and closed her eyes. It was very quiet; depending on how strong the breeze was, you heard different noises: scratchy or soft, the tinkling of wind chimes. He held her earrings between two fingers: a gold sliver of moon on which a little star had landed. He studied it, dangling from her ear, rubbed it the way he would rub a shell, doubting the cool smoothness of it.

"Go make us a drink," she said. "I'm not as dishonest as you think I am. I was flirting. I did it just to do it. I was pretty surprised when he found out where I lived and put all those bushes in the backyard."

They hadn't done this routine for so many years that at first Hildon didn't realize it had begun. It was what they had done long ago: belittled themselves so much that the other would be overwhelmed with positive feelings. That was the way they had so often ended up in bed. He was standing. She put her hands behind his knees and drew her forehead to his leg. He froze for a second, then stepped toward her. She kissed his leg.

Hildon started to laugh. He needed to choke back a terrible sadness that had started to overwhelm him. He sat on the couch now, leaning the tip of one shoulder against the back, and began to raise her shirt out of her jeans. He kissed her stomach. His nose tickled her, and she drew up her legs. "I didn't think he was nineteen," Hildon said. "I was just being a prick."

4

THE pickup truck that passed Lucy as she was driving to the airport to get Nicole made her feel as if she were in a time warp: it was a red Ford, and the driver had his long brown hair pulled back in a ponytail. As she passed, Lucy looked over and saw a thin, round-faced blond girl sitting in the passenger's seat. Wedged between them was an Irish Setter. Where would all the Irish Setters of the world be today if there had been no hippies? Lucy saw the bumper in her rearview mirror and cut back into the lane. Her mother would have said, "Where can they be going?" Her mother was always mystified by the sight of people casually dressed, couples together at two in the afternoon. She was not really asking a question but saying that she did not approve of people who did not work. She was still dismayed that Jane had no career, and she didn't take what Lucy did seriously. She could not take it seriously that Lucy was a teacher in the Arts in the Schools program because that was part time. She understood that Lucy got paid for the columns she wrote, but since they were a joke and very few people had made careers out of jokes, she didn't take that seriously either. Lucy couldn't argue with her there.

She listened to the radio. She was trying to get back to that. When Les left, she had stopped listening to music. He had played the radio all the time. When she had an image of Les, music accompanied it, like the beginning of a movie. The Eurythmics were on the radio. This summer's Eurythmics record was not as good as "Sweet Dreams." Lyrics didn't remind her of Les—he had loved all A.M. music, so just the sound of the radio was painful. The specifics changed, but the format never did. It was one advertising jingle or another. Music playing softly, gradually getting louder as the DJ finished talking, the number to call to name a song and win a prize, the number-one song, the big hit of summer, fast talk about worthless products, where to get tickets to this concert or that concert, whatever shouldn't be missed, and don't be late. Men at Work. Culture Club. Michael Jackson then and now. Blast from the Past, Oldies but Goodies, two hot dogs for the price of one, and a cold front moving in from the North. Then came a Möbius strip of music. All over America, people were driving around hearing a song and remembering exactly where they were, who they loved, how they thought it would turn out. In traffic jams, women with babies and grocery bags were suddenly eighteen years old, in summer, on the beach, in the arms of somebody who hummed that song in their ear. They ironed to songs they had slow-danced to, shot through intersections on yellow lights the way they always had, keeping time with the Doors' drumbeat. They might have to be reminded of many of the names of kids they had gone to school with, but once they heard the name, they could say with certainty which of them thought John was the best Beatle and which thought Paul was. They were as sure of the top ten, the summer they graduated from high school, as any minister of the Ten Commandments. It was how people kept in touch with their past. And above all, no matter how many other people had danced to it or made love to it or hung pictures of Jackson Browne or Bruce Springsteen or Van Halen in their bedroom, it was personal. Cyndi Lauper was singing "Time After Time" when Lucy turned off the radio. Bad enough that one song, or two songs, could break your heart—she had to make the mistake of falling in love with somebody who was an addict to all of it. It was like falling in love with someone and having it be your own special secret that the sun went down at night.

It was still difficult for Lucy to believe that she had spent more than ten years in New York. Every time she got in her car now, she remembered with amazement all the time she had spent on buses and in subways and being thrown around in cabs. She had had a car then, but it was impossible to drive in the city. She stored it in a carport in Hackensack, for $25 a month, with a woman who was a cousin of a woman Lucy had gone to school with. At the time, this had made perfect sense. On weekends—almost every weekend, when she got together with Les Whitehall—they drove to the Hudson Valley, or to see friends of hers in Connecticut. In retrospect it was amazing to realize that at least once a week she had been amazed that there was still a sky. She had gotten so used to the hard edges of things that she had come to think of the world as a gigantic coloring book, all outlines and shapes, so clearly delineated that there was little need to fill it in. One star. Two. A sky that looked like corridors, one turn after another determined by the tops of buildings jutting up as obstacles. The most needed crayon was gray.

Lucy had gone to New York because she thought that she would become a success. There was quite a difference between being successful, which she might have done anywhere, and being a success. Being a success meant being a personality, and New York was a big stage, always ready. The props distracted people, though, and Lucy was no exception. She began to work less; to worry more about getting enough sleep, which resulted in restless nights and dragged-out days; and as she lost ground, to fixate on what she had. By the time she doubted that she was going to be a success, it was also clear that the city had a way of keeping people. Life was so difficult that small triumphs began to look like success. Managing to keep your car so near the city seemed a real coup. The city always allowed people to fool themselves. There were statistics of people mugged or robbed or raped, but it still seemed that there was safety in numbers. There was something solid about New York that couldn't be shaken. It was a wall, and the people were Humpty Dumpty; the New York *Times*, the mayor, even signs hurriedly printed and hung on trees warned them to be careful, so if they toppled, they could only blame themselves. The king's horses and the king's men couldn't help them. The horses were for hire, trotting around Central Park with carriages full of tourists.

When she first moved to the city, the fairy-tale aspects of life there fascinated Lucy—things were so excessive, the veneer only intensified how primitive everything really was. It took awhile to realize that there was no proper ending to the fairy tale: things were simply out of control, and no one was in charge once the strobes were unplugged and the interview was over. It was people's own fault if they didn't get the joke. Mayor Koch was right there doing his best to amuse, on *Saturday Night Live*, if you wanted to tune in.

It could be scary if you let yourself focus on the chaos, so most people kept their sanity by focusing, instead, on things. Those who would still take a risk focused on people. When they did, of course they gave the people magical powers: everyone was exceptional and mysterious, romanticized out of proportion. Real people couldn't save anyone if they were in trouble, but heroes and heroines could. Since it was the tendency of many women to exaggerate men's importance and abilities anyway, men fared particularly well in New York.

Les Whitehall had led a charmed life: he was attractive, intelligent and amusing. People who didn't know him well would be slow to spot the fear disguised as optimism. He was always well spoken, an extrovert. The older generation knew to watch out for men like Les Whitehall, but in New York someone who was that together easily impressed people. What Lucy's grandmother knew to call "a smoothie" was now, at natural-food stores in the city, the name of a refreshing drink. In another town (might as well say another world) it might never have been apparent to anyone, including Les, that he wasn't achieving as much as he might. When Lucy met him, he was writing a novel, taking a course in philosophy, playing racquetball and jogging two miles a day, in addition to his job as a college teacher. He commuted to teach classes outside the city four days a week. This made him a maverick to New Yorkers, and exotic to his students and colleagues. In a town where every waitress was an actress, every cab driver a philosopher, where the construction workers were doing field work for their Ph.D.'s in psychology, and the hospital orderly sang opera, you gradually came to assume that every Nathan's hot dog was actually a dehydrated roast beef. It was taken for granted that people weren't what they appeared to be, and no matter what they were, you hoped that actually they were more than they seemed. The city was overcrowded, after all; people who couldn't swim had no excuse for setting out for the island to begin with. Nobody cared much about anyone's past. The present simply didn't exist, and the real interest was in the future. Ask any New Yorker where to get the Sunday *Times* on Saturday night.

Les Whitehall was from Carbondale, Illinois, and if he had stayed there, he would have gone into business (his father and uncle owned a hardware store), bought a cruisemobile, married and had children. He was saved by a scholarship. He went to Princeton, where he dated lanky, loquacious women. He learned early that it was better to be quiet than to speak and make a mistake. Much to his surprise, his silence was accepted as the appropriate response of a superior mind. Everyone at Princeton was assumed to be intelligent until proven otherwise. More than the people he grew up with, the people who crowded around him at college thought in terms of black and white. It seemed appropriate to Les that from then on, those were the colors in which his classmates, in their tuxedos and elegant dresses, would be dressed. He kept up with a few people from that crowd. Lucy could never feel close to any of them. She was no longer sure why she had been so impressed with Les Whitehall. His optimism was part of it. And he had simply been so conspicuous in a town where almost no one stood out that she had been taken in. He was tall but not too tall, handsome but casual, one of those men who could change the filter on an air conditioner and your perception of what kind of a day you had had with equal dexterity. In time, she came to learn that optimism was not something he really felt, but a convenience for him—something he could use as a sort of weapon. When things worked out, he would say that he had predicted it all along, and if they went wrong, he would turn that against whoever had believed in him. Until she met Les, she never realized that fear, not strength, could make people resolute. He knew that he was handsome and forceful. He knew how he appeared to other people. He was so sure of this, and of their surprised and happy reaction to him, that he would play around—the confession of weakness that lightened his conscience also made others see him as forthcoming. Anyone smart enough to suspect that what he did was tinged with bravado would probably be won over to his side, anyway: interesting, this elaborate defense system in someone so urbane. The childishness made them warm to him.

Another couple introduced Lucy to Les Whitehall, and after dinner he had taken her for a drink. Les's talk was full of significant pauses and deliberate omissions. He made people want to find out about him, but he chose carefully, selecting people who would have the good manners to question him graciously, backing off if the board creaked, tiptoeing forward when the bridge seemed stable. When they got tired (it was impossible to find out enough to think you had gotten to the other side) he would suddenly take on life. He wore them out in a difficult situation they never wanted to enter into, then gave them something—a fond look, a hand—so that when they least expected it, they were safe after all. He let them feel approved of, but in reality he did not approve of himself or of anyone else. Anyone who had less than he had wasn't worth his time, and anyone who had more was a threat. That was Les: he perceived of everything in terms of competition. He was still racing with the football, but running more slowly than he had in Carbondale, the letters on the back of the jersey replaced, when necessary, with his heart on his sleeve. The new goal was to get women.

He had gotten Lucy so completely that it took her months after he had gone to realize that it was so hard to talk about Les because in some sense he didn't exist. He relied on people to invent him. When he was quiet, she had supposed that he was thoughtful; when he was impervious to other people's pain, she had admired him for being self-contained and not easily shaken by circumstance. Women adored him, and had always been there for him. He didn't reject them, but like everyone who required such a thing, he hated both the person who provided it, and himself. It must have been frightening to him that he really liked no one. When he came close to a woman emotionally, he would move away physically. It worked out well for him that any woman he would bother with preferred an emotional revelation to a physical thrill. But these excesses were rare. Now, it was a mystery to Lucy why he had bothered to attach himself to her. Les took it easy on himself. He shadowboxed until he got his equilibrium back, and if he had trouble regaining it, he bounced from one woman to another, staying on his toes.

And Lucy had no one to tell it to. Just try to tell his colleagues with whom he had been so patient that he didn't take them seriously, that his good manners were nothing more than condescension. Try telling the lonely women in New York that Les Whitehall was a fraud. Lucy would suddenly become ungrateful or worse, just another pretty, bitter woman, a simple stereotype; and Les—because at the very least everyone would grant that he was complex—would ascend to the category of What We Must Accept Though It Is Inexplicable.

It shocked Lucy to realize that she could think such a thing. Wanting to be talked out of such ideas, she had even told many of these things to Les, because he was so good at rebuttals, when he could not otherwise rearrange reality. The more convinced she became, of course, the more difficult it had been to even raise these issues. It was, for Lucy, as implausible as walking up to Machiavelli and asking to borrow a dime. Even now she was haunted by remembering the perfect lovemaking, the all-night conversations, the gifts, the cards inevitably signed Love Always, Les. After Les announced that he was in love with one of his students and that he was leaving, she had wandered around their house, rounding up the little notes, reading the closings, trying to revert to the way she had thought at the beginning: that if he had written these words, they must be true. Finally, unsure of what was or ever had been true, she took the coward's way out: she simply turned it against herself. Night after night in the empty house, she thought bitterly that *of course* anyone else would have realized that the kiss that lasted forever would naturally become the kiss of death.

Lately, she had been getting closer to Hildon, because that distracted her from thinking about Les. She knew that he knew this. He knew that she knew. She thought he knew that at some point, probably soon, she would step back. They were always there for each other in times of trouble. When Les left her, it had reinforced something she had known all along, something she always got in trouble when she forgot: that she could not be an exception. Whatever crazy thoughts men had about other people, they would eventually have about her. If they distrusted the whole world and trusted her implicitly, they would come to distrust her; if they were not close to anyone and they attached themselves to her, one day they would just remove themselves. If you demonstrated, day by day, that you were not the person they feared, they would be confused for a while, but gradually they would stop trusting logic and become frightened. Hildon did not think that anyone was a soul mate except Lucy. This meant that one morning Hildon would wake up and realize that he and Lucy were not simpatico. She was afraid because this happened so often—she dreaded it—but the truth was that she did not fear men individually. They sensed this and opened up to her. They talked to her—most men would tell her anything. Even Les had dropped most of his defenses. He had talked to her day after day, night after night. He had given her everything imaginable to figure him out, and when he knew that she had, he left. While she thought she was explaining things, in his mind she was creating chaos: he had secretly wanted her to consider the evidence, and tell him that he was larger than life. He had not been drawn to her rational mind at all; he had been drawn to the idea of proving that she was romantic.

Hildon hated Les—hated him out of all proportion, even. That was Hildon's own insecurity: his fear that Lucy would prefer to analyze Les's angst instead of playing games with him. He might have been right, if Les and all the men like him had not exhausted her. She had actually come to like the way she felt now that she had short-circuited.

Lucy pulled into the airport parking lot. She had forgotten her sunglasses and the glare had given her a headache. A red-wing blackbird flew up and slanted away; it had the trajectory of a bullet, heading for the trees at the side of the parking lot.

She was twenty minutes early. A man in gym shorts and a

long-sleeved, embroidered Greek shirt was talking to his son, who sat on his knee. "You don't bite," he said. "It hurts when you bite." The baby, who knew he was being criticized, lit up with the Smile of the Sprite. He puckered his lips and kissed the air. "That's right," the man said. "Kisses, not bites." The baby shifted on the man's knee. "What does the cow say?" the man said. "Moo," the baby said. "What does the doggie say?" "Arby," the baby said. "That's right. Arby the dog. But what does the doggie say?" "Woof, woof," the baby said. The baby leaned into its father's face. "Cows may noise," the baby said. The baby arched back, and his father grabbed him around the waist just in time.

Lucy hadn't seen Nicole in more than a year. Since Les left, she had not seen anyone but Hildon with any regularity. She was wondering if this was the place to be anymore; it was the place Les had wanted to be. She didn't even know where Les was. When the plane landed, Nicole was one of the first off. The baby in the white baptismal dress who had once toppled into her lap was now descending the stairs, a bright pink gauze sundress blowing up around her. In spite of all the times she had watched her on television and at the movies, it did not really register that her niece could be a star. It was hard to realize that other people knew Nicole, other people saw her perform. A man in a seersucker jacket was talking animatedly to Nicole. When Lucy held open her arms to catch Nicole, he seemed rather disappointed. The man was clutching an air sickness bag that Nicole had autographed. "Oh, Lucy, it's so sad—this man's neighbor has a son, and the son has muscular dystrophy and he has to sit in a wheelchair and wear a helmet, and I'm his *favorite actress.*" The man smiled and looked apologetic at the same time. He thanked Nicole, backing away, smiling at Lucy, colliding with the man holding the baby as he walked backward. "Boom," the baby said.

"Listen," Nicole said, brushing her hair out of her face, "I hope you're not going to be really mad. The maid quit. We don't have a maid. Mom had it all worked out with Piggy that he was going to take St. Francis, but Piggy had to fly to Hawaii. Mom said you wouldn't die if I brought the dog. Oh, I love the dog so much. He doesn't cause any trouble. Piggy took us to the vet and they gave *poor* St. Francis a shot. He's in a cage. Whether you like it or not, I've got him. Mom gave me money to put him in a kennel if it will really upset you, but please say that he can stay with me. Please, please."

Lucy tried to take in Nicole's rush of words. She had brought the dog. Why hadn't Jane kept the dog? Why did anyone think she would care if Nicole had the dog? Where was the dog?

"You're going to think this is really awful, but Mom's in love. He's a tennis player, and he's twenty-five years old, and they're going to the Inn at Ojai and everything, and Mom just didn't have anyplace to put poor St. Francis but a kennel where he got *gross* fleas . . ."

"Twenty-five?" Lucy said.

"Mom said not to tell you—oh, he's sort of neat. He's taught me all this stuff about playing tennis. He's very handsome. He might be twenty-four and he's going to be twenty-five. This weekend is his birthday, and he was going to introduce me to Chris Evert, but I had my ticket and everything, and they were going to Ojai the next day and everything."

Nicole spotted St. Francis' cage. It was gigantic. She and Nicole had to tug together to pull it off the conveyor belt. "I can do it, oh, let me do it!" Nicole said. She began to unfasten the cage. When the top was lifted, St. Francis shook himself and fell against one side of the cage. Nicole put her arms around his neck. "Oh, I love you, St. Francis. You're all right. You're in Vermont now." The dog's eyes were bloodshot. He tried to stand, and thumped down again. "Is he ever going to forgive us?" Nicole said.

That afternoon, as the tranquilizer wore off, St. Francis dug up a rhododendron. For an encore, he treed the neighbor's cat and killed a frog and dropped it on the doorstep. He peed against the side of the house, under the kitchen window, and ate no dinner. He was the quintessential villainous dog. As Nicole said, he was "a good boy."

5

EDWARD BARTLETT greeted the morning by stretching through the motions of the Sun Salutation. He had brought his own juicer with him. That morning he had concocted, for the three of them, a mixture of fresh orange juice, lemon, Perrier, ice, bananas and protein powder. With his, he swallowed some vitamins in the shape of Flintstones characters. He washed Fred and Wilma down the alimentary and went out into the backyard to do aerobics. When he finished, he changed from his sweatsuit to his business clothes: khaki cut-offs, Nikes, and a recently purchased T-shirt that said: VERMONT—CAN 339,000 COWS BE WRONG?

Move over, Michelangelo: Edward Grant Bartlett III, born L.A., California, September 1, 1950; B.A. Cal State L.A.; M.F.A. Parsons School of Design; favorite hobby, dirt bike racing; last book read, *Foot Reflexology;* most admired American, Phil Spector; was (in the service of a major toy manufacturer) about to capture, for all time, on the sketch pad propped on his easel, the likeness of Nicole Nelson. Less than three months from this very day, the foot-high Nicole would be plastic perfect, dressed, boxed, and shipped—suitable toy or *objet* for any desirous child or dream-struck man who wasn't into inflatables and who didn't already have a paper dolly all his own.

As he sketched, Edward listened, through the earphones of his Sony Walkman, to a tape of conversational Swahili. As she stood in the yard, shielded by a striped beach umbrella, Nicole listened to Duran Duran through her earphones, keeping the beat by tapping the toe of her pink jellies.

Nicole had been in Vermont for two days, and already Lucy's life was in a state of chaos. Jane said that only important people had been given the number, and they had been told to call only if it was essential. So far, this morning's essential calls had come from Nicole's broker, who wanted to say goodbye before he left for a Club Med vacation on Paradise Island, and Nicole's agent, P. G. "Piggy" Proctor, who wanted to finalize plans for Nicole's dangling from the rope of a helicopter with Bobby Blue over the beach at Malibu on behalf of a campaign to raise money for children afflicted with sleep apnea. The last call was a total fluke: a woman selling the World Book encyclopedia.

Lucy was writing her column. She had pulled a stool up to the kitchen counter. Out the window she could see Nicole under the umbrella. The sun was stronger now; Edward had put on a coonskin cap and rubbed zinc oxide over his nose. He wore sunglasses with rectangular black lenses. He looked clinically insane.

Dear Cindi Coeur,

I want to be a nurse, but my boyfriend says that this will embarrass him, because nurses all have a reputation for being loose. He thinks I should be a computer programmer instead. My reason for wanting to be a nurse is that I have juvenile onset diabetes, and becoming a nurse would be a way of thanking the people who helped me all my life and of helping others. I just think my boyfriend has a dirty mind. I told him that if he had a heart attack and went to the hospital, he would be a lot happier to see a nurse than a computer programmer. Our relationship has been horrible since I said this because he thought that I wouldn't have said it if I hadn't been thinking about him being dead. Cindi, I never think about anybody or anything being dead. When I was thirteen I got in trouble with my father because I couldn't face the fact that my goldfish was dead and flush it down the toilet. I know better than to say this to him, though. I need your advice about what I should do with my life.

Diabetic Debbi

Dear Debbi,

Sometimes when you are in doubt about what you should do, it is best, before you act, to imagine the worst possible scenario that could happen. Let's say that you did become a nurse, and that you were on duty when your boyfriend was brought in with a heart attack. Let's say that he died, but before he did, he looked up and saw you, and his last words were that you should have become a computer programmer. Can you imagine keeping it together, and just going on to the next bedpan? If you can, proceed with your choice of occupation.

St. Francis had hollowed out a gully for himself in the patch of rhododendrons. Earlier, Edward had helped her put a stake in the ground so that they could chain him. He saw Lucy outside, sensed the potential for fun, and beat his tail like an otter. She went over and let him loose. He pawed the ground and ran in circles, then ran to Edward, who was still busily sketching Nicole. St. Francis did a double take when he saw the coonskin cap, obviously hoping to raise the tally on the daily death toll (so far it was at one; another frog). St. Francis sniffed the air in front of Edward, sat down, and looked up admiringly.

"So what's the story with that guy Bobby Blue?" Edward said to Nicole, stepping back from his easel.

"His real name's Bobby Bluestein. He had his nose done and his cheek bones pushed up. He's a real mama's boy. His nickname's Bobby Blueballs, because he's never with a girl."

Edward smiled. "I like that," he said.

"I think Derek McAndrew is cute," Nicole said.

"He your fave rave?" Edward said.

"What's 'fave rave'?" Nicole said.

"They used to say that in the fifties," Edward said. "It means the guy you're really crazy about."

"Nobody wants to care about a guy that much," Nicole said. "Nobody's into that anymore."

"Come on," Edward said. "You think a lot about McAndrew, I bet."

"He's good-looking, but he's kind of dumb," Nicole said. "He's always saying how he's going to quit the business and become a doctor. Sure he is."

Edward went back to his sketching. "So who else besides McAndrew do you like?"

"Oh, I don't know," Nicole said. She leaned over, running

her hands down her shins to her ankles, then straightened up again. "Don't say any of this to a reporter," she said.

"I wouldn't," Edward said. "I'm just curious."

"McAndrew gets it on all the time," Nicole said. She looked at Lucy, who was sitting on the grass, patting the dog, looking at her. "Not with me," she said. "With Kate. She just got canceled from the show. They never ate lunch with anybody. They were always off getting it on."

"Come on—she must be forty."

"Why do you think she got canned?" Nicole said.

"What? They didn't know how old she was when they hired her?"

"She won't do anything to make herself attractive," Nicole said. "I think she's on some self-destruction kick. The studio sent her to that place in Sweden to get her face done, and she flew all the way over there and freaked out. She came back looking just the same, but she was walking around the set in clogs. Clogs are so gross."

"Maybe she thinks she's found true love if McAndrew wants to get it on with her all the time even though she's old."

"They're making it because they're on the show together. A lot of people get hung up on that for a while. I'll bet now that she's off the show, he'll never see her again. I heard he was pretty weirded-out that she didn't get her face fixed."

"You go out with McAndrew?" Edward said.

"I don't know. He calls me, and stuff. We've gone to a couple of premieres. We don't really hang out or anything."

"Too young for him?"

"Oh, gag me," Nicole said. "You know, he's in a lot of trouble with his agent for hanging around with Kate. I don't know why they care if it gets out. It's usually the parents who care if that stuff gets around, but he doesn't even have any parents. He lives with his brother. His brother's a real thug. I think he's dropped too much acid. He got in trouble with the cops for smashing some woman's face in—just some woman who hit his car from behind out at the beach. Everybody was teasing Derek, saying he wasn't enough of a star for his brother's name to make the papers."

"You do acid?" Edward said.

"Acid's gross," she said. "Sometimes I like poppers."

"Maybe we ought to suggest to the toy manufacturer that they stuff the Nicole Nelson doll's purse with them," Edward said.

Nicole laughed.

"Who else do you like?" Edward said.

"How come you don't tell me who you like?"

"I don't go out with anybody famous," Edward said.

"Oh," Nicole said.

In the house, the phone was ringing. Lucy decided to let it ring. Since Nicole was staying through July, she should have a separate telephone number. All of the people who called from the Coast simply began talking when she picked up the phone. At first she thought they might have mistaken her voice for Nicole's, but that didn't seem to be it at all. They simply assumed that she would relay the message—that, like a secretary, she was to pass the word along.

St. Francis was stalking a bird. Just as he got within pouncing distance, the bird flew away. St. Francis had a little temper tantrum, sniffing the ground where the bird had been, then digging up dirt until Lucy told him to stop. A jogger in green shorts passed by on the dirt road. It was a breezy day, but graying over as if it might rain. The sky, mottled with dark clouds, looked like an enormous x-ray that had been hung out to dry. St. Francis settled down in his gully beside the rhododendron bush and closed his eyes. When another runner came by, the dog sensed it and his head shot up. He dropped his head again as the runner panted by.

Edward made them tabouli burgers for lunch. He had brought these, frozen, in a cooler that said It's Miller Time!, from Los Angeles.

Over lunch, he gave Nicole pointers on how to be popular. "First of all, if you're lucky enough to be an object to people, you can't go wrong. They just care about what you look like—they don't want to hear what you have to say, and they don't not want to hear what you have to say. So with them, you're just talking to amuse yourself. I find that two things are very useful when you want to put yourself across. The first one is to know about a dozen pieces of misinformation, and then to know what the correct information is. Take this for an example: Most people think that Humphrey Bogart said, 'Drop the gun, Louis.' What did he really say?"

Nicole frowned. "Lauren Bacall was married to him, wasn't she?" she said.

"What did he say?" Lucy said.

"He said, 'Not so fast, Louis.' " Edward looked at Lucy. "Now here's what you do to make an impression. You work the conversation around to Humphrey Bogart, and when somebody comes out with a famous line—everybody loves to do their Bogart routine, so you're usually in luck—you mention that he didn't say that at all, but that it's always misquoted. Say it casually, so you don't seem like a snot. Tell them the right line. And this part is crucial: if they ask you where you found something out, never tell them. Make them think that you always knew it. You have to be nice about that, too, or they'll think you're a snot. Obviously, you can go wrong with this routine, so you've got to be careful."

"Do you do this stuff?" Nicole asked.

"If I have to. To tell you the truth, it works better for women than for men. But the other thing I'm going to tell you will work for anybody. Everybody talks about the weather, right? And if they don't, it's the easiest thing in the world to make them talk about it. So what you do is you really know something about the weather. Say you're with a bunch of people and a wind blows up. Or there's no wind at all—you can still use it. You get the subject around to the wind, and then you mention the Worcester tornado of 1953. You lead up to it, actually, by not naming it so officially, so that people think you memorized some arcane information. You say, 'This reminds me of that tornado in Massachusetts," and of course somebody'll ask what you're talking about. Tell them the one that happened in the early fifties. That's the trick. You let them draw you out, so that you become progressively more specific. Then whatever you say will have a real impact. Then you move in for the kill: you tell them the thing cut through Rutland, Barre, and Worcester and killed more than sixty people. You don't want to have too many facts. You don't want to tell them how many were injured. Also, you don't want to mention the weather more than once in one night. It can also make people very nervous."

"I don't know," Nicole said. "Last year I had to memorize all these Shakespearean sonnets that didn't make any sense. The guy had some good ideas, but he was always going off . . . it was like the teacher expected you to remember what some guy said when he'd tied a couple on. Now you want me to memorize things about tornadoes?"

"Forget education," Edward said. "The difference between what I'm telling you and education is that this stuff will help you. Memorize it, then get loose, make it seem natural that you know about disasters."

"Maybe being smart would distract me. I don't want to be frustrated when I get roles and be like Kate and some of those people who think their characters never know enough, and they should be so intelligent and everything."

"Hey, you're playing the game," Edward said. "You've got to know some things to talk about so you can stay on top. You've got to figure out a way to stay on top, whether you're a phony or a real person."

Well, Lucy thought, maybe this was, after all, just a strange version of summer camp she was running in the backyard, where the big kids gave the little kids pointers about proper behavior in deep water.

6

AT eight o'clock on the Fourth of July, Hildon and Maureen, Lucy and Nicole, Noonan and his newly acquired lover Peter, pulled into the Birches to pick up Edward. They were going to drive into town and have a drink on the patio outside the inn, then walk down the hill to see the fireworks. Peter's car was a repainted, refurbished Checker cab. It was silver, with a black roof. The jump seats were upholstered with leopardskin; there was a black bear rug on the back floor. It was the sort of car any cop would give his eyeteeth to stop.

Peter specialized in *in utero* surgery: According to Noonan, he made vasts amounts of money, which he also invested wisely. He had bought into Coleco pre-Cabbage Patch and sold pre-Adam. Currently, he had been buying stock in a company that produced herbal vinegar. He felt that the vinegar market was always expanding.

Maureen was wearing a white T-shirt, patterned with red stars, and navy-blue culottes.

Hildon had opened a bottle of Dom Pérignon, and was pouring it, badly, into plastic cups.

Even with the windows open, marijuana smoke lingered in the air; it was enough to give anyone a contact high.

Noonan was singing "Yankee Doodle."

Nicole said, "I'm glad that there's some life in this town."

Peter was turning around one of the rotaries. It was filled with petunias and marigolds. Life in this town? Obviously, Nicole meant that they were lively, inside the car: they were passing the Ben Franklin, the church, and other cars, with couples in the front and babies in back. Some days Lucy felt as embarrassed not to have a baby in this town as she had felt in high school when everybody else had a little ladybug pin on the collar of her blouse. It was as though the rest of the world paid attention to detail, lived by it, and she was the outsider, not bonded to anyone by any discernible symbol. A bee that had buzzed in one window flew out the other. Everyone ducked. That was why she had thought about ladybugs and Ladybug blouses. Not because she felt like an outsider, but because the bee flying through the car . . .

"I just filled it two seconds ago," Hildon laughed. He clapped his hand over her knee. It steadied her, and that felt absolutely wonderful. In the three seconds that he had his hand clapped over her knee, Maureen had looked at Hildon, while Hildon was looking at Lucy's legs. Then Maureen had caught Lucy's eye. Lucy had been looking at her.

In the front seat, Peter said, "For instance: basil repels mosquitoes. So when you add basil to vinegar . . ."

"I'm so glad I changed my life," Noonan said, massaging Peter's neck.

"I'm going to be a millionaire," Hildon said, drinking the last of the champagne straight from the bottle.

"I don't even believe what people on the East Coast are like," Nicole said.

Before Nicole came, Jane had told Lucy that in preparation for her trip, Nicole was reading *Main Street.* While she had been reading the *Enquirer*, Nicole had been reading Sinclair Lewis.

Already, firecrackers were exploding, Peter parked in a crosswalk, across from the inn.

"Just think," Edward said. "Next year at this time, little girls will be taking their Nicole Nelson doll to the fireworks. They'll be combing her hair and losing her little shoes and crying. Their baby sisters and brothers will be teething on her head. They'll save their allowance to buy a poodle for Nicole to walk on a leash. They'll all want to grow up, shrink, and be plastic."

"Oh, gross," Nicole said.

"Maybe we can get them to package the doll with a St.

Francis dog. The dog can go on search and destroy missions for Barbie," Edward said.

"Ken is a wimp," Peter said. "He gives homosexuals a bad name."

"Who's Ken?" Maureen said.

"The Ken doll. He has a little chef's hat that he's supposed to wear out to the barbecue pit. It makes him look like one of those paper-frilled lamb chops."

"I don't even *believe* that you guys keep up with Barbie and Ken," Nicole said.

"Hildon," Lucy said, in the brief moment she had to speak to him privately, as he held open the back door for them to get out, "Maureen is looking at me."

"So am I," he said.

A college girl in a scooped-neck green dress with ruffles around the neck and hem gave them a table on the side patio. The sky was chalky, and a band of pink was widening on the horizon. A Japanese tourist took a picture of his wife, who was sitting on the stone wall that wound around the patio. He handed the camera to his wife and stood in front of the wall, hands straight at his sides.

Another girl came and asked what they would like to drink. After Edward ordered a Rémy, he pushed his chair back and went over to the tourists, who seemed to be trying to get their waitress' eye to take their picture. They both seemed very happy when they realized Edward was volunteering to do it. Edward raised the camera to his eye, then lowered it.

"You have a fisheye lens on here," he said.

"Thank you very much," the man said. He put his arm around his wife's shoulder. His fingertips rested on the wing of a large, embroidered butterfly. She was brushing his hand away when Edward clicked the camera. The man smiled and rushed forward.

"Let me take one more," Edward said. "I caught you just when you were moving your hand."

"Thank you," the man said.

"One more," Edward said, holding up his finger. He pointed to the camera.

"Thank you," the man said, walking back to where his wife stood. He stood beside her, as rigid as a soldier standing beside a tree. Edward took the picture.

"Thank you very much," the man said, taking the camera from Edward and walking back to his table.

There were small Wedgwood bud vases on the tables, with a pink tea rose, a daisy, and a bachelor's button in each. The scalloped edge of the yellow and white striped canopy blew in the breeze. In the street, five boys were yelling and playing wheelies with their bikes. A little white dog ran along the curb, yapping at them.

The Japanese tourists were deep in conversation, staring at their table but looking away when anyone at the table looked at them.

The inn didn't have Perrier, so Nicole ordered ginger ale. It came with a cherry and a slice of orange on the rim. The waitress put another brandy snifter in front of Edward, and frozen strawberry daiquiris in front of the rest. "Shirley Temple," she said, as she put Nicole's drink down.

"What?" Nicole said.

"You know what that is, don't you?" Edward said.

"I don't even know what you're *talking* about," Nicole said.

"It's what they call that—ginger ale. No alcohol."

"Is he putting me on?" Nicole said.

"No," Lucy said.

"Bobby Blue's mother collects Shirley Temple stuff. She has cups with Shirley Temple on them and dolls and all. When Bobby was a baby, he had golden hair, and she used to curl it like Shirley Temple's. I think Shirley Temple is gross."

"What's wrong with her?" Maureen said.

"When she was a kid they used to tie a tourniquet around her breasts so she'd still look like a little girl. That's so sick."

"They did that to Judy Garland," Peter said.

"God," Nicole said. "No studio would do that now. They just tell lies about people's age and stuff. That's really pointless most of the time—like, they're really not going to find out your age if you went to Hollywood High, right? Sure."

"To Gary Hart," Noonan said, raising his glass.

"Who?" Nicole said.

"You're kidding," Maureen said.

No one pursued it.

"No wonder those kids that were in the movies back then went crazy. It's really sick to tie down people's tits. I'll bet you that doesn't happen to anybody now," Noonan said.

Nicole took a sip of her ginger ale. "I know a girl who had silicone put in her calves so they'd be pretty for this beach movie she was making. Something went wrong and all the stuff fell into her ankles and she had to have an operation."

"Excuse me," the Japanese tourist said. His hands were clasped over the front of his camera. He bowed his head so that his chin almost touched his hands. "Excuse me: I am Stephanie Sykes." He lit up with a smile and nodded his head again.

"Stephanie Sykes," Hildon said. He looked at Nicole.

Nicole smiled. She had been recognized.

"Doctor Cooper!" the tourist said.

"Me? No. I'm not on the show. I'm an artist. A photographer," Edward said.

"I'm a photographer," the man said.

"You're a photographer too?" Edward said.

"I'm a photographer," the man said, smiling and pointing at Edward.

"Oh, I am," Edward said. "Yes."

"Thank you very much," the man said.

Lucy caught his wife's eye, across the patio. The woman smiled at her. The man reached across the table and she shook his hand. "I am good Stephanie Sykes," he said.

"Thank you," Nicole said.

The man smiled and bowed and went back to his table. At the table next to theirs a man who looked familiar to Lucy sat with a tall blond woman and a curly-haired little girl. The little girl was pleading with them to buy her a Duran Duran album. "Is he the one who dresses like a girl?" the man said. "That's Boy George. Everybody knows that," the little girl said. "What's the story with Boy George?" the man said. "Does he do break dancing?" It was the man she had seen at the airport, with the baby. The next time she looked, both the woman and man were looking at their table. Lucy smiled. Under the table, Hildon rubbed her knee. Peter removed a piece of lint from Noonan's shirt. In the distance fireworks were exploding. The waitress came to the table and asked if they wanted another round.

"I think we'd better move on down the line," Hildon said.

"Just bring me one more Rémy to bolt down with the check," Edward said, handing her his gold American Express card.

"No, no," Noonan said, reaching for his wallet.

"Expense account," Edward said.

The little girl from the other table got up and walked away. The woman looked at the man and sighed. "You shouldn't tease her so much," she said. "She sat still this afternoon when you explained what the different birds were. She doesn't have any particular interest in birds, you know. You wouldn't like it if she pretended she couldn't keep a crow straight from a swallow."

"I wasn't putting her on that time," he said.

"Pretend to be a little interested, even if you aren't," the woman said.

"I listen to this stuff night and day. How am I supposed to keep it all straight?" The man finished his drink and took a sip of his wife's wine.

The waitress came back to the table with the bill. There was a little piece of paper with "Stephanie Sykes" written on it. Edward looked surprised. He handed it to Nicole. Nicole read it and shook her head. She handed it to Lucy, seeming slightly embarrassed. "I am just a dishwasher," the note said, "but I love Stephanie Sykes. I will treasure your ginger ale glass always.—Harry Woods."

Maureen read it over Lucy's shoulder. "It must be the strangest feeling to be recognized. Especially if you don't even know who's watching you," Maureen said.

"Really," Nicole said. "I mean, you have to think about it because there are a lot of guys like that guy Hinckley."

"Don't even talk about it," Lucy said.

More fireworks exploded. Maureen laughed nervously. Hildon rubbed Lucy's knee under the table, so hard that the top part of her body swayed. Maureen saw her moving, and Lucy looked down, pretending that she had been moving intentionally and that something was wrong with the seat of the chair.

"Jodie Foster was so great in *Taxi Driver*," Nicole said. "It's too bad he couldn't have picked somebody obscure to give her career a boost."

"That's thinking business," Edward said, raising his empty brandy snifter to Nicole.

Nicole said, "It's getting breezy. I wonder if we're going to have a tornado."

"A tornado?" Edward said. "That isn't likely. Of course, I guess people never expect a tornado. Do you really think they cause as much destruction as people make out?"

"Are you crazy?" Maureen said. "Of course they do."

"There was that one in New England," Nicole said. "That one in the early fifties in . . . Worcester. Sixty people died, and there's no telling how many were hurt."

"Did your family have friends in Worcester?" Maureen said.

"No," Nicole said. "That was just one of the most damaging tornadoes, so it was the one that came to mind."

As they walked away from the table, Maureen said to Noonan, "Imagine that. She'd never heard of one of the presidential candidates and she knew about some tornado that hit New England before she was born. You've got to wonder what kind of an education kids are getting nowadays."

Noonan put his arm around her shoulder and squeezed. He was smiling ear to ear.

"What?" Maureen said. "I'm being stuffy?"

With his free hand, Noonan reached in his pants pocket. Noonan had stolen the ashtray.

7

THE newspaper assigned Myra DeVane to write the *Country Daze* story. There was no background information on any of the staff, so for most of the story she was going to have to rely on interviews. She wanted to do a good job, because she wanted to move on from Vermont to an important paper like the Boston *Globe.* She needed some more impressive press clips before she applied for a job like that though. If this group of people was anywhere near as interesting as their writing, it wasn't going to be difficult to write a good story. The new publisher, whom she had spoken to in person, had about as much class as John Belushi, doing Samurai Swordsman. She couldn't wait to see what the editor was like.

On Monday she went to the *Country Daze* headquarters, a remodeled turn-of-the-century house off the main street. Tomato plants were staked on the front lawn. It had been recently painted, but the yard, with patches of burned grass and bushes in need of trimming, made it look a little run down.

The law office to the left had a neat privet hedge across the front and window boxes filled with geraniums. The window boxes on the *Country Daze* house were empty. Perhaps this lack of concern with exteriors indicated that real work was going on inside and there was no time for perfecting their image. If she liked them, she would mention that in her lead.

Downstairs, as she came in, was a young woman in her twenties. Her bangs looked like overcooked bacon. The rest of her hair was pulled back in a bun. She was typing on what looked like the horizontal control panel of a jet plane. The typewriter looked particularly out of place next to the telephones, both circa 1950 black, that sat beside it on the desk. The desk was a round oak table. There was a straight-back oak chair pulled up to one side, as if someone might be dropping by for tea. A two-foot-high plastic pig carrying a red suitcase stood at the front of the desk, in lieu of a bud vase. It was studded with memos. As she answered the phone, the secretary took messages and peeled pieces of paper off a pad, which she stuck to the pig. Someone had put a little toupee between the pig's ears.

The secretary led her up the stairs to Hildon's office. He had on white gym shorts, a black T-shirt, socks, and running shoes. His feet were on his desk. He smiled at her when she walked in, and kept talking on the phone. "Quote, He'll be right with you, end quote," the secretary said, and turned and left.

Myra had seen him before but she couldn't think where. He was too handsome for her to be mistaking him for someone else. She felt herself stiffening, going on guard against someone who exuded such confidence. She found out his background: an only child from a middle-class family who went to prep school and to Yale, dodged the draft, was admitted to law school at the University of Virginia and dropped out. A year as a reporter himself, for the Detroit *Free Press.* Married, no children. Got tired of city life, moved to the country, turned a profit selling real estate and decided to start a magazine. According to Hildon, he had just been in the right place at the right time; instead of the Let's-Open-a-Restaurant dream, he had started a magazine and put a lot of his friends to work. He saw the magazine as an extended family, a continuation of the life he and his friends had led in college. Obviously they were beating the system, and while he didn't think he or this bunch was representative, he was sure that they all felt very lucky and grateful. The staff had been expanded—no, no one had left, except for one reporter who was going to leave, but that was because he had decided he wanted to be on the West Coast; it had nothing to do with dissatisfaction with the magazine. Social satire was perhaps too vague a description of what they did, really; some of it was satirical, but much of it he simply thought of as eclectic. The magazine, then, was really what he was inclined to publish—something that had to do with his own concerns and the things that amused him? Yes, but he didn't think that he was unrepresentative either, and in a way the success of the magazine proved that: he wasn't the only one who cared about social issues and who also had a sense of humor. While he didn't want to seem to wave the flag, he didn't think that a lot of stereotypes about Americans pertained anymore; most Baby Boomers were well-educated, united by their opposition to the Vietnam war, people who had had their consciousness raised about nutrition and ecology . . . he really thought that there was a large thinking population out there, and he was pleased that they were pleased with *Country Daze.* Could he characterize his audience? Well—he did not think that many farmers wanting advice about what fertilizer to use took the magazine home after flipping through it on the stands. Something for coffee-table flipping in New York? Well, they got a lot of mail and it wasn't all from New York. Look at what a cross section of the population tuned in to the Prairie Home Companion. Snob appeal? He hoped that it was promoting a sense of mutual amusement, a sense of camaraderie, rather than being something taken up by an elitist minority. The mail suggested . . .

She asked if she could see some of the mail later.

Of course.

If he preferred to talk in the office or whether he would have time for lunch.

Fine, if she had time herself for lunch.

Surely he must be aware that the magazine was seen as a rather cultish . . .

Oh, because people were devoted to something, he would not jump to the conclusion that they were a cult. Perhaps, too, she was overestimating the influence and even importance of the magazine, which was only natural because of the nature of her assignment: when she had to take it out of context, that always focused a lot of attention on something, whereas . . .

Johnny Carson didn't bother to put it in context, when he referred to it in his monologue the other night. Something like that elevated the person or thing mentioned to . . .

And did *she* think of *herself* as cultish for watching the *Tonight* show?

Well, that was hardly something only the cognoscenti knew about, after all these years.

Still: couldn't she see *Country Daze* as something that united people, instead of—as she implied—something divisive?

Could he describe himself as a counterculture Johnny Carson, then?

He wouldn't be happy with that. He wasn't a public figure, and that was as it should be.

Didn't he think that as the magazine circulated more, he was going to have to deal with personal fame?

No no no; movie actors were glamorous, not writers and editors.

Clark Kent.

That was so clearly a figure of masculine authority that it was rather irrelevant that he had been a mild-mannered reporter. What that was *really* about was macho defensiveness, a maintenance of the status quo by showing that even the meepiest, most inconsequential man can dash . . .

He excused himself, and changed into more formal attire (jeans) for lunch.

If he couldn't have predicted that the magazine would be such a success, maybe his sense of a large, homogeneous group of Americans wasn't as sure as he said.

Luck was a factor. It was certainly less of a gamble than Pet Rocks or Trivial Pursuit. He realized he was taking a gamble and he hoped that it would work; this success was just very gratifying.

But he did feel that he had his finger on the pulse . . .

Well—since he had mentioned Trivial Pursuit, was it really the case that those guys, sitting around brainstorming in a bar, thought that they were brilliant sensors of what people wanted at just that moment? Didn't they just decide that taking a long shot would be worth the gamble?

He had an Amstel Light. She had a glass of white wine. They were sitting at a sidewalk café with red tablecloths and uncomfortable chairs. Her knee kept hitting his by mistake.

Was it true that Garry Trudeau was doing the comic strip, under a pseudonym?

No. Cameron Petrus did it.

Quite a few people loved that strip. They liked the fact that the main character always had such a bad time that he dropped dead in the last frame. Wasn't this a serious social comment, disguised . . .

Have to ask Cameron.

But taken all together: the inevitable death in Petrus' column, the unhelpful, off-the-wall advice given by Cindi Coeur to people with problems, the—what would you call it?—fantasy fiction in which people killed IRS agents and their landlords . . . Did he really think that the people who liked those things were just having a lighthearted laugh, or wasn't it possible that people actually felt alienated and angry, and that out of their despair . . .

She'd be talking to people about their reaction to the magazine. What she found out would be telling, of course.

But people weren't good at psychoanalyzing themselves.

He ordered spinach ravioli. She ordered an avocado stuffed with crab. One more Amstel. One more wine.

He was always amazed at how much people would tell writers. They probably *would* try to analyze their reactions for her. Wasn't she amazed at what people would say, for the record?

Yes. But that might have to do with the fact that she was a woman, and in spite of knowing that she was a reporter, they didn't quite take her seriously.

People had always told him things for the record when he had been a reporter. It was almost suicidal.

She asked whether, apropos of his earlier remark about psychoanalysis, the column Analysts Say the Darndest Things was made up, or whether people sent in these howlers.

It started as a made-up column, but the readers began to send in true stories that were better than the things the staff had been thinking up.

The cooking column?

That was made up. And he must say, the suggestions for preparing field mice . . .

What magazines did he read?

The New Yorker, the *Atlantic*, *Time*, *Geo*, *Connoisseur*, *Paris Review* and *Architectural Digest*.

What did he do when he wasn't working on the magazine?

He really worked very hard putting out the magazine.

He had a wife, didn't he?

She enjoyed gardening.

What about Cindi Coeur?

Lucy? He had known her for fifteen years. Since college. An extended family, indeed. It was too bad Myra had missed the annual staff party. But she might want to come to the Friday meeting and see if she could line people up to talk to afterward.

He picked up the check. She asked if she could go back to the office with him—try to get a feel for the place, keeping out of the way, of course—perhaps take a look at some of the mail if that wouldn't be an inconvenience.

Last sip of beer. He paid the bill in cash.

Who put the pig on the desk?

Instead of a water cooler, they had Bennie the Seltzer Man deliver. It wasn't Madison Avenue, after all.

Had he ever been tempted by that?

Madison Avenue? Of course not.

What if *Country Daze* hadn't been a success?

He'd probably be doing what she was doing: a reporter, somewhere.

Who *did* put the pig there?

Noonan. And from time to time he decorated it: a scarf in the winter. That was a merkin on its head right now.

A what?

You're the reporter.

Must be nice to work in a casual environment. Did he get along with Matt Smith?

A great guy.

He had sold the magazine at quite a profit.

Yes, he had.

Was there a new project on the horizon?

He was very happy editing the magazine.

He certainly did present himself as being complacent, happy, grateful—somebody who had just been very lucky.

He had been.

What about the other part?

He hoped that he was a little more complicated than that.

If the staff felt as grateful to be escaping Madison Avenue and the system in general as he did, they must be quite devoted to him.

There were disagreements. No matter what business you're in, there will be disagreements.

It was an unusual success story. She didn't mean to suggest that things were other than what he said—it was just a very untypical situation.

He started the car.

"Where are you from?" he said.

"Washington, D.C. I grew up there and in Alexandria."

"My roommate at Yale came from Alexandria. His father owned some restaurants around Washington. Ever eat at La Toque?"

"I took my mother there for her birthday!"

"Still live there, huh?"

"They're divorced. My mother lives in Old Town. My father lives in Paris."

"Visit him in Paris?"

"Once. In London, actually. I was in London for a week, and he flew there to see me."

"I spent a year in Europe when I got out of college. The dollar's so strong now, I wish I had the time to go back there. Even Paris is cheap."

"At least you're not a nine to fiver. You've got so much freedom. People must envy you."

"Some people think I'm a bum. They don't understand that you've been awake all night on deadline night if they catch you out in a rowboat the next day."

"Lake Venue?"

"I've been there a few times. It'll be better next week, when the mosquitoes disappear."

He had taken a Valium before lunch, because he knew he would have to speak to a reporter, and the effect of the pill and the beer was drowsiness.

The silver Checker was parked in front of the driveway beside the *Country Daze* building. They parked a block away and walked back. Remembering the Fourth, Hildon thought what a welcome thing a hit of grass would be, to smooth things out even more. With his luck—with Myra DeVane in tow—Noonan would be there smoking a joint, as casually as George Burns out on the porch, smoking a cigar.

When they walked in, Noonan was walking out the door. "You the reporter?" he said to Myra. "I'm Noonan, the one who holds everything together here. Off the record, this man is a Communist and is planning to run for office as a Republican. I'm on my way to lunch or I'd tell you more." Noonan continued out the door.

The secretary had on earphones. She smiled when Noonan started talking, but did not stop typing. A month ago, when Hildon had gone to bed with Elena, she had not removed her earphones. She had been listening to a tape of a Jerry Lewis Telethon. Hildon noticed that the pig had epaulets of memos, and its stomach was entirely covered with white paper. He cocked his head and read a few of them without removing any, and walked up the stairs, with Myra behind him.

He gestured for Myra to walk into the mailroom. There was a Victorian sofa he and Lucy had bought at an estate sale the year before, and he had brought some lamps from his house—things Maureen didn't want when she redecorated. It was a comfortable room; sometimes at the end of the day Hildon went there and stretched out and read mail. There were more letters stacked in trays marked "In," "Out," and "Coitus Interruptus." There were several letter openers on the table.

"Make yourself at home," Hildon said. "Come and get me, or go downstairs and get Elena if you have any questions."

When Hildon left, she walked to the window and looked out.

It was a view of town she hadn't seen; a few stories higher up, she could have looked down on the domed roof of the bank. She looked into the empty window boxes. A squirrel ran up the trunk of a dead elm, then ran down again, circled the tree, and dashed into an alleyway.

She had only read half a dozen letters in the In basket when she came to one that interested her so much that she read it again, and then transcribed it:

> Dear Cindi Coeur,
>
> My problem is my former lover. She writes an advice column for messed-up people, but the joke is, she is very messed up herself. She has never broken the tie—or made a real connection—with the man who is now her boss and longtime on-again, off-again lover. Years ago, I thought that if we left New York and moved to Vermont, they could confront the situation (Vermont is also where he is in hiding from being a serious person) and find out for themselves what was real and what was a delusion. Are they hedonists or masochists? Nothing has made them figure it out, including my leaving. Don't you miss me? Aren't you tired of avoiding yourself and of parodying somebody who does care about people's problems? Now that you don't have me to analyze anymore, have you spent any time trying to figure yourself out? I'll tell you one thing: you're a hard act to follow. Can we see each other?
>
> Love Always,
> Les

8

LIKE the heroine of her favorite novel, there were many things that Maureen would never do: drink tequila; give blood; do volunteer work; put into practice what Hildon had taught her about changing a tire; sharpen her own knives; read Proust; bargain for lower prices at the vegetable stand at the end of the day; have oral sex; learn the metric system; snorkel; have a conversation with a Jehovah's Witness; do acrostics.

She had just done one of those things, and it was the most horrible thing imaginable.

Maureen had decided that she needed to change her life. She had lost her sense of herself, and she had to regain it. It was not that she had been Hildon's wife too long, but rather that it did not seem that she was anybody's anything. When she decided to be Matt Smith's lover, she thought that would spite Hildon, but actually doing something like that was self-destructive: she was only being spiteful to herself.

She did what people always did in the movies when they were having a crisis. She looked in the mirror. Even trying as hard as she could, her face was so familiar to her that she did not know how objective she could be.

She was at least attractive. It might make her prettier if she had her hair streaked, lightened around the face. She might go back to buying and wearing the candy-colored clothes she had liked as a student at Mary Baldwin College. She might affect that southern accent again, slightly. None of it would do any good if she continued to be surrounded by the bizarre, self-indulgent people who had been part of her life since Hildon's magazine became such a success. But before she could meet new people, she would have to restore her self-confidence. And today, Davina Cole, for a mere $50 an hour, was going to help her to be the best person she could be.

As Davina explained it, her approach was part psychotherapy, part whole body reconditioning, and part assertiveness training.

In preparation for their session, Maureen, as Davina had instructed, had tried to get a good night's sleep and had had mineral water with orange juice for breakfast and eaten lightly. Davina had had a photograph of Maureen enlarged, cut out, and backed with cardboard. She leaned it against the wall as they talked. This black and white Maureen was almost life size. It was quite eerie, having it there in the living room: Maureen in her sarong, smiling.

"When you look at that, what do you see?" Davina said.

Maureen looked at it a long time. "I don't know," she said.

"You see an attractive woman smiling, don't you?"

"Maybe I look silly."

"Please don't think of the statue as 'I.' Try to tell me only what you see."

"I think I see a woman who isn't especially attractive. Just an ordinary woman."

"What is the part you think is most attractive?"

Maureen thought about it. The legs were nice; the calves thin and shapely. The hair was long, thick, and rather dramatic. She knew that her eyes were probably her best feature, but the blowup had almost obliterated detail, so that they were oval, muddy pools. "The hair," she said.

"Good," Davina said. "Concentrate on that for a few minutes."

Maureen tried to concentrate on her hair, but her attention kept drifting. She was more worried about Hildon coming home while this was going on than she had been the time she went to bed with Matt Smith.

"Reach up and stroke your hair," Davina said. "Say out loud: 'I have lovely, luxurious hair.' "

"I have lovely, luxurious hair," Maureen said, stroking her hands down the sides of her hair.

"Do you believe that?" Davina said.

"Well, of course, many people . . ."

"We aren't interested in many people. We are interested in you. Do you believe that this is true of you?"

"Yes," Maureen said.

"Society has taught us to turn aside compliments, which is wrong enough in itself, but which is very harmful if we take a simple fact to be a compliment. Now, tell me something else about your hair."

"My hair is long."

"Your hair, then, is the most impressive thing you notice about yourself; it is luxurious, lovely, and long. That's very good, and easy to remember, because it alliterates."

Davina opened a canvas bag she had brought with her. She took out a white towel, went over to the statue, and draped it over the hair.

"Find something else to admire," she said.

Maureen smiled; with the sarong tied around her and the towel thrown over her hair, it looked like she had just come out of the shower.

"The legs," Maureen said.

"What about them?"

"They're shapely."

"Fine. What else?"

"You mean what else are my legs?"

"Yes."

"They're not muscular."

"Not what they aren't, what they are."

"They're smooth."

"Fine. Your legs are shapely and smooth. That's going to be very easy to remember, also, because it alliterates. Are you a writer?"

"I'm nothing."

"That's why I'm here: to prove you wrong. Your identity is not what you do. It is the wholeness of you. Your essence, which we will get to later. But today we are already noticing that the statue has some attractive features. Let me cover your legs and see what else you can find for me."

She reached in her bag and took out a piece of material and two thumbtacks. She tacked it over the legs.

"Nothing else in particular," Maureen said.

"Nothing here?" Davina said, pointing to her arms.

"They're just arms."

"And here?" she said, pointing to Maureen's breasts.

"I think they're ordinary breasts."

"Here?" Davina said, pointing to her ribs.

"Nothing really. I'm not fat, but you just want to hear what I am, not what I'm not."

Davina stood there a minute, considering the statue. She took off the material and the towel. "All right, then. You are not conscious of your face or of your arms or of your chest or torso." She reached in the bag and took out a clipboard, flipped through, and removed four pieces of paper. She handed them to Maureen. They were exercises for those parts of the body that, Davina said, would help make her more conscious of them. She was to exercise, as the little diagrams instructed her, and tell Davina the following week whether she did not feel a new awareness and more positive response to parts of her body. She was also to develop and improve the parts she admired; Davina thought that streaking her hair would be a good idea. She thought that mesh stockings would indeed accentuate Maureen's shapely legs.

"Do you believe that you have rights?"

"What?" Maureen said.

"Do you believe that you have rights?"

"Yes, of course, but . . ."

"Maureen: are you *certain* that you think that *of course* you have rights?"

"Well, yes."

"What are some of these rights?"

"I have the right to be happy."

"Specific rights, please. Not general rights. I don't want to hear you recite the Declaration of Independence. I want to hear what your specific rights are, in your life."

"It is my right to tell people when they call and I am sleeping that they have awakened me and that they shouldn't call so early."

"Very good. Tell yourself that you will do this the next time someone interrupts your sleep."

Maureen nodded.

"Out loud."

"When I'm sleeping and somebody wakes me up, I'm going to tell them that they have disturbed me and that they should see what time it is before they call."

"What other rights do you have?"

"It's my right to tell my husband that I insist that he stop having an affair with Lucy Spenser."

"Don't be ridiculous," Davina said. "No one can stop men from having affairs. This brings up a crucial point: it is impossible to have rights when you have no power. When you truly know the power you do have, you will spend less time worrying about the power you don't have."

Davina's watch alarm buzzed.

"I know he's sleeping with Lucy Spenser. Don't you think it's my right, even according to the Ten Commandments, which forbid adultery . . ."

"Maureen, please: it will do us no good if you continue to think in terms of the Declaration of Independence and of the Ten Commandments. Naturally, on the Fourth of July, or on Sunday when you are in church, they may come to mind, but you cannot let them determine your thinking. You must concentrate on what is truly the case or likely to be the case, and increase your power so that you can deal forcefully and effectively."

Davina was taking a piece of plastic out of her purse, and a hanger. She slipped the hanger in a groove on the back of the statue, held the top of the hanger, and lifted it. Maureen dangled. She moved Maureen to the sofa and slipped the plastic over the statue, and tied the bottom with a twist-o-flex.

"I should tell you," she said, as she walked toward the front door, "although this is probably premature, that if you continue to be troubled by your husband's infidelity, it is your good luck that I have an ex–sister-in-law who practices witchcraft."

9

"LIGHTS! Camera! Action!

"Who says that? Nobody says that. Let's take it from the top. People *do* say that. It makes sense, too. Think about all the people who are tempted to take it from the bottom.

"That was a bad joke.

"Hello, sweetheart. For one trillion zillion dollars and all the love that will fit onto a microchip, can you tell me who's talking to you?

"Look! Up in the sky! It's a bird. It's a plane. It's irrelevant if you're farsighted. You don't have to see to know that it's Piggy Proctor, talking to you via TDK cassette. What you see as you hear my voice, no doubt, is a bird taking flight, and if there's a plane, it's a coincidence. You never looked up thinking you'd see Superman to begin with, did you? There you are, enjoying the beauty of nature in the country, and the real Superman is off making babies with his longtime love, Gay Exton.

"I can just hear you now: what do you *want*, Piggy?

"What's to want, except your continued success. Never doubt me. As sure as they'll never put fluorescent lighting in the Polo Lounge, Piggy Proctor lives for your continued success.

"*Su casa, mi casa.*

"I am calling today with very good news. Just as you were beginning to feel like a yacht without water, what should happen but that the heavens open, and rain pours down for however many days and however many nights, and suddenly there is a vast ocean on which to set sail; you are buoyed up, higher and higher, until suddenly it is September, and all around you a new ocean of possibility: you are aboard Noah's Ark, and Piggy is with you. Where will the boat dock? On NBC. And where's the beef? *Not only* have they decided to revive the series—not only have they decided to cough up under the influence of Piggy Proctor's Heimlich Maneuvering, but they are going to a *nightly* half hour if they are pleased with the results of the pilot. Our new sponsor is a company in the Midwest that makes dehydrated oatmeal that puffs up when it hits milk. A bunch of neo-hippie capitalists sell the company and they decide to *diversify*, and what do they decide to gamble on but a girl whose fame they think will expand faster than oatmeal pellets.

"The Nicole Nelson doll is being produced at just the right time. And in addition, there's going to be a novelization of the series, to the point where it left off. It's going to be . . . why isn't this on my VDT, where it ought to be? . . . going to be monologues by all the primary characters. The book is going to be called *Barren*, and under that title it says 'Passionate Intensity,' and below that on the dummy there's *you*, on a television screen—a CU slightly in profile. Your hair is windswept and you look great.

"Now: the man who's doing this novelization seems to be a very serious fellow. He wants to talk to everybody in the cast, so I'm sure you'll be obliging. The guy's got credentials that would sound good played on a kazoo. He's written another novelization, I mean a novel, that was nominated for the National Book Critics Circle award, and he wrote a book on Vietnam—scratch that: he wrote something on Venus de Milo, an article or whatever it was—you tell me why my secretary can't make simple, comprehensible entries on this disc. It looks like I've called up a fucking dream journal instead of a bio.

"I'm having the guy call you. I understand that he wants to come up, down, wherever the hell Vermont is, to interview you for a couple of days. Try to get back into the *Passionate Intensity* mind-set before he gets there. And get Lucy to send me receipts when she bills the corporation. I can't go into Llewellyn's office and talk up a hundred dollar dead animal. He thinks everything's rechanneled money for drugs. I said, 'You don't know what life is like in the country. Nicole's got a dog, it's her necessary protection, it guards her and we deduct the Alpo bills from her taxes, right? You don't think that sometimes maybe the dog makes a mistake and kills a sheep, or whatever?' Here's the good part: I said, 'Would I pull the wool over your eyes?' You tell Lucy that the next time the dog kills something, there's got to be a receipt."

A snippet of music played; Dionne Warwick's voice singing, "Don't tell me what it's all about . . ."

The next sound was Piggy Proctor's lips, smacking the receiver.

Lucy was sunbathing on a chaise in the side yard. Edward, who was expected soon, was still waiting to hear whether he was required in New York to photograph the elevator. He was still at the Birches, collecting $800 a day plus expenses. Nicole clicked off the cassette player. She had been smiling all the time she was listening, and now she smiled more. "God, am I glad," she said. "I thought in September I was going to have to sit still for school a whole day."

"Congratulations," Lucy said.

"Imagine Stephanie Sykes as the heroine of a novel."

"What makes you think she'll be a heroine?" Lucy said.

"Because she's a main character."

"All main characters aren't heroines, you know."

"I just mean that she'll look good. Like, Juliet died and everything, but she came off looking good."

"Shakespeare might have had an edge on the person who's going to write the novelization."

"What do you mean?" Nicole said. "You don't think Stephanie Sykes is going to get trashed, do you?"

"Think about the series," Lucy said. "Nobody is really a hero or a heroine; they're all confused and pulled in different directions. Almost no decision they make can be right."

"Yeah, but Lucy—don't you feel sorry for me that I was treated cruelly as a child and I got into drugs and drinking and everything?"

"Well, if anything, the woman who saved you—"

"She didn't save me just to save me. She wanted to make it

look like her marriage was normal and she and her husband were a family, and since she was a doctor and she knew about my child abuse and everything, it was heroic to take me in."

"But you just explained it: she did it for good and bad reasons."

"Luuuucy—nobody does anything except for good and bad reasons."

"You don't think that people are ever *just* good or *just* evil?"

"In fairy tales and stuff. I don't know about real people."

"Nicole, maybe we aren't understanding each other—you aren't saying that people, when they do some one thing, are doing it for a bad as well as a good reason, are you?"

"I guess it depends on how you define bad. Most bad stuff isn't so bad that it matters."

St. Francis was on his chain, resting his chin on a basketball that Edward had left at the house the day before. It was a clear, windy day, and the airplane that Piggy said might happen to be passing by was overhead now, a small plane that flew across the yard and field.

"You mean," Lucy said, trying to sound casual, "that people are both good and bad, and sometimes they're bad and sometimes they're good."

"Who doesn't believe that?" Nicole said. "Like I said, there are probably some monsters and some angels."

"And for the rest of it, do you . . . you think people are duplicitous, or what?"

"What's 'duplicitous'?"

"Deceitful."

"No. People just do stuff. They look out for themselves, and if that means they step on other people's toes, that's just the way it goes. You've got to expect that."

"Who do you know who's like that?" Lucy said.

"What do you think about Piggy? You think he's my guardian angel? That he's just there to look out for me?"

"No, of course not. But what has Piggy ever done to you that wasn't what it seemed?"

"He was going to take Jane and me to Chinois for my birthday, for example. He made a big thing about it. So we had to go that night instead of doing what I wanted to do. He had the publicist carry on about my birthday for a week. Then he wrote a note to Barbara Gerrald and sent her six dozen roses and said he couldn't see her because he had to 'babysit.' She sent me the note when he started going out with Sylvie Marlowe."

"But he might really have had a change of heart, but he didn't want to hurt you, and of course he never thought Barbara would show it to you. Or he might have been embarrassed by how fond he was of you, and saying that he was babysitting just sort of passed it off. You know?"

"You don't get it," Nicole said. "Piggy's business."

Another airplane passed overhead and disappeared temporarily in a patch of clouds. It emerged slowly, and for a second it seemed to be pulling the cloud behind it. Nicole laughed. "I'll tell you what Barbara Gerrald did that was just great," she said. "She told the carhop at Chow's, when Piggy and his wife were in there, that the flowers were a birthday present and gave him ten bucks to put them on the dashboard. It's not that original or anything, but when Piggy and his wife came out and saw the roses, he must have had a hard time explaining it."

Lucy couldn't think what to say. She felt in the position of standing up for morality, but she didn't feel comfortable in the position of a conservative adult lecturing a child, either. She had to say something.

"Who's Barbara Gerrald?" she said.

"She's Penny Holden on *Summer Nights.*"

Lucy had learned not to persist. The more she questioned Nicole, the farther away she was led from any facts that would mean anything to her. People's real names, their professional names, the movies and/or TV shows they appeared in meant nothing to Lucy, let alone who they were married to, having an affair with, or considering suicide because of. At first Nicole thought that Lucy was teasing her, when nothing she could say would define a person, but by now she had subsided into feeling a little sorry for Lucy because she was such an outsider. Nicole had liked Edward's suggestion that they have marathon sessions in which Lucy would throw her arms around the droning TV and Nicole would teach her by immersing her in the experience like Helen Keller's teacher.

Though Lucy knew that she was really talking to herself, she said, "I guess that when Piggy saw the roses he could have pretended they were there by mistake."

"That's figuring that the carhop didn't know who Barbara Gerrald was," Nicole said.

"You really think he knew?"

"I don't want to get into it, but anybody but you would know who Barbara Gerrald is."

"But it was a surprise—the guy wouldn't stand around and talk about it, would he?"

"I don't know how it turned out," Nicole said. "The thing that might have saved him was that even if the carhop did say something, it probably didn't make any sense because those guys are so speedy. What a lot of them do is drop acid before they have to start parking the cars. One night when I was out with Bobby Blueballs and his mother, the guy that brought the car had flipped out, and he thought he was in the belly of a whale. It was about a hundred degrees out, and he had the windows up and he was sweating like mad, waving his arms around trying to swim. He sideswiped a Mercedes coming up to the front door. The cops had to smash a window to get him out, and there was an ambulance and everything, and they had to give him a shot of Thorazine and peel him off the wheel."

Edward and Noonan pulled into the driveway, in Peter's car. They were picking up Nicole, and they were going into town to see the two o'clock matinee of *Gremlins.*

"Get her to tell you her story about the new Jonah," Lucy said.

"Hi," Edward said. "What story?"

"What story?" Noonan said.

"Jonah?" Nicole said, turning to look at Lucy. "Who's Jonah?"

10

In his fantasies, Hildon was a shit kicker. He honestly believed that people who were less intelligent had superior lives, and the more stubbed the toes of their Corfam boots were, the better. Someone had to keep the garages of the world pumping gas. Someone had to think that politicians were going to improve their life. Shit kickers were up front about wanting to be studs and down home with their cooking. Seeing the charcoal glowing in their barbecue grills as he drove by, Hildon felt the same sense of peace and contentment that people feel in front of the candles lit on the altar of the church. He was simply fascinated to live among them, after a lifetime in the Ivy League. He liked it that as he lit his after-dinner Gauloises, they were wiping their mouths on the backs of their hands. Although they barely noticed that he was alive, their existence pointed out to him that he was absolutely absurd. Little Hildon with the heart murmur, who had squinted over Plato's arguments until he ended up with thick glasses at twelve, now read first-person accounts in *Soldier of Fortune* of men blowing away gooks and grizzlies. He bent his beer cans before throwing them away, sent $4 for an assortment of mail-order Superstud prophylactics and spread them out over his kitchen table with the reverence of someone laying out the Tarot. The summer before, he and Lucy had driven to another town to go to a summer street festival, and Hildon had totally indulged his fantasies. He had worn a Born to Lose T-shirt, torn jeans, pointed-toe boots with spurs and walked along paring his nails with a file clicked open from his knife. He ate hot dogs without spitting out his gum.

He wanted to stop at a bank to apply for a loan to buy a dishwasher. That was the point at which Lucy put an end to it, and drove them back in the borrowed pickup, with Merle Haggard singing Bob Wills's songs on the radio and a smile on Hildon's face as though he had just gone to heaven.

Today Hildon stood next to Lucy at the horse auction. He had on a straw hat, a T-shirt full of holes, torn jeans, the boots with spurs. His face was burning in the hot sun. He should have been at work, but what the hell. Who was going to point a finger? The pointed finger was never feared anymore; if anyone saw anything so silly, it was *meant* as an impossibility come true: E.T.'s magic finger aglow, not the demanding Uncle Sam Wants You point or the crooked finger of the Wicked Witch.

It was Hildon's theory that nobody was doing what people assumed in the afternoon—that whatever he was doing, millions were doing with him. Nothing erotic happened at night, but everywhere, all over, all day, people were pretending to be Tinkerbell or Mr. T or marine sergeants or Godzilla and being hung by their thumbs and checking into motels with their lovers to put on diapers and play patty-cake until they came. That was why the chief loan officer wasn't yet back from lunch, why the mechanic called in sick, why the judge threw the case out of court when the prosecutor's only witness didn't show. Doctors were checking in late for surgery, accountants were filing extensions, roofers weren't appearing to repair leaks, bakers burned the bread. All day, people were so lost in passion and fantasy that they could barely get the essentials accomplished so they weren't fired, the mortgage was paid, the children fed. Discos were a farce, and only geriatric cases ever attempted romantic weekends, following the recommendations of *New York* magazine. Everything stopped at night, and on weekends. Summer vacation you could forget entirely. At best, it was when people rested from their double, triple, and quadruple lives and took a break from the frantic fun they had all year long. Who was going to envy a cat for having nine lives when huge numbers of people had that many and didn't have to pay the price of eating Puss'n Boots. How many people were really going to go home and confess an affair? And if they did, how many weren't going to live to tell? Wives who were told their husbands were in a meeting would never know that they were off at nude archery practice. The *real* big deals of the world were five eight and blonde. There wasn't a traffic tie-up on the GW bridge—their husband was tied up, being flogged. Rapists were sleeping with their parole officers. Speeders were propositioning state patrolmen. And all the while, Jimmy Carter of Plains, Georgia, was committing adultery in his mind. Knowing how to move your fingers up and down the stem of your champagne flute was the new equivalent of dropping a glove. Platonic love was about as probable as the last game of the World Series being televised without Instant Replay.

And where, Lucy asked, did he think his wife was?

"Sleeping," he said.

They decided to leave and to eat lunch. As they walked away from the roped-in area, there was a boy, not yet a teenager, holding a pony. The pony was brown and white. It was eating clover, and the boy watched it with a real look of love on his face. Bees buzzed through the clover. In the distance, someone started a lawn mower. Many of the small willow trees that bordered the path to the parking lot had died.

They went to Montville, to the diner he liked. He ordered scrambled eggs and double-fried ham, and toast with extra butter. He was a little surprised when the waitress looked at Lucy, and she just smiled and said she'd have the same and handed back the menus. He put fifty cents in the juke box and played four Charley Pride songs. The Stanley Brothers were singing.

The waitress had a little hint of a smile this time. He thought that she recognized him. In the booth behind them, two men were talking about the train that had derailed in Burlington. "I don't guess anybody on that train is going to be in much of a hurry to get to Montreal," one of the men said. They had actually been there—seen the wreck. One of the men preferred Toronto to Montreal. The other preferred planes to trains. They ordered more coffee.

"Did what's-her-name with the name nobody can say win at Wimbledon?" one of the men asked.

"I guess I don't have time to pay attention to who won a tennis game," the waitress said.

"Aw—what would you be doing that you didn't have time to read the newspaper?" one of the men said.

"I guess picking it up off the floor," the waitress said. She moved to their booth. "Coffee?" she said. Hildon said he didn't want any.

"All right—I guess I will have some," Lucy said.

"I guess it might help if I go get a cup first," the waitress said. This time she did smile a delighted smile. She had one of those faces that looked entirely different when she smiled. Attractive, in a squarish way.

"Not gonna take up tennis yourself?" one of the men said, turning and looking over the back of the booth as she poured coffee.

"Way I move around here, it's the same thing, except I don't got a tennis paddle and a net," the woman said.

"I don't know that we could trust you with one of those," one of the men said.

"My hands are pretty tough," the waitress said. "Don't know that you'd want to trust me without one."

"I trust you," the other man said. "I was at Henry's the night you poured the coffee."

"Go on," the waitress said. "That was nothing."

"What did she do?" the other man said.

"You don't know about that? Henry put six mugs on the top of the bar and let her look for about six seconds, and then he put his bandanna around her eyes and damned if she didn't hit every mug dead center."

The waitress walked away from the booth, smiling again. In a few seconds, she came back from the kitchen with their eggs. "Nothing for you?" she said to Hildon, as she put a mug of steaming coffee down in front of Lucy.

"No thanks," he said.

Crystal Gayle was singing. The food was heavy. He ate faster, because it didn't taste good.

"It this the only lunch we're having?" Lucy said, deciding to be the one to start the game.

"Are we going back to your house?" he said.

"If you want to drive that far."

"What are my options?" he said.

"What's this?" she said. " 'Mother, May I?' "

He put his legs on each side of hers and pressed hers together. She smiled. With her knees, she pushed his apart. Finally he stopped resisting and let her part his legs. She rubbed her foot in his crotch. She had taken off her shoes. He resisted the temptation to break eye contact with her.

"Coffee?" the waitress said, passing by. He looked at the steam. It was fascinating: a cloud of white steam. It was something to look at.

"No thanks," Lucy said. She looked at Hildon. "Do we want the check?" she said.

"Are you sure you don't want anything else?" he said. She had eaten half her eggs. The toast was untouched. She had cut three bites of ham. "No thanks," she said.

"I think I'll have a piece of pie," Hildon said. "What kind of pie do you have?"

"Apple cherry blueberry," the waitress said.

Lucy's foot stopped moving. She brushed her hair back, looking at him.

"Blueberry, please," he said.

The waitress walked away. A woman with a crying child came in and sat at the counter. "Because I said so," the woman said to the child. "And you'd better quiet down and like it." The men from the booth behind theirs were at the cash register, rolling toothpicks out of a dispenser and paying their bill. Johnny Cash was singing. In all the time he had come here, Hildon had never heard the songs he selected. Even with the rules of chance operating, he should have heard Charley Pride at least once.

The waitress put down his piece of pie and refilled Lucy's coffee mug without asking. Lucy's face was expressionless, but she was looking straight at him. "Some pie?" he said, turning the fork toward her.

"No thanks," she said. "I don't think it looks good."

He cut a piece of pie and ate it. "It's very good," he said.

"And you want me to just wait while you eat it."

" 'Mother, May I?' " he said.

He took another bite of pie. It was doughy and too sweet. He smiled as he swallowed. "I forgot to tell you. There's a party at the Hadley-Cooper's this weekend," he said. "I'm quite taken with Antoinette. How about coming along so she'll be jealous?"

She nodded. She got up and went to the bathroom. A dancing elephant, pirouetting like a ballerina, was painted on the varnished wooden door. He didn't eat any more pie while she was gone. When she came back, she was smiling. She looked very pretty. Her hair was combed, and she had put on pink lipstick. She continued to smile. She folded her hands. She watched the woman, whispering in the child's ear, as he tried to swirl his stool back and forth. She looked beyond Hildon, to the old man who had just come in and who sat in the booth behind them. He puckered his lips and blew a breeze across the table. She closed her eyes slightly and smiled.

"Going off to the bathroom and snorting coke's not fair," he said.

"Cheating is perfectly fair in any game."

She thought about it. She unzipped her purse, reached in and took out a tiny glass vial with a coke spoon attached to it. The chain sparkled for a second, before he could clasp his hand over hers, so no one would see. Her hand was cold. She turned her hand in his and opened it to release the vial. The glass was colder than her skin. It made him feel colder than he was, the way putting a finger on an ice cube will freeze the sweat on your face on a hot day. He remembered the pony, light brown snout down, rooting around in the clover. The boy standing there, holding the pony. All the sun, outside the diner. He closed her hand around the vial and gestured for the waitress. The waitress came to their booth with the bill. "You have a good day now," she said, slapping the bill onto the table, even though he was holding out his hand.

"Want to have a good day?" he said to Lucy, getting up.

"Oh, I don't think so," she said. "I think I might wait until the party to have a good time."

She followed him to the cash register, but when the cashier dropped her pen on the floor and hopped down to get it, Lucy wandered out to the vestibule. Hildon looked at her, reading business cards that had been tacked up on the big bulletin board. He saw a large flyer from the ASPCA. Lucy walked out the door. He gave the cashier a dime and took two mints.

Lucy was walking ahead of him. She opened the car door and sat in the driver's seat. The news on the radio droned on. He opened the door on the driver's side. "Move over," he said. She didn't resist. She lowered the emergency brake and carefully maneuvered her way across it. Her lips were chalky pink in the sun. On the news, they were talking about the Montrealer. She sat in the passenger's seat, with her hands folded in her lap.

He dropped his hands into his lap and looked straight ahead. She caught on and laughed. He leaned over and kissed her. He unwrapped one of the mints, one-handed, and put it in her mouth. The chocolate had already begun to get sticky soft. While she was sucking on the mint, he kissed her again. This time he waited for her to end the kiss. She ended it when she had to swallow. He put his arm around her, and put his other hand around the side of her thigh, stroking his thumb across the top of her leg. Someone started a car and drove away. He leaned over farther and kissed her shoulder through the material. "Where'd you get the coke?" he said.

"I visited one of the kids in my art class, who had a tumor removed. His mother had coke. We did some in the hospital bathroom. I bought this from her later."

11

MYRA was deep into the article. She cleared the dinner dishes off the card table and went back to her desk. The chair she usually pulled up to the card table had broken, so she typed sitting on the ironing board facing the kitchen counter. She had a sudden brainstorm after a day of sitting this way: she turned it so that it was parallel to the high counter. That way, she did not feel as if she was poised at the end of a diving board, about to plunge into her Smith-Corona.

She had done all the necessary research, and all that she needed to do now was bang out the rough draft. Cameron Petrus, the hard-hitting reporter, actually lived for the time he could throw his javelin. Nigel McAllister, who took such wonderful photographs and who submitted his work to photography magazines, expressed his cynicism about photography's ability to communicate to the students whom he befriended at the community college where he taught and spent his time meditating at an Ashram. Noonan, who had made a fine art of parody, was deeply committed to campaigning for gay rights. And Lucy Spenser, the lady counselor, was apparently unable to guide her own life gracefully. Myra had found that out when she discovered the letter to Cindi Coeur from Les Whitehall.

Myra spent a few minutes analyzing herself: was she trying to get Lucy Spenser on the phone because she secretly liked the idea of making her uncomfortable? It wasn't that easy to make someone as together as Lucy uncomfortable, but the letter from Les, whoever he was, seemed sure to do it. There was no reason to mention in the article that Lucy and Hildon were lovers—it was hardly to the point—so wasn't she calling just to make cool, pretty, talented Lucy, who had a handsome, interesting lover—squirm? It was one of the perks of the job.

First Lucy's line had been busy, then there was no answer. Her own phone rang. It was her friend Mary, inviting her to a party that night. She had been seeing a man named Timothy Cooper. The party was at his mansion. He was inviting people his wife didn't know, and she was inviting people he didn't know. Myra wouldn't be embarrassed, because it was going to be a large crowd, and each would think the other had invited her.

Mary hadn't seen the house, but she had heard it was fabulous. She begged Myra to go with her. Myra was sure that Mary was just being nice; Mary knew she spent a lot of time alone and she often invited her to go along to things with her. The house sounded so interesting that she was tempted to go just to see it. Mary kept after her. Myra said she'd go. After living here for a year, Myra had very little sense of what the community was like. Probably, since there was so much money around this area, there were many enclaves like the one she was going to visit. Mary had a way of meeting men and getting around, but Myra had a dull life and lived for the day when she could move back to Boston. The men she met were taken not once, but twice; they all had wives and lovers. Myra had been her journalism professor's lover in Boston. He had agonized—ostensibly—about whether or not to leave his wife and daughter. He had even o.d.'d on sleeping pills when Myra said she wouldn't see him until he decided. And then she had found someone else. But her new boyfriend left Boston, and although they planned to get together before she left for Vermont, they never did. For months when she first moved to town she had not seen anyone, and then she had gone out a few times with a guy who played in a band. She didn't really care about him, and she hadn't seen him for more than a month. The only person who had asked her out in that month was Cameron Petrus. She didn't think he was attractive, and lied that she was involved with somebody. She had coffee with him (he had ginseng tea), and he told her about his heart attack. He sounded like the weatherman narrating an electrical storm. The whole thing depressed her so much that she reread her ex-professor's letters and thought about writing him—but what good would that do? He was never going to give up what he had. Her best friend had just married a man who made driftwood coffee tables. She tried not to think about it. If you couldn't ignore things, making a joke seemed a feasible alternative. She couldn't have agreed more with the *Country Daze* philosophy.

She wasn't in the mood for a party. She poured a shot of Jack Daniels and drank it while she watched the evening news. She decided to wear her 1940s dress: navy-blue, with bouquets of carnations and ribbons floating across the rayon. She put on her high heels. She brushed her hair and made a knot with part of it at the nape of her neck. Her mouth was still sticky when she put on lipstick. She thought that she smelled like a bourbon factory, but since she had already put on her lipstick, she didn't want to brush her teeth. She sprayed on perfume. She put on a rhinestone bracelet she had bought at the Ben Franklin. If Mary hadn't pulled into her drive, she would have had another drink.

Mary was in such a good mood, it was almost contagious. Procol Harum was singing "Whiter Shade of Pale" on the radio. The car, a Datsun 280 ZX, had been part of her divorce settlement. She had also gotten the country house, in Bristol. In the winter she went back to Boston, where she restored paintings at the Museum of Fine Arts and was studying Raku pottery. It was no wonder that men found her more interesting to talk to than Myra. Myra was exactly Mary's age, but she felt younger. Older, actually. She was just less sophisticated.

There was a man at the entranceway to the house with a walkie-talkie. He gave Mary's name—he announced Myra "and guest"—and waved them in. A peacock was strolling around the front lawn. The front door was open, and there was a roar of noise inside. Some people were playing croquet on the side lawn. Myra suddenly felt nervous. It wasn't going to be her kind of party, but now that she was here, she was going to have to go through with it. She stayed with Mary. They found the bar, in back of the staircase, and stood in line. The bartender had on wraparound, black sunglasses. Myra could not tell when she had his attention because he did not seem to be looking anywhere in particular. She stepped aside and let Mary take care of getting them a drink. The drinks were served in plastic cups, and Myra carried hers with exceptional care, so she would have something to concentrate on. She looked outside; there were faerie lights in the evergreens, and they seemed to border a pool. "Let's go outside," she said.

It was a pool. A naked man was lying on his stomach, stretched out on a green float with a turtle head at one end. The man's head was resting on the turtle's neck. A man came over who thought he knew Mary. They went through several possibilities, but it did not seem that they had met. As they were talking, someone that Mary did know—a man Myra had never met—came over and introduced his little boy. The boy had a peacock feather. "Tickle her with the feather," the man said, and the boy shyly turned his face to his father's leg. Myra had never seen so many men in white pants. Myra went back to the house and got another drink for both of them. This time, as she studied the bartender, she realized that he was blind: he knew where the bottles were, obviously; stopped pouring, she guessed, by how heavy the glass was. She wondered how many other people had realized he was blind. She took the spritzers and walked out back again. She didn't see Mary. As she was standing there holding two glasses, a man came up and said, "One for me?" "I don't know where my friend is," she said, feeling foolish. "For me, then," he said, taking the glass.

"I'll bet everybody here is dying to know who everybody else is," he said.

"Who are you?" she said.

"Somebody who's out of his league," he said. "There are people in the bushes over there, smoking opium. Who are you?"

"I'm Myra DeVane. I write for the newspaper."

"Goddamn," the man said. "Everybody's a writer." He took a sip of his drink. "I'm sorry—I didn't mean to insult you. I'm from California, and everybody there is writing a screenplay. Here, there are novelists and journalists and poets all over the place."

"Are you on vacation?" she said.

"I'll tell you the truth," he said. "I'm crashing this party. A friend of mine told me about it. I was going stir crazy. I'm in limbo, waiting to see if an assignment turns up that will take me to New York. I'm going to give it through the weekend, and then I'm just turning around and going home. Although this is suitable excitement." He raised his glass to the swimming pool. The man had gotten off of the raft and was swimming around. A woman was in the water with him. The lights had come on at the bottom of the pool, and as they moved through the water, it seemed that their limbs were unusually thin and long. Perhaps they were; if she was right, the woman in the pool was Christie Brinkley. She was holding on to the edge, sweet-talking a dog who had come to sniff.

"You're not writing about the party, are you?" the man said.

"No," she said. "I'm sort of crashing, too. I came with a friend."

She never knew what to say to men. He seemed pleasant enough, and fairly attractive; she wanted him to stay and talk to her so she wouldn't be standing alone.

"What assignment would you be doing in New York?" she said.

"Photographing an elevator," he said.

"Pardon me?" she said, leaning closer.

The dog was in the pool, swimming, and the woman was laughing.

"Photographing an elevator," he said. "Somebody put a million dollars into designing Art Deco elevators. I don't know New York very well—I can't remember what building they're in. The owner is getting cold feet about letting them print the name, because he thinks people will think he's a rich pig and blow the thing up."

He finished his drink. "Would you like me to make a run this time?" he said.

"Sure," she said. "Thank you."

Christie Brinkley and the man were playing keep away, tossing a yellow ball back and forth, while the dog swam wildly and snapped at the air. One man tiptoed up behind another and pushed him toward the pool. He didn't push hard enough to throw him in, but the man's drink spilled on his white pants. Mary came up, with a Japanese man. "Mr. Yamamoto," she said, "this is my friend Myra. Mr. Yamamoto, if you can believe it, is quite an expert on Japanese pottery. We met by the bar over there . . ."

When Myra's new friend came back with drinks, Mary and Mr. Yamamoto drifted away, into another circle of people who exclaimed with delight when they saw him.

"The tennis courts are lit," the man said. "Do you by any chance want to play a game of tennis?"

She was feeling a little high. "Why not?" she said.

They maneuvered past the large group of people gathering around Mr. Yamamoto and walked down a flagstone walkway, which ended where the grass started to get high. There was a tennis court below, but two people were already playing.

"Doubles," he said. "Come on."

By the time they got there the people were having such an energetic game that neither of them wanted to interrupt. They sat and watched until the mosquitoes started to bother her.

"There were none around the pool," he said. "Let's go back."

She could feel the bites stinging her neck. She held her cup against them. She wondered if the man felt stuck with her, but the next second, she didn't much care if he did. She realized that they had never told each other their names. She introduced herself.

"Edward Bartlett," he said.

"What part of California?" she said.

"L.A."

A crowd had gathered around Mr. Yamamoto, who was standing on his head. Several of them applauded. The wet dog was standing just outside the circle of people, peering in. A man in a ten-gallon hat, jeans, and a sleeveless denim jacket turned away, smiling, and her eye met his. It took her a second to realize that it was Hildon. The woman who was with him turned. Myra was looking at Lucy Spenser. Lucy had on a white miniskirt, a pink T-shirt, and an unzipped camouflage jacket. She had a mane of light-brown hair. She looked very much like her picture. Edward was waving. "There's my pals," he said.

"Who?" Myra said.

"Lucy and Hildon," he said. "Actually—do you and Lucy know each other?"

"Not really," Myra said. "We've talked on the phone."

"She sure has been nice to me," Edward said, still holding his hand up in greeting as they walked toward them. Myra wondered why Hildon had on . . . what else could she call it but a costume?

"Lucy," Hildon said, "this is Myra DeVane."

"I didn't realize you knew each other," Edward said to Hildon.

"Myra's writing a story about *Country Daze*," Hildon said.

"How are you?" Lucy said, extending her hand. Cool. Pleasant. Myra was never prepared for it, when a woman held out her hand. She shook her hand.

"Are you the hostess' friend, or the host's, or both?" Hildon said. His hand hovered behind Lucy's back. Lucy had kept the smile on her face too long; Myra understood that Lucy was not particularly interested in meeting her. If Lucy thought she was spying, that was outrageous. Just outrageous.

"The host's," Myra said.

"You know our host?" Edward said. She remembered that she had told him she was crashing. No way out of it now. "Yes," she said, hoping that the host—whichever one he was—didn't materialize. Someone jumped up, grabbed his knees, and cannonballed into the pool. It was getting dark.

"Well, it's good he's your friend, because that way you can say hello. I understand that our hostess left."

"She did?" Hildon said.

"She took the dog and left," Edward said. "Our host—your friend—was apparently unprepared."

"Unprepared for what?" Myra said.

"Her leaving," Edward said. He shrugged. "I was talking to the bartender yesterday, and he told me."

"You've been here since yesterday?" Myra said.

"No. I just came both days." He looked at Lucy. "Thanks for the hot tip," he said.

"Any time," Lucy said. She smiled again, and turned to leave.

Myra didn't like the way Lucy was acting. Or rather, that she let it show that she was acting: that she was being perfectly polite, temporarily. And she didn't care if Myra lived or died.

"I love her column," Edward said. "Don't you love that column?"

"Yes," Myra said. "Have you been friends a long time?"

"Just since I came here on assignment. They sent me to do sketches and take photographs of Nicole Nelson."

"Nicole Nelson?" she said. "What's the connection?"

"She's her niece."

"Her niece?" Both aunt and niece were involved in the broken hearts biz?

"I'll tell you something really off the record," he said. "Nicole's been sneaking into town to see a guy who's a dishwasher at the inn. Can you imagine? He told her his room is plastered with Stephanie Sykes pictures. That must be the strangest feeling for her." He shook his head. "You can't print that," he said. "Swear you won't."

"I wouldn't," she said. She liked it that he trusted her. He was nervous (and anybody who trusted a reporter was foolish, categorically), but he trusted her, and he was right to. It was obviously more than Lucy Spenser did.

"Hey, listen," he said. "Assuming I don't have to go to New York tomorrow, would you like to have dinner?"

"Sure," she said.

"Give me your phone number," he said, taking out his wallet and looking for a piece of paper. He found a cash register receipt. He gave her his pen. She wrote her name and number on the piece of paper, remembering as she wrote that you don't write your name: you just assume that the man doesn't have a collection of names and numbers. Of course, since he actually does, yours is always the one that stands out.

"I'll call you tomorrow," he said. "There are public courts, apparently. Maybe we can play."

"Great," she said.

He held up his hand in parting, even though he was standing two feet away. He was quirky enough to charm her. She smiled goodbye. As he walked away, she started to feel as awkward as she always did when she was alone at a party. She looked for the outside bar, found it, and got another drink. Straight wine this time. No one talked to her, so she sipped it and walked around. She saw the man and the little boy again, and wondered how it could be that the dog hadn't killed the peacock. Then again, there was such a crowd that perhaps the dog had just not encountered the peacock. What a coincidence, really, that out of this large crowd, Edward had talked to her, and that it was Lucy Spenser who had told him about the party. She walked around, looking for Mary. She went inside, finally, and looked in the living room. When she came out, Lucy Spenser was sitting alone, on the stairs.

"Lose Hildon?" Myra said.

"He's outside," Lucy said. "I'm just taking a breather."

"It's quite a place, isn't it?" Myra said. "Have you been here before?"

"No," Lucy said.

Stony politeness. What did Lucy think she was going to write? She wasn't trying to create a scandal out of nothing—she was just doing her job. It wasn't as if anything she had said or done had indicated that she was a piranha.

"It must be nice to have a friend like Hildon," Myra said. "Someone you've been close to that many years, and now you even work together."

"How do you mean?" Lucy said.

How did she mean? She meant, in English, that Lucy was lucky to have a close friend, and to have the further advantage of working with that friend. It was also nice that he was her lover, but Myra had not meant that; she had meant what she said.

"I meant what I said," Myra said. "I don't have the slightest interest in what you do with your private life. I'm not nosing around for information. It's just a coincidence that we were invited to the same party."

She saw why reporters turned mean; if everyone was that on-guard, that hostile, it was bound to anger the reporter and make her lash out, to get even. All right, she envied her. But she never intended to do a hatchet job. She hadn't said anything shitty to Lucy. She didn't deserve this. Not knowing where she was going, but wanting to get away, she started up the stairs. Much to her surprise, Lucy stood when she passed her. She was following her up the stairs. Myra stopped.

"I'm sorry," Lucy said. "I apologize. I know I was too on-guard. It's one of my problems. It's my problem. I'm sorry."

"I honestly don't have any interest in the fact that he's your lover," Myra said.

"Who?" Lucy said.

"Hildon," Myra said, pointing off into space.

"Hildon and I aren't lovers," Lucy said.

"Lucy—I know you are."

Lucy was looking at her. Her hand was on the zipper to her jacket. She was as still as a statue in a wax museum. She was just looking at her.

"Les says he is," Myra said.

Lucy's eyes widened. She dropped her hand to her side. "You know Les?" she said.

Myra had gone too far. She didn't know what to say.

"I don't know what your opinion of Les is, but mine isn't very high," Lucy said. She turned and began to walk down the stairs.

"He's sorry," Myra heard herself saying.

Lucy turned again and looked up at her.

"Listen," Myra said, "I don't even know him. I've been trying to call you. I was in the mail room. Hildon told me to go ahead and go through the mail. He wrote you. The letter is there."

"What are you talking about?" she said.

"Hildon wanted me to see the mail. There was a letter to you in the pile. It was from Les."

"What did the letter say?" Lucy said.

"It was about your affair with Hildon. He said he wanted to see you again."

"Les Whitehall wrote to inform me that I was having an affair with Hildon?" Lucy said.

"He just mentioned it. He was talking about seeing you again."

"Where is he?" Lucy said.

Myra shrugged. "I don't know him," she said.

"There wasn't a postmark?"

"I didn't notice the postmark. Lucy: *I don't care.* I just wanted you to know."

Lucy sat on the stairs. "Les doesn't care either," she said. "It's just completely out of character for him to do anything instinctively. I couldn't be more surprised."

12

POLICE Sergeant Brown was always unhappy. His partner, Sergeant Pasani, was equally unhappy, but for a different reason. He was unhappy because Brown was unhappy, and there was no reasoning with him. Many things made Brown unhappy. Pasani had told him for years that he was his own worst enemy. You just can't go around thinking that McDonald's food is going to be steaming hot. It's like expecting the hamburger to be served on a French roll. It isn't going to happen. The bun is going to be mush, and the food is going to be tepid. It's just going to be what it is, and having a debate with the cheery high-school girl at the drive-in window, even if you're a cop, and as big as a barrel, is going to do you no good. Day after day, Brown decided they should have lunch at the drive-thru McDonald's, and day after day, Brown could hardly chew for finding fault with the food. Brown also hated the car they drove around in. In particular, he hated the suspension system. "You want to be suspended, go home and get in a hammock," Pasani said to him. Brown didn't like Reagan or Mondale, and you couldn't even say Jesse Jackson's name in his presence. He liked one of his three children and so far the fourth had a fighting chance; his wife might be pregnant with a girl, and the one child Brown liked was his girl. He had mixed feelings about his wife. He had recently learned the word ambivalent. Every day, he mentioned to Pasani his ambivalent feelings about Essie. Pasani wasn't married—he had been married for less than a year, long ago; his wife had run off with the house painter—and Brown had created quite a fantasy life about Pasani, and all the women he had, and what a good time he had, and how few responsibilities he had. Pasani usually took the bait and spent long periods, every day, trying to dispel Brown's illusions, but it did no good. These fantasies were a necessary part of Brown's existence. It depressed him to have to tell Brown how unadventurous and how unmeaningful his life was, so unless Brown was really out of control, he rarely even broke into Brown's monologues anymore. He automatically pulled back the bun on top of his cheeseburger and gave Brown his pickle. This kept Brown's raving about the need for "some taste, some flavor" down to a minimum. After two years of riding in the car with Brown, he was at least used to him. He was able to guess pretty well when he should speak and when he shouldn't, and just because he was tired of hitting his head up against a wall, he had learned to be quick to make concessions. Brown was even in his dreams; the night before, he dreamed that Brown drove them over a cliff. He often dreamed that Brown shot him. In the dreams, they were always at McDonald's. Then Pasani realized that the drive-thru line ended on a steep precipice. Brown became so angry that he gunned the car, and they fell what seemed like a million miles before Pasani woke up, clutching the sheets. In the dream in which he was shot, they were again in the line, approaching the window, but when they got there Brown wasn't handed the food, but a gun. He simply grinned and turned and shot Pasani.

This day had been a normal enough day. Brown was incensed because the Montrealer was back on the tracks so soon. He was also furious at the fools who rode the train. He had seen some of them on the evening news the night before, and they just said that they were sure Amtrak would be very careful this time, so there was nothing to worry about. People who didn't look at the evidence were as stupid as people who couldn't see the nose on their own face. Amtrak would kill them all, over and over. "What starts that stops?" Brown said. "Go ahead and tell me, Pasani." "A cheap watch," Pasani said. That pleased Brown; he thought that everything that was manufactured now was junk. He changed the subject from the derailed Montrealer to the fact that the war had ruined the way the Japanese thought. The Japanese didn't care about anything anymore. "You ever see them say goodbye?" Brown said. "They stand there bobbin' like birds. Everybody's got to be more gracious than the other guy. If they put more of that energy into making their products, maybe the shutter wouldn't fall off the camera and the watch would tick. Tickee tickee," Brown said. He started bobbing his head at the steering wheel. "No clickee, no tickee," Brown said. "The world's going to hell. You know what I mean?" Brown dropped his jaw open and bobbed his head at the steering wheel again. Pasani braced himself. Brown stopped just inches short of the bumper of the car in front of him. "I ought to audition for a job drivin' the Montrealer, huh?" Brown said. Once something caught his attention, Brown usually talked about it for six months. Around Christmas, Pasani would stop hearing about the Montrealer.

"Where do you feel like eating lunch?" Brown said.

"Pull by the grill. I'll run in and get us a couple of ham sandwiches."

"Nah," Brown said. "I don't want ham sandwiches."

"What'll I get you?" Pasani said.

"That greasy spoon?" Brown said. "You're putting me on."

"I think I feel like one of those fried-ham sandwiches," Pasani said.

"They take forever," Brown said. "They go out and catch the pig first."

"You're right," Pasani said. "I'm gonna get a turkey sandwich."

"That turkey's so tough it's like mozzarella cheese," Brown said.

"That's okay. They stuff those sandwiches pretty good. What'll I get you?"

"Don't get me anything," Brown said. "I'm not going to poison myself."

Brown was speeding along. He gunned it at a yellow light and swerved into the other lane to avoid a car nosing out from a steep driveway.

"You're kidding," Brown said. "You really want to go all the way over to the grill?"

"Sure," Pasani said.

"We never go there anymore," Brown said.

"Today's the day," Pasani said, smacking his hands together.

Brown pulled off the road. There was a half-circle that went into the woods just at the bottom of the hill. Brown liked to hide in there and catch speeders. The shopping center with the McDonald's was two miles straight ahead. They had given a woman with a car full of kids a ticket one day, and when they pulled into the McDonald's later, she was in the parking lot, with her head on the wheel, sobbing. The doors were thrown open, and a lot of children stood on the grass. Some of them were crying, too. Others were trying to get them to stop. A few were trying to coax the woman out of the car, and one of them climbed up on the trunk and curved his arms, jutting out his jaw, hunching his shoulders, and walking toward the back window like a gorilla. There was still complete pandemonium when Brown and Pasani drove through the line and looked over their shoulders, driving out.

No one was speeding. Car after car came down the hill with the brakes on. Brown was getting mad. Another car passed by, at a snail's crawl. Brown raised his eyebrows at Pasani. "What?" Pasani said. "You think I'm sending them telepathic messages or something?"

Three cars came down the hill. None were speeding. Brown pulled out abruptly and rode the tail of the last car for about a mile.

"We're almost to the McDonald's," Brown said. "What do you say we grab a burger and fries?"

"That's an idea," Pasani said.

"You like that blonde that looks like Farrah Fawcett, don't you?" Brown said.

"I don't like young girls."

"You don't like young girls," Brown said. "Sure you don't like young girls."

"I can't stand them. They're all idiots," Pasani said.

"What?" Brown said. "You interested in spending an evening chatting?"

"Yes," Pasani said.

"That's a good one," Brown said. "You hang out the flag first?"

Pasani said nothing.

"Aah," Brown said. "You had a flag, you'd use it for a sheet."

"I'd never do that to the flag," Pasani said.

"Not if you were sober, you wouldn't."

"I stay sober. Otherwise I can't get it up."

Brown turned and looked at him. "What's with this wacko mood today, Pasani?"

"Brown—you know me. I'm the same every day."

"Better save your sweetness for Farrah Fawcett," Brown said. "I wouldn't mind sucking those fingers she runs around in the french fries."

"They don't put their hands in the food," Pasani said.

"When nobody's lookin'? You think teenage kids shovel fries in a bag with that dipper?"

"What do you think they do?"

"Use their hands."

The car in front of them pulled away. "The usual?" Brown said.

"Yeah," Pasani said.

"Hey, let me have a quarter pounder and two cheeseburgers, one large and one small fries, two milks and a large Coke," Brown said.

His words echoed above the roar of the kitchen—it was probably canned noise, Pasani thought; at the window, you could see into the kitchen, and it was relatively quiet. The woman repeated their order. She asked if they wanted hot apple pie.

"Gotta keep my trim figure," Brown said.

He zoomed to the window. If he got there fast, the order wouldn't be ready, and he could watch the girls. The girls were always energetic and cheerful. Pasani recognized all the faces now. The girls jumped around instead of walking. "There you go, thank you, sir," one said, hopping to the window. She handed the two containers of milk in separately. Brown turned on the siren, and she jumped. "Accident," Brown said. "Sorry."

"Don't do that," Pasani said. "I hate that." As they pulled back onto the highway, he removed one cheeseburger and a small french fries. He put them in the space between the seats and took Brown's food out of the bag and folded the bag the way Brown liked, and handed it to him. Brown put it in his lap. Pasani handed him a napkin. Brown tucked it under his collar. Pasani opened one of the milks. Brown took it and drained it. Pasani put the container, and the wad of napkins, on the floor. A car streaked past, going ninety. Brown shook his head. The car slammed on its brakes, barely avoiding a car that was in the left turn lane. "Jesus," Brown said. Pasani handed him the other carton of milk. He drank half of it and put it on the dash. Pasani steadied it with his hand and unwrapped his cheeseburger one-handed, removed the pickle, and handed it to Brown. "Thanks," Brown said. He unwrapped his own cheeseburger and peeled back the bun. He put the pickle in. He ate the cheeseburger, occasionally putting it on the paper so he could eat some french fries. "Good fries today," Brown said.

Pasani looked out the window. There was a beach ball in the weeds beside the highway. A little farther on, there was a dead skunk in the gravel. This part of highway had been repaved; bright black tar glistened in the sun. None of this road existed two years ago. It used to be forest.

"Shit," Brown said. "I was gonna duck into the K Mart. My kid dropped his frog in the toilet. I told him I'd bring another frog home."

Pasani finished his cheeseburger and had a sip of Coke.

"You hear that Kermit and Miss Piggy got married?" he said.

"I didn't know that," Pasani said.

"Well, that's the kind of stuff I hear all night," Brown said. "All the six-year-olds think it's great that she tricked him."

"How did she trick him?"

"She pretended they were acting or something, and then she switched a real minister."

"Why couldn't you get the frog out of the toilet?" Pasani said.

"I got the frog out of the toilet. My kids are into going to the bathroom double-decker, so the frog was down there in a mess. That's really what I want to do at night—fish out a frog that's drowning in a bowlful of shit."

"Where are we going?" Pasani said.

"We've got to check the politician's place, and then I think we ought to try to catch some speeders."

The house they were checking faced the lake. It had been robbed earlier in the summer. They got out of the car and walked around it, trying the doors. Brown backed up and looked at it. It made him angry just to see it, because he thought that modern houses were a blight on the landscape and that only fools would buy them, when there were so many houses to fix up. The house was tight. Pasani walked up the flagstone walkway, back to the car. Pasani hated the McDonald's smell after he had eaten the food.

Brown started the car. At the bottom of the hill, he hung a right. He was going to another one of his favorite hiding places. This one was actually a dirt road that cut through a patch of woods. Brown liked to take the half-circle at top speed and screech to a halt. The trees were so lush this time of year, because of all the rain, that when they parked they had to peer through branches to see the road. When they got there, Brown slowed to turn, then held the wheel hard and accelerated. When he saw the big car parked on the dirt road, there was no way he could stop in time. He cut the wheels and, scraping branches, bumped off the dirt into mud. Miraculously, he had avoided hitting the car, but what the hell *was* it? It looked like something out of a Zap comic.

"You all right?" Brown said.

The wheels on the passenger's side were clearly sunk in mud. Pasani's arm that he had used to brace himself throbbed.

"Yeah," he said.

The back door of the big car flew open, and a girl jumped out. She looked terrified. Pasani was going to leave it to Brown to discuss it with her. Brown actually looked nervous. He got out of the car.

"Hello," Brown said, walking forward. There was movement in the back of the car. Brown froze, then put his hand on his holster. There was a minute in which both he and the girl stood there. The girl was holding . . . Pasani couldn't see through all the branches crisscrossing the windshield. He bumped into Brown's seat and stepped out the door.

"Hold it," Brown said, walking forward.

It was a camera she was holding.

Pasani could hardly believe his eyes. The man was naked, trying to pull on his pants. The girl—she was only a girl—was crying.

"Get out of the car," Brown said. "What's going on?"

The man started to get out. He had his hands in the air, as though Brown had told him to do that.

"What in the hell is this?" Brown said, turning to face Pasani.

"We're taking pictures. We're not doing anything," the girl said. "You can search the car and everything. We're not doing anything wrong."

"Pictures?" Brown said. He saw a bear head and jumped back. It was a rug. The man had put the wrong leg in his pants and had to step out and try again. While he was doing this, the girl put her hands over her face and started to cry. Pasani's heart sank. His fingers hesitated on his holster. This was serious, whatever it was. Nothing could be worse, when he was with Brown, than having something happen that Brown hadn't seen on TV.

13

IT was late at night on Monday when Lucy got home and got the call from the police station. The first thing she did when they hung up was to try to call Hildon; as she feared, Maureen answered the phone. "Lucy," Maureen said, "I must tell you that you have disturbed my sleep. This is not a proper time to make a phone call, and I am within my rights to hang up." She hung up before Lucy could say anything.

Lucy cursed and reached for her car keys. They were not on the table. Of all times to lose her car keys. She took a deep breath and tried to remember where she had put them. As she was moving piles of magazines on the table, the idea hit her that she could get someone else to call Hildon. She called Noonan and woke him up. "This is important," Lucy said. "I can't explain right now. Do me a favor: call Hildon and have him call me. Will you?"

"Why can't you do it?" Noonan said.

"I just can't. I'm sorry to bother you, but this is very important."

"Hang up," Noonan said.

She put the phone down and waited. It hit her for the first time that it might be wise to call a lawyer. She sat on the sofa, still without the keys, and wondered who knew a lawyer that she could call. A bee buzzed up and down the window glass. Looking at the bee, she saw the keys, partly hidden beside the television. She snatched them up. Her hand was trembling. She pounced on the phone when it rang.

"What's the game?" Noonan said.

"What game?"

"I called Hildon's, and Maureen answered, and she had a little speech about the polite hours to place phone calls."

"She wouldn't put Hildon on?"

"No."

"Shit. She did the same thing to me. That's why I had you call."

"Is everything all right?" Noonan said.

"I've got to get Hildon," Lucy said.

"Call her back and yell if it's important."

"I can't do that."

"I don't understand anything about the way heterosexuals relate to one another," Noonan said. "I never have and I never will."

"Listen," Lucy said. "Can I come over and pick you up? I've got to go to the police station and I'm afraid to go alone."

"What is it?" Noonan said, his voice changing entirely.

"According to Nicole, it's nothing. It's—it seems awful. I can't keep talking. She's waiting for me."

"I was asleep," Noonan said. "I took a sleeping pill."

"You're awake now, aren't you?"

"I don't know," Noonan said.

"I'm coming over," Lucy said. "This is important. Jesus—this had better be as easy to explain as Nicole said. She was off parking with Edward, apparently. You don't think it was anything other than that, do you?"

"Don't ask me," Noonan said. "She's not exactly naïve."

"Don't say that," Lucy said.

"The irony is, I stole these pills from Hildon and Maureen's medicine cabinet," Noonan said.

"Should I call a lawyer?" Lucy said. "Why can't I ever think what to do?"

"Don't call a lawyer. Let's go down there and check it out."

"Okay. Get dressed. I'll be right over."

"You already said that. Hang up," Noonan said.

"Oh God, I hope this isn't something awful. If Jane finds out about this, she'll kill me. I'm ready to kill Nicole myself."

"Goodbye," Noonan said.

"That goddamn California artist manqué," Lucy said.

"Are we having a general discussion about your feelings, or are you going to come over?"

"If he's done anything to Nicole, I'm going to make sure he ends up behind bars."

"What do you think about Mondale having a woman Vice President?" Noonan said.

Lucy hung up. It was cold outside. She started back for her jacket, but suddenly she didn't think she had a second to spare. Forty-five minutes had elapsed since she got the phone call. She must have been in shock. She would tell the police that she was in shock. No: then maybe they wouldn't take her seriously. If Edward had done something awful to Nicole, she was going to have him killed. She should have known that grown men don't pal around that way with fourteen-year-old girls. All the times he said he had been driving her into town, it must have been a lie. All the movies they said they saw . . . He was a pervert—he got the assignment from the toy company on purpose, and she was too stupid to figure it out. He wasn't cooling his heels until he found out whether he was going to New York; he was lusting after her niece. None of it made sense, suddenly. She must have been mad to believe it. She couldn't tell whether she was shivering from fear or from the cold.

She pulled up in front of Noonan's. The smell of honeysuckle caught in her throat. The wind was blowing through the small willow trees Noonan had bought at the nursery. She pulled into the gravel driveway. Noonan ran out of the house. The second she saw him she wondered why she had stopped. She was picking up a crazy person to take to the police station with her. As he ran, Noonan flapped his arms like a bird. He threw open the car door and thumped onto the seat. He was clutching a washrag, pressed to his forehead. "Hay fever," he said. "I put so much Afrin down my nose, I should just chew a cherry at the same time and skip the evening drinks."

"Jesus," Lucy said, on the verge of tears for the first time, "this is just awful."

"She's all right, isn't she?"

"I talked to her. She seemed to be all right. Why wouldn't they let her come home? Isn't this unlawful detention?"

"Bite your tongue when you get there and listen," Noonan said. "Don't make them mad."

"If he's done anything to her, I'll kill him."

"You want me to drive?"

"No thanks."

"Then please slow down. I feel like we're coming in for a landing."

"Do you have a cigarette?" Lucy said.

He reached in his pocket and took out a silver case. He removed a cigarette and handed it to her. He rummaged around in his pocket, then pushed in the car lighter. When it popped, he pulled it out and held it toward her. She ducked her head and lit the cigarette.

"Did you get a discount on the trees?" she said.

"Yes, thank you," Noonan said. "I did what you said: I found the most attractive boy there, mentioned your name, and he gave me a ten percent discount."

"If he did anything to her, I'll kill him."

"The boy at the nursery?"

"Edward."

"Oh. Well, I need to ask you something. Do you want me to go ahead and ask, or just let it prey on my mind?"

"I don't know what you're going to ask," Lucy said.

"Something about Hildon."

They were in front of the police barracks. She was signaling to turn. Cars passed her in slow motion.

"What about him?"

"Have you been having an affair all this time?"

Lucy faltered. Another group of cars approached, and she couldn't turn. He was squeezing the washcloth over the bridge of his nose. He reached in his pocket, took out the Afrin, and sprayed. He pinched his nostrils closed. "Oh God," Noonan said, exhaling through his mouth.

"What makes you ask that?" Lucy said.

"Nigel does that all day long," Noonan said. "If you ask him what time it is, he asks you why you want to know."

"Why did you ask?" Lucy said.

"I already have my answer," Noonan said.

Lucy turned off the ignition. The long cigarette ash fell on her leg.

"Yes," she said. "Don't tell anybody."

"I can't understand why everybody is suddenly so up front with me. Is it because I'm leaving for California?"

"No," she said. "For some reason, I've just started to appreciate you. Why did you ask?"

"After we spoke, I called back. What Maureen did was outrageous. I demanded to speak to Hildon. I said it was an emergency. And do you know what she said? She said, 'I think it's quite awful for Lucy Spenser to call in the middle of the night asking for Hildon, just to throw me off, since I obviously think he's with her. It's another thing entirely that you're pimping.' "

"She said that?"

"She says outrageous things all the time. At the staff party, she told me that the people who worked with me thought I was murky."

"I don't think that," Lucy said.

"Thank you," Noonan said.

"I just think that when people express their true feelings, it embarrasses you, and you say things that are crueler than you intend."

"I don't intend to say anything cruel to you," Noonan said. "You've always been a real friend."

"Thank you," Lucy said, reaching across and putting her arm around his shoulder.

"It's disappointing that I don't have a heterosexual impulse in my whole body," Noonan said. He kissed the top of her head. "I'm glad Hildon is covering the bases," he said. "Are we going in or not?"

"Did you hear what you just said? And I *know* you didn't mean it to be insulting. By implication, I was part of your metaphor. And how do you think it feels to be thought of as a base? An inanimate object? A sandbag?"

"Spare me a feminist lecture," Noonan said. "I'm about to

keel over. I feel like somebody's got a blindfold over my eyes and is pulling."

"What do I do when I go in there?" Lucy said. "I'm terrified."

"Try to act normal. See what they want you to do."

"Who will I say you are?"

"A homosexual who writes for a magazine," Noonan said.

Lucy got out of the car. Noonan got out his side.

"Leave your washcloth in the car," Lucy said.

"Sorry," Noonan said. He went back to the car and put the washcloth on the dashboard.

"You don't think anything happened, do you?" Lucy said.

"You got mad at me when I answered that question before."

"You do?"

"It seems probable," Noonan said.

"What's going to happen?"

"I'm sure they'll tell you."

"I'll kill him," Lucy said.

"Stay calm," Noonan said.

Noonan reached around Lucy and pulled open the door. They were in a small square room, with a high desk to the left. They walked across the dirty linoleum floor to the desk. Lucy smiled. Noonan stood behind her.

"Mrs. Spenser?" the policeman behind the desk said.

On the radio, Cyndi Lauper was singing "Time After Time."

Instead of the usual anger she felt when she was called Mrs. Spenser, Lucy felt herself growing taller. She hoped that her attempt to look unshaken would not be mistaken for imperiousness. She forgot that Noonan was standing behind her and walked behind the desk. "What is it?" she said.

"Mrs. Spenser, your niece is fine. Did you understand what officer Brown said to you on the phone?"

"Where is she?" Lucy said.

"She fell asleep. She's fine. We think that you should talk to officer Brown."

"Where is Edward?" she said.

"You know the man?" the policeman said.

"I'm acquainted with him," Lucy said. The minute she said it, she realized that it sounded absurd.

"Mrs. Spenser," the policeman said. "Please have a chair."

"Isn't this unlawful detainment? What is the charge?" Lucy said.

"Mrs. Spenser, we are not trying to make a charge at the present moment. We are concerned because we need to determine whether there has been foul play."

"I'd kill him," Lucy said.

"Mrs. Spenser, we need your consent as legal guardian to have your niece examined."

Lucy put her hand over her mouth.

"Mrs. Spenser, please. Your niece is fine. Do you want to see her? She has fallen asleep. Let's get her, so you can hear her version of the story."

The policeman looked at Noonan. "Mr. Spenser?" he said.

"I'm a friend of the family," Noonan said.

"Mr? . . ."

"Noonan."

"Mr. Noonan. We're going to let you hear her version of the story. Are you a lawyer, Mr. Noonan?"

"A journalist," Noonan said.

"That's the same thing," the policeman said. "Mr. Noonan, please step this way with Mrs. Spenser."

Noonan began to have a sneezing fit. He was about to fall asleep, so he found it hard to keep his balance when the sneezes shook him. Lucy was walking down the corridor in front of him. He ran to catch up, sneezing violently.

"Where is she?" Lucy said.

Noonan began to sneeze convulsively. He reached in his pocket for the Afrin, threw his head back and squirted it in each nostril. "God help me," he said.

"If he's done anything, I'll kill him," Lucy said.

The policeman threw open a door. Nicole was asleep on a couch, a pile of uniforms on top of her.

"She's sleeping," Lucy said stupidly.

"Mrs. Spenser. We want you to talk to her. We need your permission to have her examined. I must tell you that if you refuse permission, we will begin proceedings to obtain permission."

Noonan began to sneeze wildly. Nicole heard him and shot up. She saw Lucy and was disoriented. Then she reached out and tried to grab Lucy, but she had no muscle coordination; she had been roused from a dead sleep. "Lucy?" she said. "You believe me, don't you?" Nicole started to cry. "Can we go home?"

Suddenly Nicole seemed shorter and thinner than Lucy remembered her. She was just a little girl, lying on a sofa. Lucy turned and stared at Noonan.

"Hi," Noonan said, holding up his hand.

"Hi," Nicole said.

Nicole struggled to one elbow. "We were just taking pictures," Nicole said. "You believe me, don't you?"

"Why were you taking pictures?" Lucy said.

"I made him do it. Oh, it's not his fault. This girl in California was jerking him around, and I thought he should send her some funny pictures. We just got in the back of Peter's car—"

"God, *no*," Noonan said. "Peter's car?"

Nicole turned toward him. "I was taking silly pictures of Edward on the rug," she said.

"Do you know the person the car is registered to?" the policeman said.

"What were you doing with Peter's car?" Noonan said.

"I must tell you that the person who owns this car may be in a lot of trouble," the policeman said.

"We borrowed it for the afternoon. We just wanted to take the pictures," Nicole said. "The cops are crazy. They almost killed us. They pulled in behind us at about a hundred miles an hour, and we weren't doing anything. We weren't doing anything but taking pictures—to send to his girlfriend. This is crazy," Nicole said, starting to cry.

The policeman was staring at Noonan. Noonan said, "I know the person who owns the car. Yes."

"And did the person realize what the car was being used for?" the policeman said.

"What happened?" Noonan said to Nicole.

"I was only taking pictures. I told you. Why are they making such a big deal out of this? They were going to be funny pictures for his uptight girlfriend. Nobody could see us. He was on the floor of the car."

"Mrs. Spenser," the policeman said. "May I speak to you in the other room?"

Lucy left Nicole crying on Noonan's shoulder.

"Mrs. Spenser," the policeman said, preceding her into the corridor, "we found a naked man in the back seat of a car with a minor. There are charges that pertain to this situation. When the film is developed, if we find any pictures of your niece . . . For your own peace of mind, I am sure that you want to ascertain whether or not there was foul play. We have confiscated the camera and film. Tomorrow, when the lab opens, the film will be developed. If there are pictures of your niece nude, I am afraid that the charge is going to be much more serious. Mrs. Spenser: perhaps you already see why we request a medical examination of your niece."

"Don't you believe her?" Lucy said.

"Mrs. Spenser, I don't believe anything anybody tells me," the policeman said. "Mr. Bartlett is in the lockup, and he tells me he should be released."

"Keep him there," she said.

When Lucy went back into the room, Nicole was calmer. Noonan was sitting with his arm around her shoulder.

"Nicole," Lucy said. "At any point, did you have your clothes off?"

"Why would I?" Nicole asked shrilly. "They were pictures for his girlfriend."

Lucy looked at the policeman. He looked back, as if he pitied her. Lucy wondered if she was crazy.

"You do realize that you were in a car in the woods with a naked man?" Lucy said.

"It was just Edward."

The policeman showed his surprise. He looked at Lucy.

"Let me talk to her privately," Lucy said.

The policeman looked doubtful. Then he left without saying anything. Noonan looked at Lucy and she nodded. He followed the policeman out of the room.

"Don't tell them who I am," Nicole said. "They don't have any idea who I am."

"Do you see the trouble you've caused?" Lucy said, so frustrated that she was close to tears.

"And don't tell Piggy. I'm not just saying that to protect myself. If Piggy finds out, your life is going to be miserable. I'm telling you. He's crazy about stuff like this."

"What 'stuff like this'?" Lucy said. "This is pretty bad, Nicole."

"I swear to you," Nicole said, "it was just a joke. They want to charge him with all sorts of things that are ridiculous. How can it be indecent exposure when we were in a car? Nobody was around."

"Apparently the police were."

"They almost killed us. They came tearing into the woods and almost hit the car. They were driving crazy. Lucy: you've got to believe me."

"Whose idea was it to take the pictures?" Lucy said.

"It was mine. I swear it was mine."

"Terrific," Lucy said. "Think about it. Don't you think that's rather odd, that you'd have that idea?"

"I never said I was normal. You've got to talk to the cops. You'll see tomorrow. There's nothing of me on the roll. I told that guy over and over. Nothing happened."

"Enough happened to ruin my night," Lucy said.

"Lucy, please say something to that cop. Get me out of here. Come on."

Lucy was getting angry now. "You're fourteen," she said. "Fourteen-year-olds don't get in the back seat of a car with a naked man."

"It was for a *joke.* It was *Edward.*"

"You're fourteen years old," Lucy said.

"Come on, Lucy," Nicole said. "That's not fair. You know nobody ever thinks about that."

14

NICOLE was upstairs, and Lucy was having trouble talking her into getting out of her nightgown and joining them. The day before, Nicole had called Lucy an uptight asshole. She thought that Lucy should talk to the police and force them to drop charges against Edward. He had been freed on bail, after the results of Nicole's examination at the hospital, and was back in California. Nicole was embarrassed to be a certified virgin. She had taken the television up to her room and watched it for three days. On Friday the man writing the novelization of *Passionate Intensity* was supposed to come to the house, but if Nicole was still sulking, Lucy would have to think of some excuse to cancel it, and Piggy be damned.

Actually, Lucy sympathized with Nicole, but she didn't want to let on. Of course she didn't sympathize with Edward, or with Nicole's preference for rape over being made to feel an embarrassed child, but what Nicole had said about being fourteen had cut to the quick: they *didn't* think of her as a child. She was one of them, and it seemed everyone had forgotten that she had less sophistication, less resources, and sensitive feelings. Nicole had such a good act going that she had convinced all the adults. Or perhaps, like Piggy Proctor, they didn't care that that was the case; they just wanted to keep the performance going so they could clap, whatever happened.

There was wild applause on *Hollywood Squares.* Bess Myerson had just said something funny. The camera switched to Tony Randall. Nicole didn't even look up when Lucy came into the room.

"We're going to take St. Francis to the waterfall," Lucy said. "Come on. We want you to go with us."

"I don't want to," Nicole said.

"You can't spend the summer in your room," Lucy said. "You love the waterfall."

"I don't want to drive all the way to Bristol," Nicole said. "You and Hildon get along fine without me. Go without me."

"I know you're mad, but I don't deserve this," Lucy said. "I didn't instigate anything with the police; *I'm* not pressing any charges. I just don't give a damn what they do, or what happens to him. He should have known better, even more than you should have. It's over now. Come on, Nicole. Let's make up and go out and have some fun."

"It's really a lot of fun for me to drag along with you and your lover," Nicole said.

Lucy sighed. She sat on the foot of the bed. Bess Myerson said something that broke them up again. X's and O's lit up on the big screen.

"You can tell him to tell you about the woman he's in love with. He'll tell you all about Antoinette Hadley-Cooper. He's not in love with me, if that's any consolation," Lucy said.

"Oh great," Nicole said. "So you let a friend of mine get in trouble with the cops for doing absolutely nothing to me, and you go with a guy who not only steps out on his wife but doesn't even love you. That makes a lot of sense, Lucy."

"Nicole, that isn't fair. I didn't tell you to go off in the woods with Edward, and I didn't tell the cops to go find you. Just because you had bad luck doesn't mean you ought to blame me."

"I'll agree," the contestant said.

"And the answer is, *Ronald Reagan* gets *more* mail than Boy George."

"Do you mind if I turn that off?" Lucy said. "I'd at least like to talk to you. I'm not angry, you know. Most people would be."

"You're not most people. You're my aunt. You're supposed to be on my side. If you cared about how I felt, you'd talk to the cops about Edward."

"This is silly," Lucy said. "They're not going to do anything but fine him. That's no big deal. I don't have the power to make cops do anything or not do anything."

"You're just concerned about having a proper image."

"If that was true, then I'd be mad at you, wouldn't I?"

"You are mad at me. You just won't admit it."

"I'm only mad that you're acting so stupid. You're not punishing anybody but yourself lying in bed all day. If you'd cut it out, we could drive to Bristol and have a nice day. Come on, Nicole."

"Go without me. I don't want to come." Nicole turned on her side and put on the radio. Some man was explaining how Peabo Bryson got his name. Peabo Bryson started to sing "If Ever You're In My Arms Again."

The radio. Lucy thought about Les and felt like crying—lying in bed next to Nicole and crying until somebody came and did something about it. She took a deep breath and exhaled. She looked at Nicole. Nicole looked very much like Jane at fourteen. She could remember how old they thought they were when they were Nicole's age—how old, and how misunderstood.

"Is there anything you'd rather do today?" Lucy said.

"I'd rather be left alone. This is my vacation," Nicole said, the corners of her mouth turned down.

"How about miniature golf?" Lucy said.

"Jesus," Nicole said. "Next it'll be a ride on your shoulders and a hot fudge sundae."

"Come on," Lucy said, getting up.

"The whole world does what it wants without me," Nicole said. "How come you won't?"

"Because I'm your aunt."

"I don't want to go," Nicole said. "It won't be any fun."

"You thought it was fun the other time."

"I thought it was pretty. I didn't think it was fun."

"It is pretty. Come on."

Nicole didn't answer. "Come on," Lucy said, getting up and walking out of the room. "We'll be waiting for you."

She went downstairs. Hildon thought that Nicole had no right to sulk. He was dismayed about what she'd done and he was even more dismayed with Lucy because he thought she was ignoring the situation. There were also problems at the magazine: Matt Smith had been calling, wanting to have jokes explained to him. Hildon did not have the time or the heart for it. Who enjoyed explaining a joke? He usually avoided the calls or made up any plausible explanation. Noonan was leaving on the weekend for the West Coast. He hadn't found a replacement. Many bright, young, half-crazy people had applied. It made Hildon feel old. It made him feel like an anachronism that he thought of so many things for the magazine without even being high. Old, anachronistic, and probably much crazier than those kids. The romance with Antoinette Hadley-Cooper wasn't going well. She was seeing a lot of other people, and she was either avoiding him or just expecting that he'd stand in line and take his turn like the others. Living with Maureen had become impossible: she had been spending a lot of money on clothes—clothes that were bought from the rack already rumpled and looking as if they had been half inflated with an air pump. They were full of strings and pockets and zippers. The dresses looked like something a person would wear to jump out of an airplane. Maureen was also concerned with her energy. She had been shaking lecithin granules in the spaghetti sauce and serving "shakes" for dinner that were bitter with brewer's yeast. She dropped seaweed in with yogurt and orange juice in the blender to make salad dressing. He mentioned Adele Davis' death from cancer. "That's an old story," she said. Maureen was studying acupressure, taking an aerobics class, and being counseled by some misogynistic crank who went around giving women instructions on how to be obnoxiously aggressive. Hildon poured himself a glass of orange juice and sat on the sofa hoping to get a laugh out of Lucy's latest column.

Dear Cindi Coeur,

My problem is that my fiancé loves to dance, and it's hard to make him be still when I need to have him concentrate. We are going to be married in the fall. He wants us to do the hand jive at our wedding and have break dancing at the reception. He says that dancing is healthy and fun. I love disco dancing, but I'd rather have old-fashioned dancing at my wedding reception than have people down on the floor. It's going to turn into an all-male thing, because the girls aren't going to get down in their dresses. Also, we disagree about many important things. I want a water bed, but he wants to buy a trampoline. When we go to the mall, he embarrasses me by popping his joints and doing the splits while I'm buying my trousseau. My mother says that he's in a world of his own, and that he is a bad bet for marriage, but I really love him. Can you think of anything I can do?

Boxstep Betty

Dear Box,

Many times problems go undetected because of the frantic pace of our world, which we have come to accept as normal. Have your fiancé checked for pinworms. This may be the problem.

Lucy sat on the floor beside Hildon. He smiled and handed her the column. He was in a bad mood, and she didn't think it was the time to tell him that an agent had called from New York, wanting to represent her. She found it strange to think of herself out there with Hints from Heloise and the Bhagavad-Gita. There was no noise from upstairs. She thought about asking Hildon to go up, just because Nicole knew Hildon less well and his nagging might have some effect.

"Maybe it's hard for her, not having any friends around. I think she's a little jealous of the two of us," Lucy said.

"Tell her to call some of her friends and cheer herself up."

"I wonder why she hasn't," Lucy said. "That must be it. Edward was sort of her property. They hung out together all the time."

"I wish I could have taken a swing at that guy before he got out of town."

"Oh, Hildon. He didn't do anything."

"You sound like Nicole."

"Well," Lucy said. "She sounds like an adult."

"She needs an education," Hildon said. "She ought to have a tutor or something. She's never learned anything."

"She's very bright."

"She knows lyrics to songs and she knows what people are talking about if they say something dirty and she knows who's who on television. She doesn't know anything about the world."

"Hildy—what is this sudden Puritanical outrage?"

"If you care about the kid, you ought to get her around some people who have a brain."

"She's around us," Lucy said.

"You just proved my point," Hildon said.

She hit his arm and got up. St. Francis, lying on his side panting in his sleep, opened one eye, saw that nothing was moving that he could kill, sighed deeply, and went back to sleep. Lucy went into the kitchen and opened the refrigerator. There was some white wine. She poured a glassful and went back to the living room.

Dear Cindi Coeur,

I am a struggling artist, but lately I have had more than my share of struggle within my own family. I am a painter, and recently my wife has begun to eat my art supplies. At first she gnawed the bristles on some brushes. I thought this was a nervous tic, because she had given up smoking and was trying to give up chewing gum. Then, my pastels began disappearing, or I would find stubs of them, wet at one end. I know that for a long time she has eaten bits of charcoal. The other day I saw Burnt Umber smudged at the corner of her mouth. I am worried that this is harmful to her health, but whenever I try to discuss it with her, she pretends that she has accidentally rubbed up against some paint or that she mistook a nub of charcoal for a loose chocolate chip. Do you have any advice about how I can solve this problem? I am now a

Reluctant Rembrandt

Dear Rem,

Forgive me for reciting contemporary cant, but I do believe that we are what we eat, and your wife must believe this also. The problem is simple: she wants to make herself into a work of art. Consider the relationship between *palate* and *palette*, and you will immediately understand your wife's symbolic quest. She obviously feels that you have concentrated too much on your work and not enough on her. It is, of course, a problem with all artists that they tend to become very self-involved. Think about having a romantic evening together regularly, with wine and candlelight. You might take the occasion to admire her, and perhaps suggest

> that she stand against the wall. When she feels more secure and feels that she occupies at least an equal part in your affections along with your artwork, you can confront her with your findings and tell her that she has been framed.

"I'll go tell her to call some of her friends, and we'll take the dog to the falls, okay?" Lucy said.

"Okay," Hildon said.

She went upstairs. Nicole's door was closed. The TV was on again. Lucy knocked on the door.

"What?" Nicole said.

"Are you serious about wanting us to go without you?"

"Yeah," Nicole said.

"Can I open the door?" Lucy said.

"It's your house," Nicole said.

"Nicole—when have I ever said that it was my house, or done things because it was my house?"

"So open the door," Nicole said.

Desi Arnaz was beaming on the television. The contestant put her hands over her mouth and jumped up and down in her seat. Bells rang, and everyone was screaming at once.

"Are you feeling lonesome?" Lucy said.

"Why would I feel lonesome?"

"Would you like to call some of your friends?"

"What friends?"

"Friends in California. You haven't talked to anybody in a long time, have you?"

"I don't know where Jane is," Nicole said.

Lucy didn't know what to say. "But you could call some friends," she said.

"I don't have any friends," Nicole said. "If I knew Edward's phone number, I'd call him."

"I didn't say you couldn't call Edward."

"Information did. It's unlisted." Nicole rearranged her nightgown. "Surprised?" she said. "I was going to call him to apologize for the crazy way everybody acted."

A monkey was playing the drums on television. It was dressed in overalls and a straw hat. The hat fell off as the monkey beat the drums. Loud canned laughter filled the room. The monkey jumped onto one of the drums and started swaying. "Oh no!" someone screamed.

"I know you think we're boring," Lucy said. "Why don't you call some people and talk to them? It's better than watching this idiocy all day."

"Who am I gonna call? Blueballs? And hear about how he's got the hots for Tatum?"

"No. Call somebody you really like."

"Lucy—I don't have any friends. You know who I hang out with all the time? Mom and Piggy."

Lucy tried to think of the names of Nicole's friends, but she could only remember names she had read in the tabloids. It wasn't possible that Nicole didn't have any friends her own age; L.A. was full of kids, even kids who were actors and actresses.

"Boy, you really look weirded-out," Nicole said, smiling for the first time. "What did you think? That those guys I show up places with were my friends? We just show up together to make each other look good."

"Are you telling me the truth?" Lucy said. "Don't you want friends?"

"I don't need any more hassles," Nicole said. "You've got to do things for friends. They jerk you around. It's all I can do to keep Piggy cooled out."

Lucy sat on the bed. "You must at least like some of those guys you're photographed with."

"Boy, this really interests you, doesn't it?" Nicole said. "People don't have friends when they're my age and they're in the business. It's a thing from your generation that people have friends."

"You had friends when you were a little girl," Lucy said.

"Playmates?" Nicole said. "We were just a bunch of kids that our mothers parked together. We got along all right. We had to."

"I guess I'm naïve," Lucy said. "I guess that on some level I bought it: the exciting life. That every teenager has an exciting life, I mean. Not just you."

"Big excitement. Go out to Spago or something and don't eat

anything because you'll ruin your figure and your skin, and if you drink—you can't do *that* in public until you're almost out of your teens. You just get all dressed up and hang out for a few hours with some kid that's real vain, or a fag, and then they take your picture and you go home."

"What do you do around the house?" Lucy said. She suddenly realized that she knew very little about Nicole's life.

"Exercises and stuff. Watch TV. Deal with the phone. Think about what places you should show up. Read scripts."

"What does Jane do while you're doing that?"

"Exercises. She goes out and swims in the pool. She's got friends, so she talks on the phone. She obsesses about her relationships with guys."

"Don't you think that's boring—what you do?" Lucy said.

"I could jog or go sky diving or stuff like that. Maybe not sky diving because of Piggy. What am I thinking of? You know—it's just passing time. What does anybody do?"

"But Jane—but it depresses your mother."

"I don't know what she's got to complain about. She's got Piggy around her little finger."

"But, I mean, you realize that you're in a special environment, don't you? That other fourteen-year-olds aren't like you?"

"Oh, sure. They eat pizza and hang out at malls and have two-dollar allowances, or whatever they have. Everybody's just hangin' out, Lucy. I don't think people go around having friends. Like, they've got to sit still with fifty other people in school listening to stuff all day, so maybe they know those guys better, but they don't keep them for friends." Nicole was warming to her subject. She shifted on the bed. "It's pretty much the way I'm telling you. You know, what would I talk to kids about? We all know the same stuff. I know kids I talk to about movies and what's happening down at the beach and all that, but I wouldn't make a phone call to tell them. If you really want to know what somebody else thinks about a movie, you can hear people talking around the lot, or you can read a magazine. You've got to have something to talk to people about when you're thrown together, so you talk about the movies. Or maybe if you're a guy, you play video games. Talking's not a very big thing."

"The kids around here who are your age have friends. They talk to each other. I know they do."

"I'm not saying that people don't talk. Look—it's a small town. You've got to act nice around here. These kids are snowed in half the year, right? You can move around L.A. It's a different thing."

"But don't you want to learn things? That's the thing about friends—you find things out, you . . ."

"Right. You find out they want to borrow money, or they tell you about their boyfriends. Around here, maybe they tell you about restaurants. There's not much disagreement about restaurants in L.A."

"I don't mean trivia when I say that they can tell you things. I mean that you can bounce ideas off of each other. You have somebody you trust. You help them and they help you."

"What do I need help with?"

"Whatever you needed help with."

"If I need something, or I need to find something out, Piggy gets it for me or has somebody find out and tell me."

"What would you do if Piggy died?"

"Lucy: it's business. If Piggy dies, there's another Piggy. This is a whole different system from the way you operate. It's just different."

Lucy wondered how much of what Nicole was telling her might be true—how little she might need or desire any closeness with other people. As crazy as it was to envy such an attitude, she did envy it, a little—she had even envied it in Les, whose ability to know when to withdraw was as flawless as having perfect pitch. Unlike Nicole, though, Les had developed his strategy for a reason: he thought he was out of control. That was why he chose his career—so the students would adore him; that was why everything he said was put forth in the best possible light—to insure people's approval. But all the undeserved adulation and applause only intensified the problem. It made him question himself more, spend time thinking about improving his act so that he wouldn't be found out. If they didn't find him out, he didn't respect them; on the other hand, he was grateful. So when Les left people, he left them warmly. They were surprised that he had abandoned them and had no idea of what had gone wrong. Long after they had picked up the pieces and gone on with their lives, they wrote bewildered notes on their Christmas cards. They called late at night, hardly able to articulate what was wrong. They kept in touch, because they didn't understand that the tie was irrevocably broken. He had stayed around so long to give them every chance; he didn't want to face the fact that they had failed, either. He switched on the answering machine to take care of late night phone calls. He never sent cards or letters. Actually, he did write them but he tore them up. It was a game. He played alone—a very private person, everyone agreed, but they did not discuss it and come to any deeper conclusions. The cardinal rule was that he did not introduce his friends to one another.

Lucy didn't know what else she could say to Nicole. Somehow, by osmosis, Nicole had to learn how people related to each other and what they did for each other. It really was good that Nicole had gotten away from her environment for a while. Lucy was going to try to have her spend more time with people. She had always thought it was a natural impulse to reach out to people, but Nicole obviously disagreed. In spite of all the activity in her life—all she did and saw, all the travel and things expected of her—Nicole was obviously isolated. Lucy had seen this in adults, but as a fear reaction. It was possible that Nicole was disguising her fears with a mask of coldness, but Lucy didn't think so. Nicole, amazingly, had the sense that everything was programmed: she knew what she was supposed to do, and she did it; she knew what other people were supposed to do, and if they didn't do it, they were fired, and people who would do it were brought in. And the sad thing was, Nicole wasn't even cynical—she didn't get the mean sense of satisfaction some cynic would get from living in such a world. Nicole wasn't angry. But she also wasn't inspired. She was complacent, and Lucy found that scary. There was no smugness about the complacency, so it was hard to try to attack it without seeming to be a flag-waving fool. Lucy was going to have to figure out how to deal with it.

When she went downstairs she was depressed to realize that subconsciously Nicole had gotten to her: there was Hildon, hanging out, and now he'd start talking about how hopeless Maureen was, and expecting help.

She looked at St. Francis, and was pleased—almost gratified—that he was a monster, pure and simple: he lived for fun, and fun meant carnage. He was devious when he meant to be and direct when that was the best course to take. They would take him to the waterfall and he would love it: people to sniff and threaten, wildlife to chase, rocks to bark at in the clear, shallow stream. He could swim in the deep part and get out and shake all over everybody, and it was hard to get mad at him because it was natural. How shocking to think that Nicole's natural state was to do what she did, with no real pull toward excess or passion or even the belief that something might be fun.

15

THE night before Myra DeVane turned in her *Country Daze* piece, she got a phone call from Edward, in California. She was surprised: kissing and not calling seemed to be the operative mode these days—every bit as popular and a more pleasantly passive version than the tried-and-true kiss and tell. They had gone out to dinner on Sunday, and then she had gone to bed with him. They had gone back to his room after dinner, where wallpaper printed with Golden Eagles replaced the clichéd etchings. An etching would have been welcome; she felt as if they were making love in a gigantic bird's nest and that she might be plucked away at any time. The eagles glowed in the dark, and seemed to swirl around the room as she and Edward moved on the bed.

When she heard that he was in California, she softened a little. He had probably had to leave town on short notice, as he had always said he might. She had had the phone unplugged most of the day before, when she was at home working. She was making excuses for him before he made them for himself.

What he had to say was even more interesting. He obviously assumed that she knew something she knew nothing about. Jail? Nicole? The car in the woods? She had no idea what he was talking about, and said as much. And then he leaped to his defense, not believing that she was serious. "Have you written me off?" he said. "Without even hearing my side of the story?"

She asked to hear his side of the story. She said again that she had no idea what he was talking about. No, it wasn't in the paper. Yes, she was sure. No, the front page was all about the mass murders at McDonald's. Then he turned the subject to police corruption. He had paid a bribe to keep his name out of the paper, taken a long shot. Was she telling him that it had worked?

Maybe she was wrong, but she hadn't read anything about it in the paper. She had been in town that day, and nobody was talking about it. What exactly *happened?* she asked him. He began to describe two cops who sounded like something from a Marx Brothers movie. Two cops, one of whom he swore was stoned, who had nearly crashed into a car he had borrowed for the day. The crazy cop had insisted on arresting him, and in the cop car, he had made it plain that money would be just the thing to hush this up. He had talked about how much toys cost these days, saying that he bet his son would be very pleased to have as many Kermits as money would buy. Edward, terrified and trying to console Nicole, had to listen to a long talk about toilet training on the way to the police station. There wasn't anything about . . . indecent exposure in the paper?

The closest thing to that was a news item about Miss America, whose nude pictures were in *Penthouse* and who might have her crown taken away.

He told her the story, conveniently changing some of the facts. He and Nicole (what an irony that he and a dishwasher were the only people who put themselves out for Nicole; how lonesome stars really were) had gone to the woods, where he was going to take more photographs of her. They had decided to go for a swim, and just as they were stripping down to their underwear (okay, in retrospect he realized that that was chancey, but why did people have to have such dirty minds?) a car had zoomed into the woods and veered off into the bushes . . . He could try to describe to her where to look; surely the mess would still be there. He stopped talking, amazed at how well he was doing so far.

"I don't understand," she said.

The cops had gotten hysterical. They were hysterical to begin with. What cop who thought he had a pervert in the car would drive him to a K Mart and go in with him and load a shopping cart full of stuffed frogs? The *cop* was a pervert. Edward thought he might be so crazy he was dangerous. He had his credit card with him, so what the hell: hush money for fifty frogs.

"This didn't really happen," she said.

"It did!" he said. "You've got to find out about this cop and get him off the force. It's your civic duty. He's a madman. Not capable of helping anybody."

"Go on," she said.

"It happens all the time," he said. "Cops burglarizing houses, running drug emporiums . . ."

He said that he didn't know what the cops had said to Lucy, but she had even refused to see him in jail, apparently. He had been given the word, when he finally got in touch with a lawyer who got bail posted and sprung him from jail, that under no circumstances should he go anywhere near Lucy or Nicole and that he should go back to California. He had his camera, and all the photographs, but the easel was still at Lucy's house. The whole sketch pad, with the drawings of Nicole.

"What do you think I can do about it?" she said.

"Do you think there's any way you could get it?"

"I've never been to her house," Myra said. "Let me get this straight: you and Nicole were going swimming, and then you were going to take pictures. Wouldn't her hair be a mess?"

Action shots. The toy manufacturer didn't want studio portraits.

"Listen," Myra said. "This is pretty crazy. I don't really know what to say. But there's no way I can help you."

"She's not there a lot of the time. She never locks the door."

"You're insane," Myra said. "You think I'd go out to her house and steal something? Can you imagine keeping that out of the papers? The Robber Reporter?"

She should really do a piece on police corruption . . .

Not her territory.

This was important. Worth talking to the higher-ups at the paper about. He would take a *lie detector* test saying that he had been forced by a policeman to buy every Kermit frog at the K Mart.

She believed him. It was just one crazy story after another. Day after day.

Lucy was having an affair with Hildon. They went off together at least once a week, and always on Monday.

Not a chance in hell.

He'd helped her out. Introduced her to Lucy. Confided in her about Nicole and the dishwasher.

She met him at the party by chance. By chance he knew Lucy, and Lucy was at the party. He hadn't had to stretch far to do her the favor. And she didn't care about Lucy and Hildon or Nicole and the dishwasher. It wasn't that kind of story. It was an article about *Country Daze* magazine.

That was the problem everywhere: only little stories got told. They were misleading. No one would know that the cops were madmen. No one was willing to listen to his side of the story, and he could explain everything.

Oh: did he want her to write what he'd just told her?

He thought that he could confide in her. He didn't think of her as a cold-blooded reporter, but as . . . a friend.

Who would break into someone's house.

It was unfair! He had done nothing wrong.

He was lucky he wasn't still in jail.

That was true.

Well: it wasn't the phone call she expected, but it was nice to hear from him, and she hoped he would have a good summer in California.

"Wait a minute," he said. "The job photographing those elevators in New York came through. I'm going to be there in a couple of weeks. I don't have any desire to walk back into Looney Tunes, but I'd like to see you again."

That got a slight smile. He couldn't see that, of course. She said she didn't see how that would happen, but she was glad they had met. To have a good summer.

"I'm serious," he said. "You could get a flight from Burlington to New York for twenty-seven dollars. I'm going to be in a room at the Plaza."

"I don't know," she said.

"Think about it," he said. "I'd like to see you again." He gave her his phone number.

When she hung up, she got a Coke out of the refrigerator and sat on the kitchen counter to drink it. It was very cold, and so strong that it burned going down. She thought about hopping a plane and going to the Plaza. It was such a nice idea that it made her realize how unhappy she was in Vermont. The *Country Daze* piece was finished, and she had no other big assignment. She was owed a week's vacation; she could go to the city and stay for a week.

She went out to the driveway, to take the piece in to work. She had not written anything about Hildon's affair with Lucy Spenser. She had nothing in it about Nicole Nelson being Lucy's niece, or about Nicole having a crush on a dishwasher at the inn. She did not intend to pursue the story Edward had told her about the police, or to include mention of the fact that the publisher's grandfather was a jump rope baron. She did not think there was any purpose in creating scandals where there were none and worried that writers who did were going to beat her to the best magazines and newspapers. It probably was an odd notion for a journalist to have: that many things were what they seemed, or less than they seemed. Myra saw it as a condescending attitude toward your subjects that their sex lives had anything to do with their performance at work. It was easy to turn things into a comedy: the lonelyhearts adviser whose own life was a shambles; her niece pining for a dishwasher, but involved with a man found naked in the woods; her boss cheating on his wife with her; Lucy's former lover writing letters from afar that were half pleading and half accusatory. Any other reporter would have stooped to making Lucy a person living a ludicrous life, and it bothered Myra that Lucy did not even feel she owed her a face-to-face interview, let alone a debt of gratitude. Even Lucy's dog, she remembered hearing, was on parole: one more dead sheep and the police said they were going to look the other way when the farmer shot him.

Taking the back road to the office, she stopped while a herd of cows crossed the road. In Boston it would be twenty-year-olds with stringy hair, backpacks and Shakti sandals. Here, it was cows. The day was overcast; another day that threatened rain. As she started to drive again, she rolled up her car window halfway and braked for a flock of birds that she did not think could possibly swoop above the car in time. She put on the radio and listened to an official from the Miss America pageant who insisted that they were justified in removing Miss America's crown. Myra spent a few seconds imagining what the letter from Miss America to Cindi Coeur would read like, and what Cindi Coeur would write back. Myra had always known girls like Lucy; girls who were in the right place at the right time. It was too stuffy in the car with the window rolled up and too cold with it rolled down. She decided to leave it down. She felt as if she could drive this road with her eyes closed. She passed Honey House, a small old farmhouse painted yellow, with a beehive painted on the front door. She couldn't see the hive now, because the door was open and a screen door had been put up. There were hand-lettered signs, pointing down the driveway to the garage, telling people where to go to buy honey. She had never bought any. Someone had told her that the farmer's wife wore an apron with swarming bees embroidered on the front and earrings with clusters of bees dangling from them. Not far from the Honey House was a wide dirt driveway that led to half a dozen pastel-colored trailers. A small American flag that had been anchored, somehow, in a birdbath, flapped in the breeze. Myra pulled quickly to the right; while staring at the flag, she had drifted to the center of the road, and a truck was coming at her. She heard her tires in the gravel and held the wheel steady. To the left and right, now, were acres of land that had been plowed. A dog trotted along the side of the road. A woman in a plaid skirt, holding a little girl's hand, walked behind the dog. What did these people do with their lives? What did they think? Depending on her own state of mind, Myra thought they were either desperate or utterly content. She was feeling low today, so it was a day when she was certain they had it all over her: that they cleaned the lint off of the washing machine filter with the same care she used editing her prose, and that both tasks were equally worthwhile. In fact, if she really wanted to feel sorry for herself, these people had appliances and she didn't—no dishwasher, no washing machine, no dryer—not even a blender after she made the mistake of leaving an iced-tea spoon in hers and turning it on. An iron. Everybody had an iron. It was like having a spine. To cheer herself up, she reminded herself that while everybody had an iron, not everybody had an ironing board. Ironing boards were among the most improvised household articles since coffee tables made out of wood cartons, and cinder block bookcases. She had removed the top board from her bookcase and put it across her table/desk to iron on, when she first came to Vermont. She realized that it was pathetic to equate having an ironing board with being a real adult. That was probably why she often used the ironing board as a chair.

People's little secrets. The things they would not even think of as being secrets, until someone, say, asked to borrow an ironing board.

She went over the high bump that led down a steep slope to the newspaper's parking lot. It was Saturday and there were only two cars in the lot; out of habit, she pulled into her space, facing the Leglan River. Before the paper moved into the big brick building, it had been a medical facility; the doctors' assigned parking place signs were still there. A friend on the paper who had gone to Disneyland had put a cavorting Minnie Mouse decal over hers. Previously she had been Dr. Trigowski. The water was muddy and almost flooded the banks. It had been a rainy summer. The dampness was still in the air, and the sky still looked like rain.

Nate Wells and Herb Walsh were in the newspaper office. Herb had pulled his chair up to Nate's desk and was shaking his head, much amused by something, as Myra walked in. Nate held a hand up in greeting and picked up his cigarette from the ashtray (another non-ashtray ashtray: a brick with the center gouged out) and took a puff before continuing with what he was reading. There was a picture on Nate's desk of his wife and child. His wife had left him and was remarried to Nate's cousin. His child had gone on a camping trip in the Grand Canyon and never been heard from again. There were also two separate photographs of collies. Nate now lived with two collies. At Christmas he had sent out cards with a photograph of the two collies sitting and facing the camera, one with a red bow around its neck and the other with a green bow. Below the picture was printed Greetings from Our House to Yours.

"Read this, read this," Herb said, taking the piece of paper out of Nate's hand. "This woman made up her own press release. This sounds like a story for you, Myra." Herb loved to be amused. He often brought the *Enquirer* in to work. He especially liked the test in a recent issue that people could take to find out if their co-workers were space aliens.

Under a line of exclamation points, *Bulletin* had been written in calligraphy. It was an announcement of the founding of a feminist commune, subtitled *Deep Breathing Can Destroy the Enemy.* As best Myra could make out, it was a holistic approach to man-hating. Since she found these things more depressing than Herb, she was just about to sigh and hand it back when she caught the list of members. The first name on the list was Maureen Hildon's. Myra's eye went back to the text. The leader, Davina Cole, had recently acquired the long-abandoned old post office building, and by September 1, would be ensconced with ten other women who wished to *save mankind from man. Mankind* could best be saved by *womankind,* but the *first step necessary* was to *recondition* through *relaxation. Self-awareness = satisfaction.* Apparently, through talking to yourself, hyperventilating, and examining your breasts, the *enemy* could be *subverted.* Potential members were urged to send a full-length black-and-white photograph or, preferably, negative, and $30 to Davina Cole. *Space may be limited,* Ms. Cole warned, though *psychic sisterhood is expansive.* There was a drawing in the lower left-hand corner of a woman with fingertips that looked like talons on her breast (nipple mid-center, like a bull's eye), and an arrow around the breast, moving counterclockwise. *Women now embrace destiny not douche bag,* it concluded.

Myra handed it back to Herb, frowning. It was beginning to seem downright lethargic not to tackle the true story of the *Country Daze* staff. Whatever it was.

Herb fell over in the chair, laughing.

"Uh-oh," Nate said. "We've offended her feminist sensibilities."

"This is the wife of the editor of *Country Daze*," Myra said, pointing to the piece of paper that Herb was now weeping into, like a handkerchief.

"You're kidding? His wife belongs to this thing?"

"What do you think I ought to do?" Myra said.

"Infiltrate," Herb said. "Oh God, look at this thing."

"Run a side-bar," Nate said. "Spill the facts and get some shrink to comment."

"How about Joan Rivers?" Herb said.

"I'm serious," Myra said. "These people are a *lot* stranger than they seem."

"The poor guy," Nate said. "What can he do about his wife being a lunatic?"

Myra looked at him. He meant it; he felt sorry for Hildon. And if she told him that Hildon was having an affair with Lucy Spenser/Cindi Coeur, he would shrug and say that was nothing. Men really did stick together. That was true.

It suddenly occurred to her that she hesitated to analyze people's messy lives because that would be hypocritical. When had she analyzed her own? Nothing much was happening in her own life right now. She was waiting for more: a bigger city, a more prestigious job, some romantic involvement. That old, familiar complex that seemed overwhelming—the last thing she'd want to admit to people. It was as though it was a personal failure, a sign of weakness, not strength, to have effectively kept the world at bay. Going to New York would be a way to try to change that.

Herb called her a sissy and said he was going to infiltrate.

She left her piece on the editor's desk, with a note asking him to call her in the morning to let her know if she could take off at the end of the week.

16

WHEN she heard the back door close, Nicole turned off the television and sat in the silence of her room. Though she would never let on to Lucy, she thought that she was beginning to figure out what quality Lucy had that she herself lacked. It was difficult to put into words. It was partly what Jane always said: that Lucy was solid. Lucy would make a good actress, because she really had a foundation; she didn't have to invent one. Piggy always said that Marilyn Monroe was a great actress because people could tell that she was someone underneath, and the more she giggled and pursed her lips, the more real the hidden someone became.

Nicole envied her. She kept her own hours, didn't have to dress any particular way, didn't seem to care what people thought about her. Dropouts were interesting to Nicole (that was what her grandmother called Lucy and Jane): they didn't have a lot of hype surrounding them; they were just out there, like nudists.

She remembered sitting in a screening room with Piggy, watching Marilyn Monroe movies. When Marilyn smiled, Piggy would point out how much sadder that made her look. When Marilyn cried, you knew she was going to pull through. Piggy also had photographs of Marilyn Monroe in an album: when she was half naked she looked ladylike; when she was dressed in a suit she looked like a sex object. Piggy was hoping that Nicole could grow up to be more like Marilyn Monroe. If she didn't, he wanted her to try to fake it. As far as Nicole was concerned, that was impossible. Even Marilyn Monroe would have found faking it too much of a chore. She thought that a lot of it had to do with how close the camera came in. That made people's eyes look large, and when people saw big eyes, they assumed that there was depth. It was a trick. It was probably a more interesting world for people who were myopic.

Nicole was feeling sorry for herself. Her mother hadn't called for days. Edward was back in California. He had been a friend, and look what happened: people butted in. He probably wouldn't have been around much longer anyway. It wasn't like she was going to New York with him. He wasn't Jerry Lee Lewis.

She went downstairs. Lucy's new column was finished, so she read that:

Dear Cindi Coeur,

My husband has pet names for everything in our trailer, but he often has trouble remembering our son's name. This has so disturbed Elbert Jr. that he has repeatedly questioned me about whether Elbert Sr. is really his father. What can I do to make Elbert Sr. take the time to care?

Honeybuns

Dear Honey,

There may be a psychological (psy.cho.log.i.cal: having to do with the mind) reason for what Elbert Sr. is doing. Think about what a terrible name Elbert is. Hardly anyone would name their child Elbert if they wished him success. Elbert Sr. is probably maladjusted because of his name, and he may be displacing his resentment or anger onto your son. You do not say what your own name is, but I notice that "honeybuns" refers to a part of the female anatomy that has obviously caught your husband's attention. Perhaps he is so taken with your derrière that he is unable to concentrate on his son. Try sitting down when your husband comes home from work, and then see if he has his wits about him to greet your son by name. Also, you do not give your husband's age. It is possible that he is suffering from Alzheimer's disease. Often, when people's faculties start to go, they have an awareness that this is happening, and they become afraid. Probably your husband would not admit that this was the case, even if you confronted him with the evidence. It might be a good idea to suggest to him that you move to the South, where it is still very much the style for everyone to greet each other as "honey."

Nicole got her Walkman, found the Madonna tape, and put it on and went out into the yard. Lucy's house was on top of a hill, but everywhere Nicole looked, it was flat. It wasn't late enough in the afternoon for the cows to have been herded into the pasture, so Nicole could see in all directions, and there was nothing in sight. It was windy and overcast. Lucy and Hildon were going to be cold at the waterfall.

Nicole tapped one foot on the chaise, keeping time with the music and keeping a fly away at the same time. She began to tap both feet. The sky brightened a little. This early in the day, the moon was already visible. The moon had been full, huge and orange over the weekend; it looked like a special effect, something seen through the window of a spacecraft, instead of the real moon seen through the windshield of Lucy's car. Nicole missed driving. That was the one thing Bobby Blue had taught her to do: he had taught her to drive. His chauffeur, really. Out at the beach. Not on the freeways or anything. She tried to think of Bobby as a friend. She actually liked the chauffeur better. He was going to be an actor. When he got off work he hung out, waiting to be discovered. He had turned her on to Madonna long before Madonna had a hit song; he was a friend of hers, and he'd recorded her. Now, he said, she wouldn't even speak to him.

A butterfly flew past. It was a Monarch butterfly. Nicole knew that because she had read for a part in a TV movie called *Monarch.* She lost out to some kid who wasn't even around Hollywood six months later. Somebody said she cracked up, but Piggy's wife said she'd heard she went back to Montana. Maybe it was the same story, but Piggy's wife just filled in the detail.

She wondered what it was going to be like, living with her mother and Steven when she got back to L.A. She hoped her mother wasn't in some lovey-dovey mind-set.

When the tape was over, she got up and went in the house. Brooke Shields was on the cover of one of Lucy's magazines. Nicole couldn't imagine why they didn't make her pluck her eyebrows. Nicole flipped through the magazine. Brooke Shields with Michael Jackson. That was about as convincing as

Liberace with Farrah Fawcett. She carried the magazine, and a couple of others, upstairs. She started the water in the tub and dropped in champagne bath beads. She probably should have gone to the waterfall. There was nothing to do.

Nicole rummaged around in her Sportsac. She took out a cigarette case Piggy had given her years ago. She liked it because it had a mirror inside, and because of the inlay: a mother-of-pearl Christmas tree with rhinestone lights. The engraving beneath it said: "Merry Christmas, 1960—Michael and Ginger." Nicole kept her joints in it. She took the radio into the bathroom, put it on the back of the sink, and turned up the volume: Cyndi Lauper, singing "Girls Just Want to Have Fun." It was weird, Nicole thought: what would be background noise in L.A. was noticeable in the country. Out the window, what looked like a funnel of butterflies spread out and flew away. Nicole looked down at the ground, but there was nothing. After a few minutes a swallow swooped low over the lawn and shot away. Nicole dumped the little pink conch-shaped soaps out of the clamshell-shaped soap dish and used it for an ashtray. Naturally, the minute she took the pack of matches out of the cigarette case, struck one, lit the joint and sat down, static started on the radio. The radio station was playing "Here Comes the Sun" throughout the day, and the first listener to call when it began would get a bottle of orange soda. Through the static she could hear Walter Mondale saying that he did not think he was unexciting.

She stretched out in the tub, raising her toes under the stream of water. She wondered who Piggy was going to vote for in the election. Piggy always said that he supported whoever buttered his bread. Piggy's way of talking made the whole world seem like an enormous restaurant.

The talk with Lucy had upset her. She turned off the water and slid forward until her shoulders were under water. She puffed on the last of the joint. She was remembering an episode of *Passionate Intensity* when Cora, her adoptive doctor-mother, took her aside and told her that she was being given an award at the hospital. She wanted Stephanie to go, but she had to think of a way to leave Gerald at home: the constant acclaim was too much for him—he needed friends of his own, not her friends. Gerald was lost in his fictional world; he didn't know how to deal with people any longer. And Cora was beginning to feel guilty; of course her lover would be there, and she didn't want her big night spoiled by having to shun him to protect Gerald's feelings. Pauline, who played Cora, was always catching flies, wringing her hands and improvising—anything to hog the camera. In real life, she was having an affair with the main scriptwriter, so she always had monologues anyway.

Nicole slipped lower, turned her head to the side and blew bubbles in the water. She could not remember why it was, exactly, that she had been drunk in the bathtub when Cora was dressing in her strapless evening gown to go to the awards banquet. They had done so many takes of the bathtub scene that her skin had gotten shriveled. Also, she had to sit in the tub in a flesh-toned body suit, which felt gross. There wasn't enough hot water, but the director said her shivering just made her look more drunk. In real life, Henry, who played Gerald, was writing a novel. He was also seeing a psychiatrist, to figure out if he was writing the novel because he was genuinely motivated or because he strongly identified with his character, who was a wimp and a failure. The doctor suggested that these issues were fascinating and that he write a nonfiction book about them instead. He came to talk to Henry every day during the lunch break. The psychiatrist was overweight, and spent much of the time trading jokes with the cast and eating ham sandwiches and olives from the buffet table set up on the side. Henry was beginning to wonder aloud to the cast whether the doctor was bucking for inclusion in his book. His nickname for the doctor was Brine Breath.

Nicole cupped her hands over her breasts. She was too afraid to examine them, and although she realized that it was unlikely she would detect anything by placing her hands there, she hoped that somehow, mystically, her wish to keep her breasts would be transmitted through her fingers. While putting on her evening gown, Cora had found the lump in her breast.

"Cut! Cut! That screaming's not in the script!" the director had said. "If I want an Indian uprising, I'll say so. When I don't, I don't want to hear screaming. Get the camera back to the bubblebath."

"I think that's in keeping with what my character would do," Pauline said.

"Pauline," the director said, "women don't scream when they touch their bodies. They don't even scream when men touch their bodies unless they're whores in a Bangkok whorehouse, faking it. Get camera two back on those goddamn bubbles."

Nicole stubbed out the roach in the soap dish. She closed her eyes. It wouldn't be long before she was back on the show, with Pauline in a state and Henry whispering things under his breath about her uncalled-for hysteria. Nicole would again be staggering and hitting up against walls and unable to get out of bed. It was a lot better than sitting in a chair and hearing about the bombing of Pearl Harbor.

Nicole got out of the tub and wrapped a towel around herself. She dumped the roach and ashes down the toilet and flushed, then rinsed the shell and put it back on the sink with the little soaps in it. Even though Nicole was probably the first to hear "Here Comes the Sun" on the radio, the prize didn't seem worth the trouble of running downstairs and dialing the number. Instead, she sang along as she dried off. She opened the bathroom cabinet and decided on powder instead of lotion. A sure sign that Lucy used a diaphragm. No woman over the age of twenty powdered her body—the stuff was only around if there was a baby. She hadn't found the diaphragm yet. She wondered if Lucy had taken it with her to the waterfall.

Nicole sprinkled powder over herself, feeling relaxed and light-headed. It was really her good luck that Piggy hadn't sent a tape or called. Tomorrow was the day she was meeting the guy who had . . . no, that was Frankie Avalon who wrote "Venus." Or had Piggy said that the guy was a scholar who had written about the real Venus? Venus was some love goddess or something. Since America had the hots for Stephanie

Sykes, vamp and victim, it was appropriate that the guy who had written about Venus was now writing about Nicole. Or whatever Piggy had said, babbling away on the last tape.

Her hands were still dusty from the powder when the Federal Express truck pulled into the drive. Did she know Piggy or did she know Piggy? "Oh, gag me," she said to herself. She hollered "Wait a minute" from the bathroom window, pulled on her bikini pants and dress and began to run down the stairs. Her hair dripped down her back and felt awful. On the stairs, she had the feeling, for a second, that she was on an escalator. Just as she opened the door, a bee buzzed in. She jumped back. The deliveryman jumped to one side.

"Signs of summer," he said. "Nicole Nelson?"

She signed for the package. The usual blue and white envelope. Piggy's wit and wisdom inside.

"Do a lot of people tell you that you look like Stephanie Sykes?" the delivery man said.

"I am," she said.

"You're her? You can't be her. You're in Vermont."

"It's a show," Nicole said. "I'm a real person. I travel."

"You're putting me on."

"Give me a quiz," Nicole said.

"What happened when . . . nah, you watch it like me. You'll just pass the quiz, and that won't prove anything."

"Well," Nicole said, shrugging. "I mean, it's not important to me if you believe it or not."

"Hey," the man said. "Are you really?"

Nicole nodded.

"Nah," the man said. "People think you're her all the time, huh?"

"This is from my agent," Nicole said, slapping the envelope against her palm. "My agent usually sends me cassettes instead of calling me. Then he can nag me if I don't remember everything he says. He wants me to play them over at night before I go to sleep. No kidding. Want to hear?"

The man was starting to look perplexed. "Well—if you are Stephanie Sykes, you sure are good on that show," the man said. "My wife Betamaxes it and I watch it at night. Have a couple of beers and check out what's new, you know? Good show. Sorry it was canceled."

"It's going to be back on in the fall," Nicole said.

"Yeah?" he said. He stood there, not saying anything. "What did you say you were doing here?" he said.

"It's a secret house where I rendezvous with Michael Jackson," she said.

"Nah," the man said, shaking his head. "Now I know you're putting me on."

"How do you know?" Nicole said.

"Because he's on tour."

"His double is on tour. Michael Jackson is upstairs in the bathtub."

The man frowned. He looked past her into the empty house.

"Have a good day now," he said, turning to go.

"One second," she said. "Just one second. I'm going to prove it to you."

She went into the living room and got the cassette player. She went out to the front stoop—the man backed up so far he almost fell down the steps—and put the player on the little table. She opened the package, took out the tape, and clicked it in. "This is my agent, Piggy Proctor," she said.

He stood on the first step, smiling nervously. The truck was idling in the driveway. The tape started.

"Hello, cream puff," Piggy said. "I feel as far away from you as cellulite is from Jane Fonda's thighs. Just a few words of information before the writer gets there . . . some Piggytalk to psych you into Sykesdom—"

"See?" Nicole said, clicking it off.

"He does this instead of calling you?"

Nicole nodded.

"And Michael Jackson's upstairs?"

"I was kidding about that."

"Jesus," the man said. "I'm glad. My wife's not gonna believe this as it is."

"Would she like my autograph?" Nicole said.

"Oh, *would she!* She was an abused child herself, and she lives and breathes Stephanie Sykes. Her stepfather locked her in closets and threatened to push bees in through the keyhole. Hey, what she doesn't know from suffering. She worships you. Would she like it? You bet she'd like it."

Nicole went into the house and ripped a piece of paper out of Lucy's tablet. There was another Cindi Coeur column. Nicole would have to read it later. Lucy was really pretty funny.

"You know, the other show she really loves is *All My Children.* She wrote a letter to Phoebe Tyler Wallingford one time, and she wrote her back. You know, in real life her husband was an alkie, and she had to leave him because they had kids."

"What's your wife's name?" Nicole said.

"It's . . . jeez, her nickname or her real name?"

"What name does she go by?"

"Well, her name's Patricia, but everybody calls her Poodle."

"Maybe she'd like it if it was informal," Nicole said. She wrote: "To Poodle—may you always be top dog. Best wishes, Stephanie Sykes."

"This is fabulous," the man said. "This is really fabulous. You just thought of that? Right now?"

"Sure. Actresses have got to think on their feet, right?"

"Hey, that's amazing," the man said. "I sure am glad I mentioned that you look like Stephanie Sykes. Man, who'd believe it? I ring the doorbell and there you are. Pretty unbelievable."

The thought of listening to the rest of the cassette was more than Nicole could bear. "Do you think you could do me a favor?" Nicole said. "My aunt was supposed to give me a lift into town. I don't know where she is. Are you going that way?"

"Oh, sure. Glad to. The only thing is—jeez, I hate to ask a star this, but a guy got fired about a year ago. If you can sort of duck down so nobody sees you—"

"You got it," Nicole said. "Just one sec."

She ran upstairs, got the cigarette case, her makeup bag, and her purse. She threw them all in, put on her jellies, and ran down the stairs again.

"Man, Poodle's never gonna believe this. Of course, I'd better leave this part out," the man said. "I kind of like it that she's so jealous. I don't want to work her up, though. I don't know what she'd say if I told her I was riding around with Stephanie Sykes."

Nicole hopped in the truck. High off the ground, she felt more powerful. She was going into town with a plan, and she thought it was a good one.

"You know who else I really like? Liz Curtis. Gloria Loring. And Priscilla Presley. I think she can really act. Can you imagine that? Moving into Elvis Presley's house when she was your age? She's really a knockout. That natural look makes women look good. She had that teased-up hair when their kid was born. She looked about ten years older then than she does now."

"I don't think Lisa Marie's as pretty as her mother," Nicole said.

"Jeez—imagine being just a baby and having your old man fall over dead in the bathroom. I've got a three-year-old kid, and he'd fall over dead with me if I was on the floor, you know? Not that it's not always rough, but when you're just a little kid and one of your parents drops dead, it's got to be bad. You know he wasn't any daddy that put bees through the keyholes. He probably pushed diamonds through, huh? They say Graceland's a pigsty now. It's a big tourist trap."

The deliveryman was speeding. Swallows flew past the truck, flying low over the road. A package slid to the floor. When they got off the dirt road, Nicole ducked low. It was too much trouble to bend over that far, so she sat up again, then slid way down on the seat.

"Sorry," the deliveryman said. "It's protocol, you know? Did you know that the Queen never carries her own umbrella? Wacky world, huh?"

Nicole nodded.

"My mother-in-law's neighbor was in a room next to Lucie Arnaz when she had her last kid," the deliveryman said. "Saw her every day. Said she was really friendly. Kept the door to her room open a lot of the time."

Nicole's thoughts were drifting. This wasn't the outfit she

would have chosen if she'd had more time—and it probably wouldn't have been the moment if she hadn't been stoned—but what the hell. She might not have friends, but she didn't have to stay a virgin, and what better place to be deflowered than in a shrine to yourself?

17

HARRY WOODS was embarrassed. It was one thing to have a Stephanie Sykes shrine in his room, and another thing to have the real-life Stephanie walk in. She walked around, looking at all the photographs he had cut out of magazines, strolling the way people stroll through art galleries on Sunday, with one eye on whatever paintings were hung, while picking up people in their peripheral vision whom they might make a move on. Nicole intended to go to bed with Harry Woods, but she wasn't entirely sure how to seduce him. She had seen enough movies to know that props would be a help, but there were very few things in Harry Woods's room. Eye makeup was also a help, but she had forgotten to put on makeup in her rush to get a ride with the Federal Express man. So she was strolling around, trying to think, vaguely assessing different images of herself. There were pictures from newspapers, from magazines, black-and-white glossies he had gotten from the studio. He would probably buy a dozen Stephanie Sykes dolls. There were stories about *Passionate Intensity* tacked to his bulletin board. There was also a large oil painting of a spaniel with a bird in its mouth, an orange and blue sky glowing behind the dog, and a man down on one knee with a rifle, on a hillside, near a patch of trees.

"Do you like to hunt?" she said, sitting in one of his director's chairs. She toed one of her jellies off her heel and, with her toe still in the shoe, flapped it.

"Nah, that was there when I moved in," he said.

"I'm glad you don't like to hunt," she said. "I think hunting's gross."

"Yeah," he said. "People come to the inn with deers dripping down their vans and stuff. Sometimes the parking lot looks like a slaughterhouse."

"That's really sick," she said.

"They say if you don't kill 'em, they starve to death," he said. He shook a cigarette out of the pack and held it toward her.

"No thanks," she said.

"Mind if I do?" he said.

"Go ahead," she said.

He lit the cigarette and sat in the other director's chair. There was a white plastic table between the two chairs. He threw the pack of cigarettes on the table.

"So you must really think it's weird and all, my having all this stuff in my room."

"I don't know," she said. "What do you like so much about Stephanie Sykes?"

He blushed. He looked at the table and tapped his cigarette ash into an ashtray.

"You don't smoke?" he said.

She shook her head no. She picked up the pack and flipped the top open and closed. Her shoe fell off her foot.

"So you must really think you're in the boonies," he said.

"Oh, I don't know," she said. "You meet interesting people everywhere, you know?"

"Where all have you been?" he said.

"Paris," she lied.

"Yeah?" he said. "Are they real nasty to Americans, like I heard?"

"Oh, I don't know," she said. "I stayed with a friend."

"Yeah?" he said. "They call streets over there boulevards. I know that."

"Yeah. Paris is really exciting."

"You speak French?"

"No," she said. "But it worked out okay, because the guy I stayed with spoke French."

"Yeah?" he said. "There's a lot of Oriental tourists at the inn this year."

They sat in silence. She put the cigarette pack back on the table and ran the tip of her second finger up and down the edge of the arm on the director's chair.

"You must think it's pretty odd sittin' here," he said.

She shrugged. "The guy in Paris has got a lot more pictures than you do," she said. "I put up pictures sometimes."

"Yeah? Whose pictures have you got up?"

"People I've met," she said.

"Yeah? You must know a lot of stars."

"I guess so."

"Yeah," he said. "There's a lot of pictures with you and Bobby Blue."

"We're just friends."

"You ever meet Brooke Shields?"

"Sure," Nicole said. "We're with the same agency."

"Yeah?" he said. "What's she like?"

"Well, you know," Nicole said. "There's nothing between her and Michael Jackson."

"I read where there's nothing between Michael Jackson and anybody."

"Yeah. I think he's messed up."

"You know Michael Jackson?"

"Not very well."

"Yeah?" he said, with more interest. "You've met him?"

"A couple of times," she said. "He's real reclusive and everything."

"Yeah."

"He's really a great performer and all, though."

"Yeah," he said.

She took off her other shoe and slid a little lower in the chair, crossing her feet at the ankles. She wished she had touched up the polish on her toes. St. Francis had run up to her and licked her foot when the nail polish wasn't quite dry; the smeared polish made her big toe look bloody. She put her heel over her toes. There was a big pink mosquito bite on her shin. Nothing she could do about that.

"So what's it like being an actress?" he said.

"I don't know," she said. "It's not hard. It's hard standing around the set while you do scenes over and over. Kind of boring." That didn't sound right. "Kind of exciting," she said.

"I bet," he said.

Another thought came to her. "Some days I feel like Jonah in the belly of the whale," she said.

"Swallowed up," he said.

"Yeah. So it's nice to be in the country and all."

He nodded. He took another cigarette out of the pack and lit it. "Hey, you don't drink, do you?" he said.

"Oh, sure," she said.

He got up. Across the room was a small refrigerator sitting on the floor, with a jade plant on top and a pile of paperbacks. He opened the door and took out a beer. "Beer or vodka?" he said.

"Vodka, please."

He went into the bathroom. "This is clean," he said, coming out, holding a glass. "The shelf's just in the b-r."

She nodded. She had had vodka before, in fruit juice, and it wasn't bad.

"I've got some orange juice," he said.

"That'll be fine."

"Yeah," he said. "That's all I like: vodka and beer. I drink Coke too. Real Coke, not diet stuff."

"You've got a great body," she said. "You don't need to diet."

He blushed again. The orange juice was in a bowl with a plastic top. He took off the top and poured the juice into the glass, which he had put on the floor. He poured some vodka in, then put both the orange juice and vodka back in the refrigerator.

"Sorry I don't have any ice," he said.

"It's good and cold," she said, taking a sip. It tasted almost like regular orange juice.

"I drank fifteen of them last month," he said.

"Yeah?"

"I mean in the same night."

"Yeah," she said. "I've done that."

"It's not legal for you to drink, is it?"
"Sure," she said.
"You're fourteen, aren't you?"
"Nah, that's what the studio says. It's sort of embarrassing that they always lie and everything."
"How old are you?"
"How old do I look?"
He blushed. "I don't know," he said.
"How old are you?" she said.
"Twenty-one."
He took a sip of beer. "How old are you?"
"Sixteen."
"Yeah?" he said, taking another sip of beer. "That's cool."
"Yeah," she said. "They lie about everything."
"What do they lie about?"
"Oh, everything."
He continued to look at her.
"The P.R. people say whatever they think they ought to say. You know, most of the dates are put-ups, for instance. Guys who don't go with girls and stuff."
"Yeah? You ever go out with one of those guys?"
"I like straight guys," she said. "I guess business is business, though."
He nodded.
"You know what they call Bobby Blue?" she said.
"What?"
"Bobby Blueballs, because he's a mama's boy."
"Jeez," he said. His face turned red. He took another swig of beer. "I stopped hanging around my mother when I went to kindergarten."
"Yeah," she said.
"So how long are you here for?"
"Not much longer."
He nodded.
"You live here all year?" she said.
"Oh yeah," he said. "This is my place."
They were in a stucco building at the back of the inn's prop-

erty. It faced a tiny stream. There were two doors. As they talked, somebody came in, whistling. You could hear everything through the walls. The person who came in turned on the water and hummed.

"They threw this place in as part of the deal," he said. "I used to room with another guy, before I got this job. I like living alone."

"It's nice," she said.

"Well," he said. "I'm not always gonna be a dishwasher. I've been workin' a couple nights a week down at the hardware store. I install doors on the weekends with this other guy. We were thinking about opening our own hardware store."

"You like this town?" she said.

"It's okay. Only I don't know if it can support two hardware stores, you know?"

"Yeah," she said. "Maybe not."

"What I am officially is an underachiever," he said. "My brother's in Juilliard."

"What's that?"

"Music school."

She had finished her drink. She put the glass on the table.

"Would you like another one?"

"Thanks."

He got up and took her glass back to the floor in front of the refrigerator.

"I thought maybe you wanted to be a chef," she said.

"A chef? Nah. I'm just a meat and potatoes man."

"So what's your favorite show?" she said.

He poured orange juice and vodka in the glass.

"Could you make this one a little stronger?" she said.

"Sure," he said. "Sorry."

He put the bowl and bottle back in the refrigerator, took out another beer and twisted off the top. He went into the bathroom and threw away the cap, then came back and got the glass from the floor.

"I don't believe you're really sittin' here," he said. He shook his head. He took out another cigarette and lit it.

"Well, that note you wrote me was pretty nice."

"Yeah," he said, blushing. "I didn't think the waitress was really going to give it to you, you know?"

"Well, I didn't say anything because of the guy I was with."

"Yeah? What guy were you with?"

"Oh—did you see who was sitting at the table?"

"I looked out the window," he said.

"The tall guy with the sandy hair."

"He your friend from Paris?"

"No. That's another guy."

He nodded. "You travel around a lot, huh?"

"More than I really want to. It's nice to just hang out."

"Yeah," he said. "I can dig that."

"I was with my aunt and some of her friends. We were going to the fireworks."

"I missed them," he said. "Yeah. I was working."

There was silence again. The man next door was singing in the shower.

"Maybe we should go in the bathroom and sing along," she said.

"Yeah," he said. "He's noisy. Bill Sinclair. He works maintenance. Cut his thumb off with hedge clippers last year."

"Oh, gross," she said.

"Yeah," he said.

"So where do you hang out?" she said.

"Raindance," he said. "You been over there?"

"No."

"It used to be on the main street, but it moved this summer. It's down past the Episcopal Church. Sort of hard to find, if you don't know what you're looking for."

"So do they have music and everything?"

"Yeah," he said. "Live bands Friday and Saturday."

"I'm always listening to music in L.A. It's been pretty quiet around here."

"Their bands are pretty good," he said.

Nicole had almost finished her drink. He was watching her.

"Did you really keep the glass I drank out of?" she said.

"I was just kidding," he said.

"I guess it's not like it had a picture of me on it or anything."

"Right."

"Well," she said. "It was nice to stop by." She put her glass on the table.

"I don't get it," he said.

"What don't you get?"

"How come you came looking for me."

"I like to meet people when I travel," she said. "I like to connect, you know?"

He continued to sit in the chair when she stood. She stepped into her shoes. It was always hard to slide her feet into jellies. She thought it would be awkward to have to bend over to pull them on. Finally she did have to bend over to pull the heel of the second one on her foot.

"So give me a call if you'd like to hear some music sometime," he said, standing.

"Now I don't get it," she said.

"Get what?"

"Do you just think it's weird having me here?"

"Yeah," he said. "It's pretty weird."

She shook her head.

"I mean, it seems like there's Stephanie Sykes, and then there's you. Not that you don't look like her," he said, laughing.

"What do you mean, there's me?"

"It's like you're a regular person. I wasn't sitting here thinking about the person you play on TV."

"Is that a compliment?"

"Just something I was thinking," he said.

She was looking at him.

"I didn't mean it as a put-down or anything. Sure; it was a compliment. I guess I never thought about you in real life."

"Yeah," she said. "A lot of me goes into my character, but other stuff goes into being me."

"It was nice getting to know you," he said. "Do you want another drink or anything?"

"I won't keep you."

"No. Really."

"No. I'm not going to keep you."

"Well, I got Eddie to take over for me in the kitchen. You might as well keep me. I don't have any more orange juice, though. Maybe we could go over to Raindance."

She knew they wouldn't serve her. Even with eye makeup, she'd never pass.

"No thanks," she said.

"Okay," he said. "Let me know if you ever feel like hearing some music."

"I'll probably be leaving soon."

"Oh yeah? Going back to California?"

"Sure. This was just a vacation."

They were both standing in the room facing each other. He put his beer bottle on the table.

"Your aunt lives in town, huh?"

She nodded.

"Did you tell her you were coming over here?"

"Why do you ask that?"

"Just wondering."

"She just figures I'm hanging out," Nicole said.

"That's cool," he said.

"I don't see any point in telling her. You know?"

He nodded his head. "You're sixteen, huh? When are you going to be seventeen?"

"Why do you care about that?"

"Wondered when your birthday was."

"September," she said.

"Virgo?"

"Yeah."

"I'm Pisces. Not a bad mix."

"I never can remember," she said. She knew that her mother was a Scorpio. Piggy Proctor was a Gemini.

"I've got a book," he said, gesturing toward the refrigerator.

"I guess I sort of believe that stuff," she said.

"It works out a lot of the time."

"Do you have a girlfriend?" she said.

"Not really," he said. He looked at her. "You've got to have friends to hang out with, right?"

"Uh huh," she said.

A breeze was blowing through the window at the foot of the bed. She walked to the window and looked out. Stretching to look as far as she could, she saw beside the inn the croquet field that they had walked through coming down the hill to the apartment. No one was there. He came over to where she stood by the window. She sat on the foot of the bed and continued to look out. He was making a move, finally, and she knew it. He must have known she was striking a pose. "Do you ever play croquet?" she said.

In the movies he would have seized her on that line.

"We could do that later," he said. He came a step closer. "This isn't some joke, right?"

"No," she said.

"Nobody knows where you are."

"No," she said. "I told you: I didn't see any point in saying anything."

"That the way you generally feel about stuff like this?"

She nodded.

"Yeah," he said, coming close enough that he touched her. "I guess it figures that you wouldn't have gotten where you are by being a dummy."

ANDREW STEINBORN, ghostwriter of *Puts and Calls for Fun and Profit*, author of *Mazie, the Mouse Who Came to Stay*, and *I Will Always Love You*, the unauthorized biography of Dolly Parton, was in reality a novelist. He had completed his first, after his nonfiction achievements, while a student at Iowa; it concerned a talented, misunderstood man who never completed novels. It was taken to be comic by his professor, and after being stunned in the conference, Steinborn decided to go along with this notion. "Evelyn Waugh couldn't have done these scenes better," the professor said. "You've created a character who has no humanity, no humor, no saving graces—but I warn you, the reviewers are going to pounce because you've been so uncompromising." The novel—the first Steinborn had finished, although he had worked on four others before he went to Iowa—was never published and never reviewed, though after a year of getting up at six to write for two hours before jogging and going to work, he had recently completed a novel called *Buzz*, which was about people at a fashionable resort in Southampton, as seen from the perspective of a mosquito.

Like F. Scott Fitzgerald, he was also waiting for the call from his agent to tell him the book was sold, so that he could use this good news to persuade Lillian Worth, the woman he loved, to marry him. She was a nurse who had quit her job at Mass. General and moved to Iowa to live with him his last six months there. Creativity was just in the air: she had written about a dozen poems. It was Andrew's idea that she might put together a book of verse for the terminally ill and dying—a realistic yet inspirational, no-holds-barred book influenced by her reading of Elisabeth Kübler-Ross and her personal experience of watching people die. She thought of them as people who had died, not, as all her colleagues did, as patients who had passed. "Passed" seemed a silly euphemism; it carried with it, for Lillian, connotations of life being a long exam, and then at the end the payoff was death.

Lillian had moved back to Massachusetts a month before Andrew left Iowa. She was almost out of money, and the money he was inheriting wouldn't materialize for two or three months. She had found out that she could get her job back at Mass. General, and as long as Andrew was now willing to move back to the East Coast, she thought that it made sense to leave early. Things had gone well in Iowa City—good but not great—and she thought he was being crazy when he talked about her departure as her "leaving him." She was going back to find an apartment during the summer, before everyone got back into town in late August to start school; her friend had a lead on a railroad flat on a street behind Porter Square. She hoped that the apartment was as good as her friend made it seem. She was sure that if she and Andrew could live in a sunny, spacious apartment, many of the problems they had would disappear; it *had* been close quarters in the converted garage they lived in on a farmer's property just outside the city.

Lillian had had no intention of seeing anyone else when she got back to Boston. When she told Andrew that, it was certainly the truth. He took her to the airport and they said goodbye. He liked public passion, and she was learning to tolerate it. He attracted a lot of attention even when they weren't touching, because he dressed in amusing suits with boxy jackets and wide legged pants. In the winter he wore a fedora.

"Don't leave me," he said, clutching her to him at the airport.

"Shit, man, be cool," a man who was stacking peanuts in a vending machine said.

Andrew loved it that the man had entered into their conversation. That was real life: just try to put that in a novel and have people believe it.

He kissed her passionately. "Never leave me," he said.

"No. All right," she said, putting her hands on his shoulders and trying to push him back. She was getting flustered. "I'll call you tonight."

"You're the most beautiful girl in the world," he said, kissing her across the forehead.

"Shee-it," the vending-machine man said, slamming the door shut.

Andrew loved that.

Finally she got on the plane. About an hour into the flight, the man sitting across the aisle from her struck up a conversation. When he referred to Andrew, he called him "your husband." She didn't correct him. He didn't seem to be flirting, but she was prepared. She had never found anyone on a plane attractive and wondered who all those stewardesses found to marry. It said something about planes that she never desired anyone when she was a passenger, but the thought had crossed her mind quite a few times in the hospital.

The man said his father was picking him up at the airport. He all but insisted that since where she was going was right on their route, she must come with them. His father: what could be the harm? As they waited for the luggage, he looked around for his father. "Maybe he parked out front," he said. Their bags finally came out, and she followed him to the door. He didn't seem to know what to do when he didn't see his father's car. "I'll call him," he said, "but you go ahead. Sorry it didn't work out." By this time she felt some loyalty to him. Where *was* his father? She stood by his bags while he went inside and phoned. He came back shaking his head. "He forgot. He just plain forgot," he said.

The man's name was Evan. He asked if she would like to share a cab. They waited in line for a cab. It was hot, and the heat was visible, waving up from the asphalt. They finally got a cab. Her back stuck to the seat the minute she leaned against it. They talked about Andrew's comic novel. Evan smiled politely but he didn't really seem amused. Perhaps, like any joke, it was better in the telling—or reading—than in paraphrase. She didn't tell stories well. Andrew was a great storyteller, and being with him, she realized that her speech was never very exciting, that she didn't say witty things, that her stories lacked punch lines. Evan had seemed interested in talking to her on the plane—it was just when she began telling him about the book that he began to lose interest. When the cab pulled up in front of Lillian's apartment building, he offered to carry her suitcase, but she told him that she could manage with no trouble. He gave her his card. "Call if you have time for coffee or a drink," he said. She felt awkward suddenly, and wondered if he did too. Walking up the front steps, she thought of her friend Anita's "Isn't She Lovely" test. The categories were often changed to protect the innocent. Sometimes Anita would just hum the first bars of the Stevie Wonder song and Lillian would find herself making up categories and scoring everyone from the man in the car next to theirs to the elevator operator. Anita didn't change the pronoun when the test applied to men. One of the first judgments made was that they fit the category. Evan got a 9 for looks, a 2 for economically feasible (he was a carpenter) and a 10 for chutzpa (he kissed her before she got out of the cab, then sat back, smiling, and let her carry the suitcase, as she said she would).

The truth was, she liked him. She thought about him, looked at his card quite a few times, and on Sunday she called. She told him, then, that it wasn't what he thought: the man at the airport hadn't been her husband, although she was committed to him. He told her the situation wasn't what she thought: he had been attracted to her, and so sure she wouldn't share a cab with him that he had made up the story about his father. His father lived in Arizona. They agreed to see each other on Wednesday. The next morning she did the cowardly thing and wrote him a note saying that she had made a mistake to call him. Much to her surprise, he didn't respond. More than a week later, when Andrew was due in Boston, she got drunk during the afternoon and called Evan. "What do you want me to do?" he said. "If that's the way you want it, there's nothing I can say." She was embarrassed, and they hung up. But that only fascinated her more: there was never, ever, a time when

Andrew didn't have something to say. When they were having good conversations, he would run out of the room and come back with the recorder, to help him with dialogue later. He wanted them to be very close, so whenever they had a disagreement, he would later say out loud what he intuited that she felt. It was scary; he would become her—when he spoke from what he thought to be her mind, even his face took on her likeness. It made her hate every thought she had, rational or irrational. She did know that he loved her madly. She had said that they would live together. So she tried to forget about Evan and what he might do. Anita called Evan "cocky" for what he had done; she didn't believe that his response had been sincere, and she told Lillian to stay posted.

Then Andrew drove to Boston. There was much celebration because they had gotten the apartment and could move into it in August. Meanwhile, he would stay with her. The first night he was there, he picked up the phone and whoever it was hung up. It happened again the next morning. The next time the phone rang, Lillian picked it up. It was a literary agent; Andrew had given her Lillian's number so that she could call if she was willing to take him on. One of the deciding factors—in fact, she was so sure of Andrew that she had already made the commitment, although she did not tell him this—was that she felt he would be the perfect man to write the novelization of *Passionate Intensity.* She was proud of herself for sounding so enthusiastic on the phone when she reached Andrew, for pointing out that the novelization would be published around the same time his real novel came out. She said that she was surprised that he had never heard of Nicole Nelson (one of the agents she worked with had filled her in about who she was). The next day, she Federal Expressed to him cassettes of four shows and a photocopy of the *People* magazine interview with the cast, plus a bio sheet on everyone. Lillian called Anita, and they arranged to go to her boyfriend Howley's house in Cambridge, while he and Anita were seeing a movie at Coolidge Corner, to watch the shows on Howley's Betamax.

"It's real," Andrew said. "You know what I mean? It's almost primitive. Like tom-toms beaten before the kill. It's just prolonged, made dramatic. So much happens. I see why this has captured people's attention."

"I've never heard of anybody who watches it," Lillian said. "It's like *General Hospital.*"

"I've heard of plenty of people who watch *General Hospital.* I've never heard anybody talk about this show."

"Don't misunderstand me," Lillian said. "I think you should take the money and run."

He looked at her. "It isn't a question of that," he said. "It's a way to stimulate my own thinking."

"About what? Abused children and promiscuous doctors? Don't you think everybody thinks the same things about those clichés?"

"Lillian—there are many layers to everything. Subtleties."

On the TV, Stephanie Sykes was locked in a bathroom, drinking from a flask. She was crying and disheveled, her eyes owllike with sadness. She heard a noise and raised the top of the toilet tank and dropped the flask in.

"Stephanie?" Gerald said. "Your mother has called from the hospital. She can't take you to the rehearsal today, but when she gets home at midnight, she wants to go over your part with you. Stephanie—your real mother is going to be in the audience on Saturday. There is no way that . . . that Cora can stop it. Your real mother is in a prison hospital now, darling. And the patients who are well enough are going to come to the performance. Do you . . . what shall I say to Cora?"

The music came up, sudden and loud enough to explain, by itself, why Stephanie, at that moment, collapsed in the bathroom.

"You must know, darling," Gerald said to the unconscious body on the other side of the door, "that Cora and I believe in you. We believe that you will go on to be a great dancer. Darling, you must know that . . . we are your real family."

More music. Lillian looked at Andrew.

"Why doesn't the person who writes the dialogue write the novel?" she said.

"I don't know," he said, "but you should never look a gift horse in the mouth."

"This isn't a gift horse—this is an albatross."

Andrew looked shocked. Then his face lit up. "What a brilliant way of putting it," he said. He put his arms around her and kissed her. "There's no one like you," he said. "When my agent sells *Buzz* and I get the money for this novelization, we're going to have the most splendid wedding in the world."

He put on the next cassette. Apparently, his agent had not sent four consecutive programs, but an assortment. In this one, some doctor was kissing Cora's toes and nuzzling her ankle. They were in an office at the hospital, and suddenly a nurse walked in. That would never happen that way. In real hospitals, what was going on was always so shocking that everyone knew enough not to open doors. It simply wasn't done, without knocking. Jane Austen's characters would have been perfectly comfortable in Mass. General. Lillian said this.

"You mean so much to me," Andrew said. "I worship that strange, wonderful mind. I missed you so much when we were apart. A writer's life is so lonely, and to have found a soulmate . . ."

When Anita and Howley came home, they were still watching.

"Another goddamn plodding movie about some guy that's obsessed," Howley said. "He's driving around, listening to crap on the radio, and thinking about this woman, and outside the car there are magnificent, snow-covered mountains, and he's so out of it, he's just whizzing by, going to meet this woman for two seconds just to have a look at her . . . I paid good money to see that?"

Howley stood in front of Lillian, blocking her view. "What the hell is this?" Howley said.

"*Passionate Intensity,*" Andrew said.

"What in the hell is happening in this world?" Howley said. "This thing looks like a soap opera."

"It is a soap opera, Howley," Anita said.

"It's like *General Hospital,*" Andrew said.

"Yeah?" Howley said, kicking the footstool away from the chair and sitting on it. "Famous people do cameos?"

"Is this the show that had Elizabeth Taylor?" Anita said, sitting on the floor, next to Howley.

"I don't know," Andrew said.

"That was *General Hospital.* I don't think she was on two of them," Lillian said.

"Make us drinks, baby," Howley said. "I'd do it just to seem liberated, but it breaks my heart to put as much ice in a glass as you like. You'd better make them."

"None for me, thanks," Andrew said. "It's not true that all writers have a problem with alcohol."

"I'll have one," Lillian said.

"Now how do you figure in this?" Howley said.

"I'm going to get inside their minds," Andrew said. "I'm going to add dimension to what's going on. I'll be enlarging those characters, subtly telling the public what they are and what they aren't."

"I can tell you what they aren't," Howley said. "They're not real. There's not a guy on this show that would spit crossing the street."

"Make drinks and don't put ice in them; that's fine with me," Anita said, hugging his leg.

"That's Stephanie Sykes," Andrew said, when Nicole came on the screen. "Look at that face. They picked her because she's got depth."

Howley turned from the screen and looked at Andrew. Lillian looked at Anita.

"Come on," Anita said to Lillian. "Help me pour whiskey in glasses."

Lillian got up. All the tumbling and talking on the screen was making her exhausted. She wanted to bolt down a whiskey or two before she had to get up and go home.

In the kitchen, Lillian and Anita heard the bloodhounds, wailing in the backyard. They let them in, and they tore into the living room. They ran to Howley, and he reached down and stroked their ears. The dogs joined the crowd, mesmerized by people crying on *Passionate Intensity.*

19

NICOLE answered the phone, so she was the first to get the news of Jane's marriage. One week after Nicole flew East, Jane had married the twenty-four-year-old would-be tennis pro. Piggy Proctor had given her away. They were married in a friend's backyard. She could not remember the names of the friends, because they were Piggy's friends, not hers. In attendance were Piggy, Piggy's wife, and Piggy's mother, who was visiting for the week.

Nicole tried to sound cold, but she had to fight back tears. "Why wasn't I there?" she said.

"It was sudden," Jane said. "It was just something that we had to do, and it seemed silly to make a big production of it and have you fly back—"

"See how you like it when I do this to you," Nicole said.

"I didn't do it *to you*," Jane said.

"Yeah. You were just feeling up and thought you'd marry that guy."

"We're all going to be happy together. Even Piggy loves him."

"No way," Nicole said. "Piggy gets it together when he has to get it together."

"You know how much I love you," Jane said. "Don't sulk."

"You're my mother, not my director," Nicole said.

Lucy was standing in the kitchen doorway. Nicole handed her the phone. A few minutes later Nicole was slumped in a chair on the side lawn. She was painting her toenails.

"Tell me about it," Nicole said. "Tell me about how great it is that I have a twenty-four-year-old stepfather. That would make him ten when I was born. I'm supposed to call him Daddy? His balls hadn't dropped when I was born."

"Nobody said you have to call him Daddy," Lucy said. She was upset, but she didn't think it would be a good idea to make Nicole any more upset than she already was. Lucy was remembering Jane's first marriage, and how she had immediately taken a deep breath and tried to keep their mother calm by pretending that everything was fine. Jane had married the first rich man who proposed. He had saved her from a dreary life as a model, living in a shared studio apartment with another girl, who was studying languages. Jane had become a cliché: the beautiful, intelligent, aspiring New York girl who lives with her expansive ideas in one room, with a full-length mink in the closet and a purebred kitten for company. Lucy had been to the apartment. Jane's desk was also her makeup table and her bureau drawer. She slept on a thin mattress, folding it so that it would fit partially under the desk and sleeping with her shoulders and head in the kneehole tunnel so that her roommate wouldn't trip over her if she went to the bathroom during the night. The desk drawer was filled with piles of pastel underwear, boxes of cosmetics, love letters tied neatly together with ribbon. The same drawer held her checkbook, her diaphragm, and four boxes of Joy which had been given to her in exchange for twenty subway tokens by a photographer's assistant who had been given the perfume by a client. Lucy had been with Jane when she made the exchange. Later, when Lucy lived in New York, too, she understood these trades: the cumulative effect of the desperation—all the things dreamed of and coveted—resulted in an atmosphere in which lesser things meant nothing. Small things were small things: to be shoplifted, given away, swapped for other small things. The two-carat diamond Jane was offered at the end of her first year in the city was no small thing, and she promptly agreed to get married. Her former roommate recited love poems in French, Italian, and Turkish. The Beatles, piped through her mother's sound system, sang "The Long and Winding Road." Under her wedding dress, Jane wore a garter she had been given by a man she picked up hitchhiking on the Cape the previous fall, with "Obladi, Oblada" spelled out in rhinestones. She sprayed on the Joy the way woodsmen apply Deep Woods Off. The shoes were Eighth Street pink satin, with three-inch heels. She held tight to Lucy's hand when she walked out of the bedroom and started down the corridor to the living room of what was by then only their mother's house. A man played "Here Comes the Bride" on a pump organ that had been brought in for the day. The best man, the groom's brother, was a retired jockey from Columbus. Jane and Lucy exchanged looks during the ceremony. Lucy had forgotten what those secret looks meant. Her personal secret had been that she did not know what was happening. Why hold herself accountable when her own sister was happy to have everything go up in dust, particularly white dust, inhaled through one nostril? Years later, in nightmares, that organ music still came back to her. Even at the time, it sounded like what would be played in a B movie when someone was drowning. And then Jane's husband had drowned.

Nicole blew on her toes. "Notice that she's too much of a coward to have told Grammy," she said. "And notice that Piggy was too much of a coward to tell me." Nicole sighed. "I mean, I bust ass so we can have this great life, and she runs off with some kid."

Except for her vocabulary, Lucy thought, Nicole sounded very much like her grandmother.

"Who is he?" Lucy said, unable to hide her distress.

"He's not Jimmy Connors, or you would have heard of him."

The cows had come into the back field and were grazing, swishing their tails and occasionally snapping their heads around, trying to scare off flies. St. Francis was tied up in his spot by the rhododendrons. He was feeling very bad after all the screaming he had had to endure regarding the incident with the sheep.

"Honest to God," Nicole said, "if you don't have Brooke Shields' mother and that set of problems, you've got a mother like mine and a whole different mess to deal with."

"Do you think she loves him?" Lucy asked.

"She hardly knows him. I'll tell you, she was getting really down because she wasn't meeting anybody interesting who was straight. She told me she was beginning to think all straight guys were like Piggy. This guy's some jock."

"He doesn't want to be in the movies, at least," Lucy said.

Nicole rolled her eyes. "Sure he wants to be in the movies."

"How do you know?" Lucy said.

"Because he got all excited about being an extra. He got to jump out of his seat and catch a baseball in some movie that never got released, and he had a still blown up and hung it on the back of the bedroom door."

Nicole had been reading magazines. From time to time she had also been reading *Pride and Prejudice*, but she thought it was too weird. She read a chapter or two, then got back to the news of Princess Di. She was on the cover of this month's *Good Housekeeping*, which was on the top of the magazine pile. Princess Di was shown in profile, the hat she wore indistinguishable from a cow pat except for the spray of feathers.

Jane had told Lucy that what she wanted for a wedding present was for her to make the call to their mother. Lucy had offered to send a silver-rimmed salad bowl instead. Jane had gone into gales of laughter. Stoned. She had made the call stoned.

Now, Nicole was walking around the lawn, aimlessly, like a small child. She was squinting in the sun, and the breeze was blowing through her hair. Standing by the car, she looked small—just a pretty little girl in summertime. She could have been happier, but the truth was that her mother's phone call hadn't been the only blow; part of her world had ended the day Ralston-Purina and Campbell's Soup canceled.

Lucy decided that the best thing to do was to let Nicole be alone for a while. She went into the house and dialed her mother. This was really her summer of doing favors for her sister.

"I have something to tell you," Lucy said when Rita answered. "It's not terrible, but I don't think you're going to think it's good news."

"Say it," her mother said, her voice almost a whisper.

"I don't really have the details," Lucy said, "but a few days ago Jane got married, in California."

There was complete silence on the line.

"She didn't tell us right away."

"Who did she marry?" her mother said.

"Well, it's embarrassing to admit, but I didn't write his name down when she told me, and I don't remember."

"What does he do?"

"I'm not sure of everything that he does, but he's a tennis player."

"If that's the best thing you can start with, I don't know that I want to know what else he does," her mother said.

"It's her life," Lucy said. "She can take care of herself."

"She'll have to, married to somebody who plays tennis."

"But it's just that I'm not sure of what else he does."

"He wants to be in the movies, if he isn't already. That's what he does."

Lucy said nothing.

"She didn't invite you to this wedding?"

"No," Lucy said. "She just called us. Nicole was hurt. I wish Jane had given her the option of being there."

"Jane doesn't think about anybody but herself."

"That isn't true."

"I'm not going to argue with you," her mother said.

"She was afraid to call you," Lucy said. "Are you going to call her and wish her the best when you get yourself together?"

"Give her my best wishes when you speak to her," her mother said.

"I don't want to be the go-between," Lucy said.

"No one wants to star in a movie that's already been made," her mother said.

"Please call her."

"Couldn't Piggy stop her?" her mother said.

"Piggy gave her away."

"What does Piggy say about this?"

"I haven't spoken to him about it."

"Is she pregnant again?"

"I don't think so," Lucy said. "That wouldn't be any reason—"

"Your sister doesn't do anything as the result of reason."

"I don't think so," Lucy said.

"Is he foreign?"

"No. Apparently he's a Wasp. She's sending pictures."

"Is he an old man?"

"Quite young."

"I assume that he isn't well off, or you would have said so."

"I assumed that if he was, Jane would have told me."

"What does Piggy say?"

"We-we-we, I want some."

Her mother was silent.

"I didn't speak to Piggy."

Lucy waited for her mother to continue. There was a long silence.

"How is Nicole?"

"We're all as surprised by this news as you are. She's taking it okay. I think she's having a pretty good time here—better than I thought she'd have."

"Are you carrying on with Hildon while she's there?"

"I don't carry on with Hildon. He's my oldest friend. We went out on the Fourth of July with a bunch of people, including Hildon and Maureen."

"God!" her mother said.

"I know that you like Maureen sight unseen because she's a wife," Lucy said.

"To feel sorry for her is not to say that I like her. If she stays married to Hildon, I don't have much respect for her."

"How is it this has turned into a conversation criticizing me?" Lucy said.

"I'm glad you realize that it's criticism, instead of just thinking that I'm commenting," her mother said. "Unless you or your sister are hit over the head, you act like I'm Dan Rather with the news."

"You know I'm not going to give up a fifteen-year friendship just to please you," Lucy said. "Try to be nice to me. I don't find it easy to break news like this to you."

"Yes," her mother said, softening her voice a little. "I can't understand why your sister pretends to be afraid of me. She does anything she wants, and she knows I have no control over her."

"How are you feeling? Is your hay fever better?"

"I have new antihistamines, but they make me too sleepy."

"It *is* her own life," Lucy said.

"I feel like she's just thrown it to the wind," her mother said. "She was that way when she was a baby, of course. She liked to be bought a balloon so she could let go of the string. She never even cried."

"Well, she's married him, and that's that."

"I'm going to go lie down," her mother said. "If the pictures are going to upset me, don't send them. If you talk to Piggy, tell him that he'd better have something good to say for himself when he calls me."

"Goodbye," Lucy said. "I love you."

"I love you too," her mother said. "Goodbye."

Lucy felt sadder than she thought she would when she put down the receiver. She could see it from her mother's perspective—that almost everything they did was strange and upsetting.

She thought about that as she left the house and drove to meet Hildon at the Hadley-Cooper's. It wasn't at all what her mother claimed—that she had conveniently found a sort of all-purpose person, a lover-husband-father in one: it wasn't that, because Hildon wasn't dependable. She could depend on him to be there, but she couldn't guess about his mood, couldn't change it, whatever it was—Hildon was still an enigma, after all these years. His recent good fortune seemed to have made him crazier instead of more stable.

She had asked Nicole if she wanted to go, knowing that it was safe to ask because, as usual, Nicole was sure to say no. She was going back to the house where she had gone to the party not long ago with Hildon. She was glad to have somewhere to go, because she did not want to think about Jane. Hildon wanted her to see the pond, with the carp swimming in it, and a statue of Richard Nixon in the center, pissing.

At the last intersection before the house, she looked carefully at the map Hildon had drawn, that she had kept crumpled in her glove compartment. She found the unmarked driveway without any trouble, and got out of the car and went to one of the stone pillars. The pinkish stone below the lantern on the left was wired so it could be pushed, triggering a device that would make the iron gate rise so she could drive through. She felt like she was in a James Bond movie as she touched the stone and it moved. The gate rose slowly.

Hildon's car was in front of the house, in the big circular driveway. The driveway looked enormous, almost empty of cars. He was throwing a yellow tennis ball for a Dalmatian in the field beside the house. The dog ran barking to the car.

"He won't hurt you. Here, Kissinger!" Hildon called.

The dog raced back to where Hildon stood, and looked up at the tennis ball, eagerly. Lucy got out of the car. It was quite a mansion. The other night, she had not noticed the large holly bushes across the front, or the urns on the front steps with Norfolk Island pines in them. It was an enormous pale gray house—almost silver—with a catwalk across the top.

"They went to North Carolina for the week," he said. "I have the key. Here's the key."

It was an ordinary key; she had expected some more dramatic way to enter the house.

"They went away and left the dog?"

"There's a caretaker."

"Who are these people?" she said.

"Just rich people. I changed a flat for Antoinette, and she asked me to come for a drink. She was very attractive, so I thought I would. They're real Cindi Coeur fans. You're going to have to come back sometime when they're here."

She noticed the inside of the house more this time. The house was traditional enough: a long Oriental runner in the hallway, a winding staircase, cherry furniture, primitive paintings of lumpy children and animals with bows around their necks. She looked at the staircase, and thought of Myra DeVane. Les.

"I've got a great afternoon planned," Hildon said. "There's some Cakebread Cellars in a cooler in the other room. You're really going to like the entertainment."

Hildon gestured to a room at the end of the hallway. Inside, black velvet modular furniture made an L-shape in front of a screen. Hildon gestured for her to sit down. He touched a button and the screen widened. He touched another button and an image came on the screen and seemed to shake itself into focus. Hildon sat beside her and put his arm around her shoulder. She could see his wide smile in her peripheral vision.

And there they were: Lucy and Hildon, standing and talking to Matt Smith. She had expected pornography, and instead she was watching Maureen, in her sarong, pouring a glass of wine. At this point, Hildon removed his arm from around Lucy, sat forward, and poured from their bottle of wine. Maureen was turning to talk to Cameron Petrus. Suddenly there was a quick cut to Lucy, dancing with whoever that silly girl had been. Hildon picked up the remote control switch from the floor. He pushed a button and the videotape stopped. Maureen filled the screen, frowning, her hand almost in front of her face. Hildon released the button. In slow motion, Maureen's frown deepened and her hand stopped in front of her eyes. That image was there as Hildon opened one button and slid his hand under Lucy's blouse, cupping his hand around her smooth breast, then moving his fingertips. Between his thumb and first finger, he felt her nipple stiffen.

20

IT was one of the few times in his life Piggy Proctor had a typical response to anything. He stood with his hands at his sides, glanced down quickly as the sheet was pulled back, looked away, and fainted.

He must have talked himself back to consciousness, because the first voice he heard was his own, saying "Oh no" over and over. He was sitting on the floor. The floor felt like a slab of ice. The doctor was keeping him from falling over by supporting his shoulders. He was standing behind him. Piggy was leaning on the man's legs, his own legs spread in front of him like somebody lounging in a chair at the seashore.

Tomorrow, if Jane hadn't been dead, she would have been on the beach in Martinique, honeymooning with her new husband, who had just killed her.

"Mr. Proctor," the doctor said, stepping back a few inches. "Do you feel able to stand?"

Even the suggestion made Piggy breathless. His heart was racing. "Sure," he said. "Let's get this show on the road, right?" He clapped his hands together. They were freezing.

The doctor was standing in front of him, helping him up. It felt like one side of his head had been crushed.

"I thought you were going to be wrong," Piggy said. "I didn't come in expecting this."

"I'm very sorry," the doctor said. "Will you come into the office and sign some forms? Is there anything I can do?"

He was holding Piggy's hand like a schoolchild. He was maneuvering him out of the room.

"Who should I call?" Piggy said. "What am I going to do?"

They were in a corridor. Piggy didn't remember the day outside being anywhere near this bright. He had been at his office, in the middle of getting his weekly shiatsu massage, when his secretary came in and said that there was an extreme emergency. She was always interrupting him, and although it was for a good reason, Piggy continued to think that the best way to keep her in line was to communicate to her that if she couldn't think of adjectives, the situation wasn't desperate. He liked to see her worked up. If he had to be worked up all the time, he liked to have company. He suspected that his secretary had gone back to her Valium addiction; she had a longer and longer string of adjectives every time, but she spoke about the emergencies very dispassionately: "A most urgent, terrible, extremely upsetting problem has arisen," she had said, then turned and wandered from the room.

Two days ago his wife had hit another car on Rodeo Drive. One of the roofers had lost his footing and had broken his hand as he fell off a ladder. Bobby Blue wanted to hang from a rope over the beach at Malibu with Tatum O'Neal instead of Nicole. His other secretary, Zeva, had misprogrammed the computer; not only had the man who was going to write the novelization of *Passionate Intensity* not written a book on Venus de Milo, but he was apparently some unheard of chump, whose name wouldn't dignify the project.

"I can't believe it. How did this happen? What am I ever going to say to Nicole?"

"Is that the next of kin?" the doctor said.

Of course! Of *course* the doctor didn't realize the magnitude of what had happened. He sat in the chair the doctor pointed to.

"That was Nicole Nelson's mother," Piggy said.

"Did she have a young daughter?" the doctor said.

"Nicole Nelson. You know, she's fourteen." The doctor's face registered nothing. "Stephanie Sykes."

"She has two daughters?" the doctor said.

"*Passionate Intensity*!" Piggy hollered.

"I'm sorry, Mr. Proctor. I'm not following you."

"You never heard of *Passionate Intensity*?"

"It's from Yeats," the doctor said.

"It's a big hit on television," Piggy said. "*Passionate Intensity* is gonna scoop *General Hospital.*"

"I've heard of *General Hospital,*" the doctor said. "I don't watch much TV."

"You've *heard* of it!" Piggy said.

"Mr. Proctor, how are you feeling? Is there anyone I could call for you?"

"You know the guy who used to be the midget on *Fantasy Island*?" Piggy said.

"Yes," the doctor said.

"Ha!' Piggy said. "You know his name, right?"

"Herve Villechaize," the doctor said.

"See?" Piggy said. "He's not still on the tube, and you know that name, right? You may not watch much television, but the unusual gets your attention. Everybody knows who the midget was on *Fantasy Island.*"

"He sat next to me on a flight to Hawaii," the doctor said.

"You mean you never saw him on *Fantasy Island*?"

"No," the doctor said.

"Then how did you know who he was?"

"He told me," the doctor said.

"You'd know Stephanie Sykes if you saw her," Piggy said. He shifted onto one buttock and pulled his wallet out of his back pocket. He flipped it open and handed it to the doctor.

The doctor looked, smiled, and handed it back. It was a picture of Piggy in a tuxedo and Nicole in a satin dress with rhinestones around the neck. The flashbulb seemed to be exploding on Piggy's forehead. Piggy looked at the picture. He hated it that he was half bald.

"You've at least *heard* of *Passionate Intensity,*" Piggy said.

"I've only heard the line from Yeats," the doctor said. "Are you feeling anxious? Is there anything I can do for you?"

"Yeats?" Piggy said.

"Yeats," the doctor said. "The poet."

"What are you talking about?" Piggy said, moving to the edge of his chair.

" 'The best lack all conviction, while the worst are full of passionate intensity,' " the doctor said.

"You're putting me on!" Piggy said. "Jack Dormett titled the show!"

"Mr. Proctor, if you're able to concentrate now, I have a couple of brief forms that I'd like you to sign, and then if you wish to use the telephone, or—"

"How could it be a poem?" Piggy said. "I don't know anything about that."

The doctor stared at Piggy.

"Give me the line one more time," Piggy said.

The doctor sighed. "It's a line from *The Second Coming*," the doctor said. " 'The best lack all conviction, while the worst are full of passionate intensity.' "

"The worst?" Piggy said. "Dormett wouldn't dare put one over on me."

"Mr. Proctor," the doctor said. "Do you understand why I cannot continue this conversation?"

"Because I don't converse," Piggy said. That was what Jane always said; that he issued policy statements, talked to himself, cracked jokes, threatened violence, and used non sequiturs the way other people shook salt on their food. That he was so frustrating he was fascinating. Jane's face was scratched and scarred from all the rocks and trees and bushes she had tumbled through when the motorcycle went off the road and plunged down the canyon. Jane was dead. Piggy put his face in his hands. He pressed his palms against his eyes until he saw yellow. As he pressed, the headache became worse. If Dormett had put one over on him, he would personally kill him. He looked up. The doctor was sitting behind his desk, his own chin cupped in his hand. He lowered his hand and looked as if he was about to speak, but he didn't. The forms Piggy had to fill out were on his desk. Piggy reached for them. The doctor picked them up, stood, and brought them to Piggy. "Feel free to move your chair forward, or whatever is comfortable," the doctor said. "I think I'm going to get a cup of coffee. Would you like a cup?"

"Thank you," Piggy said.

"What do you take in it?"

Piggy did not drink coffee. "Milk," he said.

The doctor got up. The doctor locked his top drawer with a little key before leaving. There was a phone on the doctor's desk. As soon as he finished listing days and dates, he was going to have to use the phone. The thought came to him that it would be a good idea to call someone—call Hildon—and have him be at Lucy's house when he called. His secretary had Hildon's office number, in addition to Lucy's, where important messages could be left for Nicole. He stood and picked up the phone. Someone on the phone was talking about an airline that had declared bankruptcy. He pushed a button on the bottom of the phone and got an outside line. He dialed his office.

Dora answered. "This is important," Piggy said. "Get that book with summer numbers in it and give me Hildon what's-his-name's or what's-his-name Hildon's number for Nicole."

"Mr. Proctor," Dora said, "I have extremely urgent, terribly disturbing news for you. Zeva quit. She took things out of her desk drawer and threw them all around the office and turned the desk over before she quit. It will take me a minute to find the book."

"Christ," Piggy said, "find it as fast as you can and call me back." He did not realize until he had hung up that he had not given her the number. Someone coughed, and continued by. Piggy looked at the form. He looked at the other one. Jane was dead. The worthless, reckless scum she had married was in a coma and expected to die. From measurements taken of the skid marks of the motorcycle, he must have been traveling at about the speed of sound. Jane had been thrown. She was DOA. He was alive, but just barely. Piggy did not want him to live, and if he did, he would personally kill him. From the picture Piggy had seen, the motorcycle, down in the canyon, where they had plunged, looked like an accordion with handlebars. What in the name of God was he going to say to Lucy? The newspapers were going to get hold of it, so he had better think about what he was going to say. They didn't put it in the paper until the next of kin had been notified, though. He looked at the form in front of him. Next of kin. Jesus: Jane's mother. She was already furious about the wedding—wait till she heard what they did for an encore. There was going to be an autopsy. He hated to think what that might reveal. He picked up the pen and was filling out the forms when the doctor came back in the room. Another man, probably a doctor, stopped in the doorway and said, "Did you hear that Air Florida filed for bankruptcy?" "That happened days ago," the doctor said. "There goes that smart investment down the drain," the doctor said.

Piggy was thinking about the ride on the Cyclone he had taken the spring before with Jane. Nicole was too frightened to go on it. They were on location, bored, and Piggy had rounded up half a dozen members of the cast to go with them. He could remember Jane's excitement as he closed the bar over their car. The way they were thrown against each other over and over, rocking left and right, and suddenly flipped upside down. They were both terrified, but exhilarated. His legs were shaking when they got off, and he could hardly hear. He could remember Nicole standing there, turning a pink cotton candy. She was always sulky when Jane had the nerve to do something she wouldn't do. Cotton candy made her face break out. She knew it, and was pleased to be licking the wide plume of spun sugar. She might as well have been Lolita with her lollipop.

Piggy could not remember if Lolita had a lollipop. Sue Lyon was great in that movie. He remembered the heart-shaped glasses. It was a good thing to have a gimmick. Michael Jackson's glove. Nicole needed a gimmick. As she grew up, she was going to be blow-dried into the same blond prettiness as everybody else.

The doctor handed Piggy a cup of coffee.

"Thank you," Piggy said. The ghost of Jane made him say it.

The doctor nodded and went to the window and stood there, sipping his coffee. Piggy signed the form. It did not seem possible that he could be doing this. He had forgotten the title of the poem. He couldn't remember what had happened to Sue Lyon after she did *Lolita*. A first-rate actress in a first-rate movie, and then what happened to her? He couldn't let Nicole fade away like that. She was going to have to really concentrate on her career, get it together in spite of her sadness, and go on. Jesus Christ: how could Jane have done it?

"You don't mind if I use the telephone?" Piggy said.

"Do you think you'd like something to calm you? Take a pill and wait a few minutes before calling?"

"Oh yeah," Piggy said. "Give me a pill."

The doctor unlocked his desk drawer. There were many pill bottles inside. He took the cap off one bottle and shook out a pill. He handed it to Piggy. Valium. A yellow one. That would be about as helpful as handing a child a penny. Piggy took it without comment.

"I'll let you have some privacy," the doctor said, finishing his coffee and throwing away the cup.

"Not necessary," Piggy said. He was hoping that he could still win the doctor over, so that he could turn the conversation around to that poem. Piggy's usual way, as Jane had pointed out to him, was to point his finger and demand information. Jane had tried hard, lately, to make him what she called "civilized." Piggy had found that speaking bluntly to people usually worked fine, but Jane thought he was a bad example for Nicole. He created tension that was unnecessary, and he was a bully. She had a small Evian water spray that she would take out of her purse and spray in his face, when he made non sequiturs. Now she was dead, and he was going to have a dry face the rest of his life and never learn. He thought about demanding that his wife spray him in the face. It seemed unlikely. She was too tranqued-up to push a spray bottle, and she never listened to him when he talked, anyway. The doctor was halfway out of the room.

"No, no," Piggy said. "Just a quick call. I'll do the hard stuff from the office. Please sit down."

The doctor sat in a chair. There were folders stacked on a table. He opened one and began to read.

Piggy wanted to impress the doctor favorably. He remembered to say hello.

"Hello," Piggy said. "How are things at the office?"

"What?" his secretary said.

"I'm fine," Piggy said.

"What's wrong?" his secretary said.

"Do you have that number handy?" he said.

"Mr. Proctor, is this really you? If everything is all right, say, 'I like New York in June.' "

"What the hell do you think?" Piggy exploded. "That I've been kidnapped?"

"Oh my God," his secretary said. "Oh, don't worry, Mr. Proctor, I'll take care of everything. I understand."

"Don't hang up!" Piggy hollered. "Are you out of your mind, Dora?"

"Don't do anything to make them suspicious," Dora said. "I'm dialing the police on the other line."

"I'll kill you!" Piggy said. "I haven't been kidnapped! You goddamn imbecile. Talk to the doctor. He'll tell you I haven't been kidnapped."

The doctor, looking very taken aback, got up and took the phone. "Hello? To whom am I speaking?" he said.

"Who are you? What do you want?" Dora said.

"I'm Dr. Endicott," he said. "Is there any problem?" He looked at Piggy as he said this.

"Tell her, 'I like New York in June,' " Piggy said, suddenly remembering what she had said to say.

"Mr. Proctor, if everything is all right, I'll leave it to you to chat with whoever is on the phone," the doctor said, his hand over the receiver. He took his hand away and held the phone out to Piggy.

"Well, thank God *War of the Worlds* isn't on the radio today, or I wouldn't even have one numbskull to answer the phone," Piggy said. "Will you give me that goddamn phone number?"

"I'm sorry, Mr. Proctor. I couldn't understand the way you were talking to me and I thought . . ."

"Hurry up!" Piggy said.

She gave him the number.

Piggy slammed the phone down so hard the desk vibrated. The doctor jumped. He started to say something, then looked down at the folder again. Piggy knew that he had made a terrible impression.

"Sorry," Piggy said. "I guess everybody gets a little excited when they come in."

The doctor hesitated a moment. Then he nodded.

"Christ," Piggy said. "This is a real tragedy. I'm not myself, I can tell you that."

"Is there anything else I can do for you?" the doctor said.

"I'll just—let me make this one call and then I'll be on my way," Piggy said. He picked up the phone. The doctor gave him a half smile and went back to the folder. People were talking on the phone about buying Coleco. Piggy pushed a button and got an outside line and charged the call to his office.

"Hello?" a woman's voice said.

"Hello," Piggy said. "How are you today? This is P. G. Proctor, calling from Los Angeles. May I please speak to Hildon?"

"I must tell you that I am coming down with a cold and that you have disturbed my nap," Maureen said. "It is within my rights to say that I consider my rest more important than continuing this conversation. I am going back to bed now."

She hung up. Piggy looked at the desk top. He thought he was going to explode. He felt a murderous rage toward the woman who had answered the phone, toward his asinine secretary, and toward Jane, for dying. To say nothing of what he felt toward her husband, who drove them both over a cliff. He clenched his free hand and released his fist, then hung up and sat in the doctor's chair.

"Terrible connection," Piggy said. "Have to try later."

"Mr. Proctor, are you going to be able to drive?" the doctor said. "Do you think it might be a good idea to call Mrs. Proctor, or a friend?"

"Mrs. Proctor already racked one up this week," Piggy said. "Tailgating on Rodeo. Smashed in the front of the 450."

The doctor nodded.

"Say," Piggy said, ripping another piece of paper off the doctor's prescription pad. "What was the name of that poet again?"

The doctor looked like he was about to speak, then stopped. Piggy thought the doctor wasn't going to tell him. The two of them looked at each other, across the room.

"William Butler Yeats," the doctor said. "Y-e-a-t-s. The poem is titled, *The Second Coming.*"

Piggy wrote it down. "All that money, and he plagiarizes," Piggy said.

"It isn't plagiarism to take a phrase from a poem for a title," the doctor said.

"Sure it is," Piggy said.

"No," the doctor said.

"Maybe Yeats and Dormett both came up with the same idea. Coincidence," Piggy said.

The doctor looked at him.

"Making a mountain out of a molehill, right?"

The doctor gave him his half smile again. He held out his hand. "Mr. Proctor," he said. "If you need anything, please don't hesitate to call."

"Thank you," Piggy said, folding the piece of paper and putting it in his pocket. "Hell of a day, huh?"

Piggy was confused in the corridor for a while, until he found the Exit sign. He followed it to the elevator, and rode to the basement. He had no memory of where he had parked. There were probably a million cars in the garage. He suddenly wanted to be in his car very much. He felt furious and exhausted, and he would feel better if he could sink down in the driver's seat. He walked through row after row of cars, then remembered that he had parked far down one of the rows. He began walking vertically, instead of horizontally. It took fifteen more minutes to find the car. He took out his car key and opened the door and sat in the driver's seat. A woman got in a car not far from his, started it, backed out fast and hit a car behind her. She pulled forward, cut the wheels sharply as she backed up again, and drove away. Her license plate said

Lucky-7. Piggy started his car. The radio was on. He turned it off. He drove the wrong way down a one-way lane until he got to the booth.

"Did you see which way those arrows were pointing?" the attendant said.

"You see which way my finger is pointing?" Piggy said, holding up his middle finger.

The attendant laughed. "What do I want to fight for?" he said.

"Have a real life experience. Put it in your screenplay," Piggy said.

"My screenplay's about a whorehouse in a cave in prehistoric times," the man said. "I want De Niro to play the bouncer. You think knocking your teeth down your throat would add anything?"

"I like that," Piggy said. "A man who's got confidence. You assume that you'd knock my teeth out. Confidence is the name of the game."

The man gave him his change.

Piggy unfolded the piece of paper in his pocket and glanced at it.

"You going to be the new William Butler Yeats?" he said.

"Screw that," the cashier said, as the bar rose in front of Piggy's car. "I'm gonna be the next Robert Towne."

Piggy made it almost all the way back to the office before it hit him that Jane was dead, and he had to turn off the street and dry his eyes in a parking lot. Through his tears he saw a neon burger with beads of light blinking around it. The lettuce that ruffled out from under the roll was blue. The bun was yellow. Piggy looked away, up at the sky. The sky was blue. He blew his nose. Thank God: the sky was blue.

THE day was perfect. Everything caught the light: the leaves of the aspen trees flickered silver and green as they blew in the breeze, birds and butterflies seemed irradiated—even the pebbles in the big circular driveway of the Birches glowed like shells underwater, and simple weeds seemed beautiful.

Andrew Steinborn and Lillian Worth were officially engaged. Her engagement ring, a small diamond in an elaborate platinum setting that had once belonged to Andrew's grandmother, seemed larger when it caught the light.

Andrew considered this a pre-honeymoon. They were going to be married the first of September, but since *Passionate Intensity* was due at the end of September, he wouldn't be able to take a real honeymoon with Lillian for a while. The room at the Birches was free, and Boston was hot. He had been able to persuade Lillian to come with him. Actually, she had been glad to come, because she was starting to get cold feet about the wedding, and she thought the trip with Andrew would solidify their relationship. She had tossed around the idea of seeing Evan again, letting Andrew go to Vermont alone. She was ashamed of herself; he was a wonderful person, enthusiastic about his work and enthusiastic about her, on his way to a successful career. It seemed strange to think of being the wife of Andrew Steinborn the famous writer. He might like to think of himself as F. Scott Fitzgerald, but she certainly did not envision herself as Zelda, who was clearly a vain, neurotic woman. She would not pull Andrew down, but would support him. On the ride up, she had read him plot summaries of *Passionate Intensity* programs, and when that got to be too much of a chore, she read some poems from *The Complete Poems of Robert Frost*, which Andrew suggested might put them in the mood for Vermont. The poems weren't what she expected: they seemed laconic and confusing—brain teasers, almost. Perhaps that was just because anything would pale in comparison with the plots of *Passionate Intensity.*

It would all be much easier to take if Andrew would just admit that the show was only a soap opera. Why did he insist that it was something more—that there were subtleties and hidden complexities in the characters, and that to the intelligent viewer the show was more than entertainment. If he had been a nurse as long as she had, he wouldn't have such an interest in fathoming the thoughts of hysterics.

Lillian wasn't sure what the purpose of these interviews was, either. She suspected that the actors just played their parts with no more thought about their characters' inner workings than a keypunch operator whose job it was to use a machine. But that was why he was a writer and she was not. Her job was technical, really, but it was always easy for Andrew to imagine that someone imagined something. He thought of people as existing both within and beyond themselves. He wasn't put off by people's complexity. He actually enjoyed it. He thought that people, without realizing it, were always in the process of figuring out themselves and others: there was a constant molting going on, and only the foolish wouldn't want to observe the feathers and bone exposed. It did make him, as her friend Anita said, a little too serious. Intense, Lillian thought: not serious. She wished she had been quick-witted enough at the time to say that.

They were registered at the Birches as Mr. and Mrs. Andrew Steinborn. There wasn't a phone in the room, so while she showered and changed her clothes, he went down the hall to phone Nicole Nelson. Alone in the room, she touched the wallpaper (the eagles weren't really raised; they just looked that way) and opened the closet door. When she was alone in a hotel, she never used the closet. She threw clothes over the chair or on the spare bed. She took two dresses out of her suitcase and put them on hangers. The Bermuda shorts wouldn't wrinkle. Nothing else really had to be hung up. She closed the closet door and sat on the bed, looking out the window. There were large shade trees that almost blocked her view of the Green Mountains. As they checked in, the man behind the desk had mentioned that the inn, a quick drive and a pleasant walk away, served cocktails outside, and that the view of the mountains was particularly good in early evening, when shadows started to spread. She wondered what it would be like to live in a town like this. She looked in the desk and found one postcard and one envelope. There was also a pen: black plastic, with the end cut on the diagonal, to be used as a letter opener. It struck her that she hardly ever wrote or received letters anymore.

Andrew came back to the room. "No answer," he said. He had tried to call before, from the road, to confirm the next day's appointment. Lillian could tell that he was getting worried.

"You'll get her eventually," she said.

"I hope so," he said. "I'm more interested in her than the other characters. She's really the center, you know?"

Lillian was tired of thinking of *Passionate Intensity.* She stretched out on the bed. He went to the window and positioned himself so he could see around the trees as well as possible to the mountains. He was tired from the drive and thought that a drink might help him unwind. He realized that Lillian was stretched out behind him. They had been in motels together before, but no place as classy as this. He felt like a child playing grown-up. There was something a little intimidating about playing Mr. and Mrs. Andrew Steinborn on such an elaborate set. F. Scott Fitzgerald had felt what he was feeling now: that so much was expected when you were in a high-class, adult world. Maybe that was why he liked Zelda so much—because she cut through all that, she insisted on remaining the child. Or the *enfant terrible.* He wished that Lillian would get up, come over to him. For a writer, it was strange that his imagination failed him so often when he needed it. He just wished that there was some way to connect, and not to feel awkward about it. He turned and smiled at her.

Her eyes were closed. She looked small, centered on the

nubbly white bedspread. He looked back out the window, then decided to make a little noise to get her attention. He pulled open the desk drawer. Nothing much inside. He pushed it closed. When he looked at her again, she was looking at him.

"You know," she said, "hardly anybody writes letters anymore."

"Easier to call," he said.

"But if you have a letter you can reread it."

He made a mental note: Send her letters. Love letters. It would be something private between them.

"How many letters have you actually reread?"

"I can't think of the last time I got a real letter. I guess from my mother, when I was in nursing school. I was lonesome, and I always reread those."

Her mother had emphysema. This was not a good topic of conversation.

"Want to leave the car here and walk to the inn the guy at the desk told us about?"

"Sure," she said.

She was relieved. She had felt as if they were two adults, playing at conversation. She suddenly remembered the letter she had written Evan—the last letter she had written. She wished that instead of their speaking on the phone he had written back. She thought she would be better able to puzzle out what he had said if she could look at it. Who was she kidding? His tone of voice had told her he was sincere. Anything could be written in a letter. The voice gave it away. What had he said: "There's nothing I can do about that." He was right, of course; here she was at the Birches with Andrew, in Vermont, and there was nothing he could do.

There *was* something she could do.

She was shocked at her thought. She had almost put him out of her mind, and for no reason, on the ride, she had started thinking about him again. It was because she had trouble extending her seat belt. She had had a similar problem on the plane, trying to clamp her seat belt shut. There had been a piece of cardboard in it; she had pulled it out, knowing the man across the aisle was watching, thinking that she was some dumb woman, too inexperienced to know how to close a seat belt. And that thing he had said to her about his father, who didn't even live in Boston. She had really thought that was very inventive. And it was equally unusual for him to have then told her the truth. She could see his face quite distinctly. She just had, when she was resting on the bed with her eyes closed.

Some people were playing croquet on the lawn that stretched beside the parking lot. One ball cracked against another, and a teenage girl jumped up and down, clapping. The man who was playing with her gave her a look of exaggerated dismay. When Lillian looked over her shoulder, expecting to see the man going down the slight slope to try to hit his ball back up to the playing area, she did a double take: he was standing with his arms around the girl. They were kissing, his mallet thrown in the grass.

They passed a little row of shops as they walked past the green: Aubuchon Hardware, a hobby shop, a laundromat, a pizza restaurant. The laundromat had window boxes on the side, planted with petunias and marigolds. A few cars drove by. The breeze felt good. She had gotten hot in the car, and sitting for that long made her stiff; she felt like a gingerbread man, baked and then put out to cool. There was a large white church on their right, with a tall spire. Two people sat on the lawn, talking. It seemed like a very nice town: small, quiet, pretty. She didn't think she agreed with Andrew, although he was much smarter than she was, that anything that seemed simple was really a deception. She thought that maybe you did become a different person, depending on where you lived.

They walked down the hill, and as they did, the breeze came up stronger. They walked up the flagstone steps to the front door, and Andrew held the door open for her. There was a deep-green rug in the lobby, patterned to look like it had been stenciled. The walls were white, with punched tin lights hanging every six feet or so. There was a sign, with an arrow pointing left, in front of the high front desk: Cocktails on Patio. The man behind the desk smiled as they walked by. She was sure that they looked like a married couple. When she was in college she always read wedding announcements in the paper, to figure out whether the bride or groom was getting the better deal. She looked at people's left hands to see if there was a ring. She couldn't think of the last time she had looked at the page of wedding announcements. Or of the last time she had been to a wedding.

The girl who seated them was all smiles. The deck was crowded. She gave them a table in the last patch of sun, asking if this was all right.

She couldn't stop thinking about Evan. She thought that discussing him with Andrew might exorcise him. She ordered a rum and tonic. Andrew ordered scotch and water. She looked at the engagement ring. He saw her looking, and smiled. She smiled back. Church bells started ringing just at that instant. The timing was either so appropriate or inappropriate that she continued to smile. Andrew put his hand over hers.

A man, woman, and little girl sat a couple of tables away. The man had two large dots of calamine lotion on his forehead. He and the woman were drinking a bottle of wine. The little girl was swishing her fingers in the ice bucket.

"Thirty dollars a ticket?" the man said. "I've never heard of such a thing. You can never sit close enough to see the performers, anyway. It's better to watch it on television."

"It's not on television," the little girl said.

"It'll be on television eventually," he said.

"I'm going to call the baby-sitter and let her know we're going to be awhile longer," the woman said. As she pushed her chair back, Lillian looked at her left hand, then looked back at her own table as the cocktail waitress put the drinks down. The little white napkins blew in the breeze.

"If I have half the money for a Walkman, you'll buy it for me the next time we go to Burlington, right?" the little girl said.

"I don't like the idea of them," the man said.

"But you're wrong," she said. "You can hear through them. You can hear everything everybody's saying."

"But you don't pay attention to it," he said.

"You don't always pay attention."

"But I don't have something clamped over my ears," he said. He put his hands over his ears. She looked at him awhile, then tried to tug them away. She couldn't budge his arms.

"That's not what it's like," she said, pulling. "Come on—that's not fair."

The man started to hum and tap his foot, looking off in the distance. The little girl, half amused and half angry, continued to pull his arms.

Lillian tried to think what it must be like to be a parent. She hoped that Andrew's agent's plan for having the two books come out simultaneously would launch him on a lucrative literary career, and that she wouldn't have to go back to work once their first child was born.

She thought about Evan kissing her, in the cab. She reached for her drink and drank half of it.

"Did I ever tell you about the time F. Scott Fitzgerald was riding up Fifth Avenue, and it was such a sunny, perfect day—he was on his way to the Plaza—that he burst into tears because he thought he would never be that happy again?" Andrew said.

"Yes," she said.

"You know," Andrew said, "I think that eventually we should move to New York, when I start to be well known. I think that's the place to be."

"I sort of like small towns," she said.

"I don't want to be anonymous," he said.

"A lot of famous writers live in small towns."

"Well, if you're really famous, you can do that. I think that first you have to go to New York, then move away." He took a sip of his drink. "Nothing's going on in small towns," he said. "Nobody's thinking anything new."

"What about *Main Street*? *Peyton Place*? *Our Town*?"

"It's better when things are on the surface," he said. "I like it better when all that excitement is out there, in the air."

She nodded. She tried to think of what kind of excitement she and Andrew would experience. He was holding her hand

and kissing her fingertips. He raised his eyebrows. She made an effort to smile, and took her hand away. She looked at the engagement ring on her finger.

The waitress came to their table, smiling instead of asking if they wanted another drink.

"I don't believe so," Andrew said.

"I think I'll have another," Lillian said.

"Well, all right," Andrew said. "Make it two."

The waitress walked away, her skirt blowing in the breeze. The breeze lifted Lillian's hair. She said, "I'm not sure we should get married."

His face went blank. He jerked his head and snorted a little laugh. He looked at her for a couple of seconds. "You're kidding," he said.

"We didn't get along very well in Iowa."

"We got along in Iowa," he said.

She looked at him. Her hair blew over her face, and she didn't push it away.

"We were living in a tiny little house, and I was working night and day," he said.

"I know, but that might have been romantic. We just fought all the time."

"We didn't fight all the time."

"We fought a lot."

He put his fingertips on the napkin—lightly, as if it were a Ouija board. He raised his hands, then clasped them and looked at her. She had seen lawyers do that on television, when they were puzzled.

"I think we look at life so differently," she said.

"At this moment we certainly are looking at it differently," he said. "I love you. Do you love me?"

"Yes," she said, "but I don't think that's all we should think about. I don't know how I'm going to fit into your life. I think that maybe you aren't always realistic."

"By realistic do you mean conservative? Backward thinking? Safe?"

"But you might let yourself in for a lot of disappointment if you really have this image of us as Scott and Zelda, living it up in New York. I mean, I read that book you gave me. They were both outlaws from their own lives."

"They didn't fit into the slot they'd been assigned, if that's what you mean."

"I don't mean that. I mean, they were actors. And they were so ambitious. You can't think we're anything like them."

"He was very romantic, and he was a risk taker," Andrew said. "Don't you see me that way?"

She didn't. But she wasn't Zelda, and it seemed cruel to say that she thought there was a difference between being a romantic and being a dreamer. What F. Scott Fitzgerald had done was risky, and it was partly just his good luck that it worked out as well as it did for as long as it did.

"He was an alcoholic and he died young," she said.

"You're the one who ordered the second drink," he said. "I didn't say I thought I was a duplicate. I only said that we have a lot in common. I look on him as an inspiration."

"But that's the way things were years ago. It doesn't mean so much anymore to have gone to Princeton. People don't want to go to places like the Plaza now."

"Walk into the Palm Court any afternoon at five o'clock, and you'll find it packed with people," he said. "Fashionable people."

"Maybe we should talk about this later," she said.

"You're treating me the way Zelda treated him. He and I are both genuine romantics—that's what's so sad. That neither of you realize that we don't have to be led around by the nose."

"He's dead," Lillian said. "You talk like he's a friend of yours."

"I quite realize that he's dead," Andrew said.

The waitress brought their drinks. "I'm sorry it took so long," she said.

She and Andrew reached for their drinks in unison, the way people on a lurching subway car reach for the strap.

"I can't understand why you're bringing this up," he said.

"I think Zelda was shallow," Lillian said. "She cared about

appearances, and money and success. I don't like to be compared to her."

"She was also quite adventurous and beautiful, and she wanted to have a good time. She was always up for things."

"You've ignored all the bad things about her and blown her out of proportion."

"Well," he said, sipping his drink. "You know, most women complain that men don't appreciate them. I think of the two of you as very attractive, interesting, unusual women. I think you should be glad that I feel that way."

"You keep talking about both of them as if they're still alive."

"They're very real to me, and in that sense they are alive."

"If they were alive, they'd be different. They were our age years ago, when the world was different."

"I'm telling you," he said, "the Plaza hotel is crowded to this day. Brooke Shields goes to Princeton."

It was so heartfelt that she caught herself before she laughed. She held her breath. She looked at him.

"Zelda was a bitch," she said.

"Why is it that beautiful women never like other beautiful women?"

"I don't think that's true," she said. "And if somebody's a bitch, why should anyone like them?"

"I've never heard you talk like this."

She shrugged. "You're the one who's always saying that everybody's so complex," she said. "According to you, everybody's stuffed full of complexities, like toys hidden inside a piñata."

He cocked his head. "What a brilliant simile," he said.

"Thank you," she said.

"I know what you're doing," he said. "You're doing just what she did to him. You're trying to excite me. There's something sexual about it, at the same time that it's cruel."

"*I'm not her*," Lillian said.

"You were playing a trick," he said. He took a drink and looked out over the railing. The sky was bright: gray-blue, with only a few wisps of clouds. A sprinkler rotating in a wide circle sent jets of water around the lower part of the lawn. A boy pedaled by on a bicycle.

"I met somebody on the plane," she said.

He jerked his head around and looked at her. "What plane?" he said.

"The plane from Iowa to Boston."

He continued to look at her.

"I did. I'm sure you've met people since you've known me that you've found attractive."

"You're putting me on," he said.

"I'm not. I mean, I think it's only normal. I met a man on the plane."

"Does the story get any better than that?" he said, picking up his drink and taking a sip.

"I just thought I should tell you," she said.

"Well, now you've told me."

They sat in silence. The woman who had left to make the phone call returned, finally, and sank down in the chair, complaining that the line had been tied up all that time, and that no baby-sitter could possibly be talking on the phone and watching the baby at the same time. The little girl began to talk to her mother about buying a Walkman when they went to Burlington. "Stop nagging," her father said, "or we'll leave you with the baby-sitter next time."

"Shall we go back to the Birches?" Andrew said.

"Why are you talking that way?" she said. "Why did you say, 'Shall we go back?' "

"You now find everything about me questionable?"

"What are you going to do, punish me for being truthful?"

"You've had your way. It would be a little late to punish you."

"Don't make me feel bad," she said. "What do you want me to do: hoard all my secrets?"

"Go right ahead," he said, folding his hands again. "Fire away."

"I was talking about honesty in general. I don't have a list to recite, Andrew."

"As you know," he said, "I think that only simple people

with simple lives have simple secrets. And they're usually in hospitals, being looked out for. I'm hardly shocked. I just wonder about your motivation."

"You don't want me to tell you when I'm confused?"

"As I said: Fire away."

"I'm not a submarine."

"You really are quite bright this evening," he said.

"Maybe you should give me credit for having a brain. Not just for being a stand-in for Zelda Fitzgerald."

"I do," he said. "When you act like this, I see exactly what F. Scott Fitzgerald found so painful but so energizing at the same time. If you have any doubts, I can erase them."

"Order another drink."

"I'd rather go back."

"I'm not going to make it a contest of wills," she said. "If it's so important to you to go back, we'll go back. Do you mind getting the bill?"

"You get it," he said. "Really put me down."

"For one thing, Andrew, it's not a put-down in 1984 if a woman picks up the check. You'll have to think of something better."

"I can think of something better," he said. "Let's go back to the Birches."

She had a sudden image of the room: the wallpaper, the cherry writing desk with the straight-back chair facing the window. The postcard, envelope, and letter opener in the drawer. The big bed with the white spread, the inappropriately modern goose-neck lamps on the night tables.

"On the way back to Boston, huh? We had a fight, and you met a man on the plane."

"Stop it," she said.

"Come on," he said. "I deserve it. Who am I but some unheard of writer. Don't you wonder why I think I deserve you?"

"Stop it," she said. "You're embarrassing me."

"I'm the one who should be embarrassed. I'm always telling you what's going on below the surface, and I conveniently forget that you're complex, like everybody else."

She got the waitress' eye and motioned for the bill.

"Put me down," he said. "I deserve it. But I want you to know that I can prove myself to you."

He was back to being F. Scott Fitzgerald, but suddenly it occurred to her that the routine had never quite been what she thought it was; he wanted to pretend that she was a bitch and *only* a bitch. Simple, like silly Zelda.

22

NICOLE was sitting in the living room of Lucy's house, discussing the future. Work was important to her. Work kept her centered. That was what she was telling Andrew Steinborn.

"What do you think?" Steinborn asked, moving the conversation away from her to Stephanie Sykes. "Does Stephanie feel a victim—does she realize that she's living in that house because she's useful? That in alleviating her suffering, Dr. Cora Cranston has mitigated her own, as well?"

"What does mitigated mean?" Nicole said.

"When something is made less," Andrew said.

"I don't really see it that way," Nicole said. "She got picked up by the doctor, sure, but what does it matter that the doctor ends up happier and she ends up about the same? I guess it depends on whether you think doctors are more important people than the rest of the world, and saving one doctor is more important than saving an alcoholic."

"But Stephanie Sykes has *depth*," Andrew said. "You think her salvation is important, don't you?"

"I guess so," Nicole said, "but look—not everybody's going to be saved."

Andrew cocked his head.

"I haven't read anything except the first two scripts," she said. "I don't really know how it'll go this season."

St. Francis ran down the stairs and stopped at the front door, whining. Nicole got up and took the sock out of his mouth and opened the door. He ran out onto the lawn and turned and barked. When he was sure that he had lost both the sock and Nicole's attention, he stopped and walked over to his gully by the rhododendrons.

"Chain the dog," Lucy called from upstairs.

"Excuse me," Nicole said.

Andrew followed her outside. The day was bright and breezy. The dog raised his snout and sniffed the air. Lillian had decided to sleep late. Andrew sat on the lawn and bumped onto one hip, pulling a piece of grass and chewing it. Nicole came over to where he sat on the lawn and sat down beside him. He thought that he must have challenged her too much with his questions. It was important to let her know that he cared what she thought and that he was not particularly interested in what was scheduled to happen on the program.

"How do you get inside your character?" he said, starting over.

"Oh, that's not hard," Nicole said. "She's young, so she's pretty easy to figure out."

"But you're both fourteen, aren't you?" Andrew said.

"Yeah, but I mean, she's young. She hasn't really hardened into being who she's going to be, so I sort of approach her thinking that nothing I do can really be wrong, because she's changeable, right?"

"Can you give me an example?" Andrew said.

"Well, like in the scene where she's in the bathroom, and Cora Cranston discovers the lump on her breast? I mean, there's only one way to react if you find a lump, but somebody like Stephanie, just watching, can really do any number of things. So I thought that at that point she'd really harden herself. I'd try to show her getting hard, because she has enough of her own pain, right?"

"So you see her as very self-protective?"

"Yeah. I guess so."

"Well, how do you get into that? I mean, as an actress, what thoughts go through your mind?"

"That there can't be two people hogging the camera at the same time. I mean, if I had had more of a reaction than Pauline, I mean Dr. Cranston, that would have scooped her scene, and I didn't really have the right to have the camera go to me, you know?"

"But leaving aside the technicalities of how the show is

filmed: it was a conscious decision to have your character freeze just then?"

"If I hadn't decided it, Pauline would just have made a scene."

"Is that what you think about?"

"That's just manners. I mean, when I'm stumbling blindly around the bathroom, Pauline lets me have that. If she threw herself against the door because she suspected what was going on, that wouldn't be appropriate, you know? She'd be trying to get the camera during my scene."

"I see. But leaving aside what seems to be a question of . . . manners . . . I mean, leaving aside whose scene it is and all that, what does Stephanie Sykes feel at such a moment?"

"What moment?" Nicole said.

"When you looked out and saw Dr. Cranston open her mouth in horror when she found the lump in her breast."

"I felt that it was Dr. Cranston's moment."

Andrew looked past Nicole, at the heavy clouds blending into each other. He was not communicating well with Nicole.

"I understand that," he said, "but I'm interested not in the way the scene should be filmed but in what you felt at that moment."

"You mean what Stephanie Sykes felt?"

A bee buzzed past. Andrew jumped back. The sun disappeared behind the clouds.

"You lose yourself when you're acting, don't you?" Andrew said, a little annoyed that she had called his error to his attention.

"What Stephanie Sykes would do doesn't have a lot to do with the way I'd act," Nicole said.

"Aha! But as you understand her character . . ."

"She's half sloshed all the time. She's not all there. You know?"

"Yes. Right. But she's been an abused child, torn between loyalty to her mother and the relief of being taken out of that situation, and suddenly she sees that her new life is threatened. Does this make her feel alone? Sad? Angry?"

"I guess she's all of those things," Nicole said.

"And so, in a split second, you decide that she'll look a particular way, or make a particular gesture."

"Right."

"That's what I'm trying to find out: how you intuit what she's feeling and translate it."

"You know," Nicole said, "I don't get that many CU's."

They seemed deadlocked. Andrew was sure that he was phrasing these questions wrong. Or perhaps she was just being modest, or even unwilling to share with him her deepest feelings. He opened his notebook. "Let me read you something," he said. "I was talking to Pauline. Dr. Cranston. And she said, for instance, 'When I touched the lump it was as though all time stopped, all life stopped: my own hand, my own life, was whirling around, the way protons and electrons whirl around the atom. I knew that I had but a second to communicate that sense of a human being relinquishing herself to the ultimate motion of infinity.' "

Nicole didn't say anything for a minute. Then she said, "Did she know in advance what question you were going to ask her?"

"No," he said.

"Well, this is strictly off the record, but Pauline gets a little hyper about things, you know?"

"Yes, yes, but that's all right. I want to hear about what the people on the show understand that their characters are feeling. That's the way you can best help me. I'm not interested in the sort of technical dimensions of the scene, but in what you know and how you channel it into action."

"The other thing is," Nicole said, "we aren't just up there doing what we want. There's a director and a producer, plus the script."

"At that moment, then, did you feel so restricted that you didn't introspect about your character, just because it was Pauline's—Dr. Cranston's—moment?"

"It's hard to remember," Nicole said. "I can't even remember exactly what I did."

"Well," Andrew said, leafing through the notebook again, "for example, Pauline said about that scene that you were perfect; that when Stephanie Sykes, seeing her stepmother's fingers freeze, realizes that time itself is freezing, and she is being frozen with it, she expresses her resistance by drinking and sliding slowly down against the bathroom door, much the way top-heavy snow slides and spills. It was as natural a gesture as that."

Nicole shifted on the grass. "I was supposed to get out of camera range so the screen would go black at that point," Nicole said.

"But that wasn't what you were reacting to," Andrew said. "You could have, uh . . . smashed your fist into the medicine cabinet mirror, or something, and the camera could have focused through that into blackness—"

"The show's not that arty," Nicole said. "That's a good idea, though."

"And, uh, that's what *you* did, with your consciousness. For what reason did you see Stephanie Sykes doing it?"

"Well, I mean, she drinks because she's not happy. She knows the shit's hitting the fan again, excuse me, and that's a drag, so she sinks down in despair."

"You see her as being in a state of despair."

"She's got a lot of problems and she's an alcoholic, so she just folds up a lot of the time. That's what she's supposed to do. I, with my own consciousness, feel that that is what she'd do."

Andrew was sweating. With the sun behind the clouds, his skin felt itchy as the air cooled. The cassette player clicked off. He reached for it, then thought that he might be intimidating her, even though she had had no objection to being taped. He didn't turn the tape over. He leaned back on both elbows. She was really just a child, after all; no doubt she felt that people in his position were quizzing her like a teacher, and she would be resistant to that.

"Just tell me some things you'd like me to know about Stephanie Sykes," he said. "Let's forget my questions now."

"I don't know," Nicole said. "She's pretty much the way she's explained in the press kit."

"Is it hard to play such a troubled person?" Andrew said.

"No," Nicole said.

Andrew was looking at her expectantly. She remembered something Piggy had said. "She's Everyman," Nicole said. It was her own thought to add that she didn't mean it as a sexist comment.

"Then, you don't see her as greatly exaggerated?"

Nicole remembered something else. She wasn't sure it would apply, but she decided to take a chance. "I see her as Jonah swallowed by the whale," she said.

Andrew immediately rose to a sitting position. He opened the tape recorder, flipped the tape over, and said, "You see her as Jonah in the whale? What do you see the whale representing?"

"Society," she said.

"So, uh, you see her as cut off, buried, in effect, a microcosm within the macrocosm, fighting for survival."

"Right," Nicole said.

"That's a very powerful image. Is it hard to play the role of someone you sympathize with so strongly?"

"I couldn't help her," Nicole said.

Andrew looked at her.

"I mean me. Nicole. In real life. You can't go around helping everybody you sympathize with. You can't help it that you're on top and the other guy isn't."

"You don't think of her just as a victim of fate, do you?"

What else? Nicole thought. She realized that she wasn't very good at imagining what people might be, or even what they might be doing, other than what they were and how they were acting at the present moment. She also realized that she was getting into deep water with Andrew Steinborn, and that it was better to try to end this discussion. What she wanted to say to him was that she didn't look down on anyone, real or imaginary, who kept her from sitting in a chair in school all day long, nine months a year.

"Oh, no," she said.

Steinborn let the tape run for another few seconds, then reached down and clicked it off.

"Thank you for your time," he said. "I find it important not to guess about the world, not to transfer my own assumptions, but to remain open enough to ask questions. My novel will be published shortly, and I'll send you a copy. I very much appreciate your having taken the time to discuss your role with me."

"Sure," Nicole said.

As they were walking back toward the house, Nicole looked up at the sky. "It's not unheard of to have a tornado," she said. "I wonder if we're in for a tornado." She was studying the sky, her face absolutely blank.

"Do they have tornadoes in Vermont?"

"I'm not sure," she said. "The one that comes to my mind is the Worcester tornado of 1953. It took ninety lives."

"Did your family know people who died then?" Andrew said.

"No," she said.

He nodded slowly. He looked at the sky. "You're not one of those intuitive people who are prophetic, are you?" he said, smiling nervously.

She was tired of answering questions, and she didn't want to ask again what another word meant. The ringing phone would save her. She held out her hand, but instead of shaking hands and letting her get the phone, he clasped her hand and looked at her soulfully. Even as he drove away, he was thinking that the writer's life was not an easy one, but he gave himself credit for searching for truth, instead of making assumptions. He looked at the sky through the front windshield, and then at the sky behind him, in the rearview mirror. Sometimes important information came at you in the most unexpected ways. He pushed harder on the accelerator, hurrying back to Lillian, and the inn.

By the time Nicole went inside, the phone had stopped ringing.

WHEN Andrew got back to the inn, Lillian was out. When she did return from shopping, though, she had quite a story to tell him. She had been browsing through Sweet Sincerity, a shop that carried cotton nightgowns and bed jackets from the 1920s, fans, and other pretty, old-fashioned ephemera. Lillian and one other woman were the only customers. They were both flipping through the racks of clothes when two women came into the store, asked the woman behind the cash register whether she was the owner, then suggested that she stock useful things for the contemporary woman, such as thermal underwear, body-building devices, hiking boots, and Mace.

"Women must provide for women," one of the women said. "The day of the damsel is gone. We should not nourish ourselves with refined sugar," she said, pointing to the gold boxes of Godiva chocolates stacked by the cash register, "but with healthy proteins and carbohydrates that will be transformed into healthy body power."

"Give me a break," the woman behind the cash register said. She was in her twenties, with a pink streak painted in her short, curly hair and cheeks heavily rouged a deeper pink than her hair.

"The enlightenment of women can allow for a new radiance in our society. Pectoral power, not penis envy," the woman said, hitting the counter. "I would suggest that in place of those Debbie Harry and Annie Lennox stills, you hang pictures of women such as Margaret Bourke-White and Dr. Helen Caldicott."

"Oh, shit," the saleswoman said. "I left the Upper West Side to hear this hysterical shit?"

The woman who stood beside the woman lecturing the store owner stepped forward. "Maybe you could put up a picture of Margaret Mead," she said.

"Listen," the owner said, a pink curl falling over her forehead, "I busted my ass to get the kind of store that I want, and suggestions about how I decorate it are really out of line."

"It is never too late to change your thinking," the first woman said. "Inner power will provide outer beauty. Consider Helen Hooven Santmyer." She turned toward the woman who stood beside her and raised her eyebrows.

"Sophia Loren," the woman said.

"Sophia Loren," the older woman said. "How would she be an example?"

"She's a businesswoman. She sells Sophia perfume."

"That's ridiculous," the older woman said. "She's a pawn of the media. She's a terrible example."

"I don't believe this," the owner said. "In New York they just come in and tie you up and take the money and then shoot you or not. Here, I've got to die of boredom."

A woman who had been flipping through the rows of nightgowns and who had averted her eyes through the confrontation started to move toward the front of the store. "My name is Davina Cole," the older woman said, reaching out to stop her. "I notice that you are pregnant. I hope that if the child you are carrying is female, that it will be all-powerful. You may communicate more power to the child by wearing Extra Large camouflage shirts as nightgowns, rather than purchasing any of this silly frippery."

"I'm calling the cops," the owner said. Her nails were so long that she dialed the phone with the back of a pencil.

Police Officer Brown's wife, as she walked out of the store, knew just what she was escaping. The shop owner would live to regret calling for help; she could hardy wait to hear *his* version of what happened when he got home.

There were only a few seconds in which Lillian was the only other customer in the shop. When the owner began talking to the police about the women who were causing a disturbance in her store, Lillian moved toward the front of the store to leave. Myra DeVane walked in just then, hoping to find something suitable to wear to her rendezvous with Edward at the Plaza. Almost at once she realized that there was a problem—but it was also a problem that interested her: the woman who was stacking pamphlets on the counter had to be Davina Cole.

"Masculine tumescence has caused mind-boggling tragedy," Davina Cole said to the owner.

Lillian began to wonder about her notions of easygoing, small-town life.

Myra DeVane took out her wallet and flashed her Press card. "Tell me what you're here to protest," she said.

"The subversion of women through sentimental desensitizing," Davina Cole said. "Misogyny will be overcome when women wear the mantle of power."

"My long-suffering ass," the owner said. "Everybody else closes this time of year, and I stay open. Then two dykes walk in and want to make a Christmas tree ornament into a cannonball. Where the hell are those cops?"

"And who are you?" Myra said, writing.

"Maureen Hildon," the other woman said.

Myra looked up. "I just interviewed your husband," she said.

"Her husband is involved in masculine-dominated, oppressive capitalism," Davina said.

"Is that right?" Myra said to Maureen, fishing in her purse for her recorder.

"Well," Maureen said, "the number of women on his staff is not representative."

"Have you spoken to your husband about that?" Myra said, putting her recorder on the counter, next to the pamphlets and candy boxes.

"They no longer communicate," Davina Cole said. "With new-found power, Maureen is devoting herself to maximizing her strength so that the enemy can be subverted."

"That's right," Maureen said. "But don't think of me as Sophia Loren."

"Sophia Loren?" Myra said.

"A token," Maureen said. "A creation of the male-dominated media."

At that point, Officer Pasani opened the door and, with his partner, walked into the store. Myra suddenly stiffened into the reporter who is all eyes and ears. Caught under the heel of Officer Brown's regulation black shoe was a wadded-up, regulation size McDonald's french-fry bag. "Okay," Brown said, hitching up his pants. "What's the problem on this lovely day, ladies?"

Officer Pasani removed his hat and held it over his heart, as if the National Anthem had just been struck up.

Dear Lucy,

I'm writing you on the morning of my wedding day. Even though you're not here, I feel that you are. That first wedding was such a mistake. I still get scared thinking about it. You know, I never would have gotten through it without you. I never thought I'd have a wedding without my family present. Most of all, I never thought I'd get married without *you* being there, but I didn't know how I could invite you without having Mother and Nicole. This really embarrasses me to say, but I think part of the reason he's marrying me is that he thinks I'm such a free spirit. Somehow, having my mother and daughter at the wedding would really change that notion and—truth—I've become a coward in my old age. I want him to think I'm impetuous and unencumbered. He'll find out soon enough that that's not true.

I was thinking, last night, about all the hours we spent playing pretend when we were little girls. It makes me laugh now that we thought we could have any fantasy we wanted, and the worst price we'd pay would be having Mother yell at us for borrowing her clothes or standing on the bed. Lately there are so many fantasies thrust at us in all those articles telling us there are millions of men out there if you just become perfect that I'm just exhausted. I already pretend to enjoy exercising so I'll look good, and say that I like health food instead of salt and sugar. Why not just admit that things are terrible but we have no choice?

I'm going to tell you something that I wouldn't tell anybody else. I'm doing this because I think it will keep me from getting old. I've been spending too much time doing what I ought to do instead of what I want, and this is a chance to change that. I'm tired of buying into people's notions of the way things should be. I don't want to be laid-back and supportive and the perfect little mother to the perfect little star. There are a lot of scared people out there who seized some power and started making their own fear look like logic, dictating the way things should be. But I've seen through it now, and I'm stepping aside.

Wish me luck. I love you.

Jane

Dear Nicole,

Dear child, we have never met, but my heart goes out to you in this time of sadness. When I was a girl your age my own beloved mother died, and I know how bad you must feel. There is nothing that can substitute for a mother's love. It is actually a testament to mothers that they do their caring so gracefully that we do not realize that it does not always come easily or naturally to them, but rather that they are selfless and willing to subtly convey to us that their suffering is never too great. I have always tried to emulate my own dear mother in raising Percy. He has been such a satisfaction to me that I am sorrowful it was impossible for me to have other children. He is a wonderful son, though, and that is great compensation: one task well done is worth many done poorly. I asked Percy—your dear "Piggy"—for your address so I could not only extend my sympathy but also let you know that, even to a stranger like me, your mother communicated her great love for you. We spoke of children before the wedding, and it was with much pride that she showed me the pictures of you that she carries in her wallet. As you know, the baby picture of you with your little curl is in the photo section for everyone to see, but the more recent picture of you in an evening dress (at an awards ceremony, I believe) she keeps in the slot where she places her American Express card. That way, of course, she may open her wallet without revealing to others her connection with you and inviting comment, yet still keep the older you close by, to glance at privately. Your mother and I discussed not only your beauty but your many accomplishments at such a young age.

As you must certainly know, your name is the female version of the Greek Nikolaos, which denotes the "Victorious army." You are a girl, then, among other Nicoles (for you are never alone), who represents her people. I am sure that you will show strength in dealing with your sad new burden, but the young and resolute shall lead us all, and you, I am sure, will be at the front of the line. This sad occasion has made Percy seem even more precious to me. Please know that he loves you and is there for you. We are always our mother's children, whether or not our dear mothers are with us in fact, or but in memory. Just as Percy draws strength from me, and I draw strength from my own dearly beloved deceased mother, let me urge you to continue to draw strength from your mother, who is ever with you. My dear, take strength in the fact that someone with your resources can and will triumph over the ebb tide of grief and be carried out to deeper water.

My sincere sympathy.
Mrs. Robert (Edna) Proctor

Dear Everybody,

Forgive the impersonal quality of a Xeroxed letter, but time is short, and if I can't reach everybody by phone, I just wanted to be sure to say goodbye. I will write to each and every one of you personally, as the faith healers say, but right now I've decided to leave for California with Peter[1] and come back Aug. 25 for the house closing.

For reasons that I can't even understand myself, my life had gotten so much better[2] in Vermont lately that it is now with some regret that I find I won't be living among you any longer. This is a big move, and it's perfectly possible that I'm more scared than I realize. I'm very glad that at last I have another person to love and to share my life with. You're all welcome in S.F. any time. It'll be hard for that group of people at my new job to top you. I hope that you will all think of me as the same person, just happily stepping into a more honest, natural identity. (Sounds like a clothes ad, I realize.) As Peter was saying to me this morning, thank God that man who blew away all those people in McDonald's left his *wife* in the apt. when he did it. Let the press deal with heterosexual behavior for a while.

Peace be with you, as you pursue a piece of whatever action you want. Golden Gate bridge postcards to follow.

Noonan

[1] Lucy—he likes you the best of all of them and wants you to visit. You always were nice to me, and I'm glad we got closer lately.
[2] Leaving aside Maureen. Just heard the news. Good riddance!

Dear Nicole,

I read the story in the paper about your mother. I know that you must feel very sad. I remember telling you that I got away from my mother as fast as I could. I think boys try to do that more than girls and also she wasn't a very good mother. She hardly ever fixed meals and she expected us to do things that were impossible like fix the car when we didn't know any more about how to fix a car than she did. I guess you haven't been real unhappy so it must be a rough time for you. Probably it's easier to leave than to be the one that's left. If you were still around, I'd try to cheer you up, but I read that you've gone back to California for the funeral. I thought I'd write this to you c/o your aunt at the paper anyway because it could get forwarded. I don't know if anybody will open it first or not. Thanks for the game of croquet.

Your friend in Vt.
Harry Woods

Dear Lucy,

When I got back from a week's vacation I found out about your sister's death. It was a tragic accident. There are so many near misses on these Vermont roads that all winter I have a sense of my mortality. Having this happen in summer seems doubly shocking, for some reason. I cannot imagine how difficult it must be for you. I'm glad that Nicole was with you when she had to get such awful news, but it must have been very difficult for you to be the one who had to take care of things. I have even found it difficult to be temporarily apart from all my friends. I imagine that the news must not even seem quite real.

You don't really even know me, but I have thought often about the brief conversation we had at the party awhile ago. I was probably more intimidated by your presence than I realized, and I think I overcompensated by trying to appear cool. You handled everything beautifully, including my bubbling over and blurting out information about Les Whitehall. I guess that I have been thinking about how graceful you were, and although it is none of my business, I wondered whether you might not be paying a price for being that way. I have nowhere near as much composure as you. I also turn aside insults and smile through things that are painful, but I pay a price for doing that. It was probably naïve—and convenient—for me not to realize that you must, too. People want to have an easy fix on other people, and since you are Cindi Coeur, it's easy to assume that someone who satirizes our shortcomings has set herself above us. I guess that the reason I'm writing is to say that if you ever want to step down—that's wrong; step aside—that I am no more the hard-nosed reporter than you are the high-and-mighty advice columnist looking down on everyone. If you ever feel like talking, I would like to have another chance.

Sincerely,
Myra DeVane

Dear Lucy,

I want to extend my apologies for any trouble and worry I have caused you. Naturally, if I had imagined that there might be so many repercussions from the plan Nicole and I had to solve my problems with my lady friend, I would have saved myself, as well as others, the misery we have all had to endure because of the picture-taking incident. Now that it is clear beyond any doubt that nothing was amiss between Nicole and me, I hope that your feelings toward me will once again be kind. As you know, I left my easel and sketch pad at your house. Of course shipping the easel would be too much trouble, but I would appreciate it very much if my sketchbook could be sent to me. The sketches of Nicole are important, and the project must go on quite apart from our personal problems. If you would send the sketchbook to me, I will send you a check by return mail to reimburse you for your trouble. I hope that you are having a pleasant summer.

Best wishes,
Edward

Dear Lucy,

I've been trying all summer to get up the nerve to ask you out, but I've never been able to do it. I thought that maybe you thought I wasn't your type, because I work at the nursery. I do know that you were flirting with me the day you and your friend were there, though. I hope I don't insult you by saying this. What's wrong with flirting, after all. I was very interested and I guess it's a sign of how much ego I have that I thought you'd come by again, or maybe even call. I did meet your friend who wanted to buy trees for his front lawn because he wanted to make his house, which was up for sale, look nice. I told him to say hello. Maybe he did.

I suppose I should write Cindi Coeur instead of Lucy Spenser, but that might be a little too cute. I thought you could answer my question just as well.

I guess I'm writing you because I think you'll give me an honest answer. Did you also feel good energy between us, and if so, is the reason you stayed away because you're involved with someone else or because I was an employee at a nursery? I'm going to confide in you: I need to know, because my luck has been lousy lately. My father is quite rich, and I always felt that if I didn't do something real with my summers (I realize that working in a nursery isn't meaningful, but other summers I've done things like work at a camp for handicapped kids), I'd become just another one of those kids who lounge around their parents' summer house, doing some perfunctory little things the gardener or whoever doesn't do, and sipping gin and tonics with the folks at night. I don't mean to present myself as some prince in frog's clothing, but it would help me to know whether you think I never will meet someone who's right for me outside of the world I was brought up in.

I realize that this sounds like I'm accusing you—like I expected you to be a bloodhound or something. I don't mean that at all. I just want to know if I'm right that the attraction, at least, was mutual, and whether you might have stayed away because you were interested in someone else, or for some other personal reason. It would help me to know. I guess, rereading this, that I wouldn't have written you if you didn't do the Cindi Coeur column, after all. I never write letters and don't know how I got the idea. Or the nerve. At any rate, enjoy the rest of the summer. There's a present you'll have found by the time you get this.

Sincerely,
Don Severs

Dear Nicole,

Everyone on the show is terribly sorry about what happened. It is shocking news about your mother's untimely death. I think that I am particularly moved by what has happened because I have always been a kind of stand-in mother. I want you to know that you can still count on me.

As we all know so well, the show must go on. You will have to hide your own sorrows to effectively portray the sorrows of Stephanie Sykes. Really, though it seems small consolation at a time like this, it does make one pause to remember how many gifts and resources we have been given to draw on. Hard work will help to heal the wound. I am sure that you can triumph over this, as Stephanie has gradually managed to master her alcoholism, etc. Remember that you are not just a teenage girl who has lost her mother, but a character in your own life, and that your life is under your direction. Hard work and dedication will put you over the hump.

I have read someplace that when someone has trouble, vague offers of support are often not very helpful, however sincere. I thought that we might meet and talk about anything you like the first Monday of every month at the Polo Lounge. My treat.

With good wishes,
Pauline

Dear Miss Spenser,

I have in my possession a check issude from the Starlight, Star Bright Corp, in the ammount of $90. Down at the bottom of the check, where there is a memo line, it says Dead Sheep. I do not know, if this is the way you are accustomed to doing things, but anybody with desent manners would know that this is no suitible apology. My wife and I have been country people all are lives and we know that an acident like this is a thing that happens. But you did not right or call to say that you were sorry that your new dog had done this. As it happens that particulur sheep was old ect. but with a dog like that it is dangerus, also on are property there are valuble sheep and if he got at the two pigs there would really be trouble as we have been fatenning them well for a long time and no money could repay us. We also have such pets as a cat and a parot out on the front porch and having seen how that dog lungd at the sheep I don't even no that I cunsider my bird safe. I would think that you would have handled this matter difruntly than just to have someone send us money like that. I also have something else to say to you. You taught my daughter drawing last year and when they drew the animals in the teraryum you put stars on her work for bringing home things I am embarased my wife saw because they fetured a part of the annatome that I would not even right in this letter to a lady, the part of the annatome was pronownced and exageratid. It should have been X'd out by you when that part was their at all let alone a part almost as big as a lizurd itself. Letting children draw this is not art. If your dog comes on are property again I would feel within my rites to shoot him.

Your negbor,
Mr. D. Wiegand

25

THE morning after the funeral in Los Angeles, Lucy went downstairs to Piggy Proctor's living room. She was the first one awake. She had forced herself to get up even though it was very early, because being awake and tired was better than being asleep and enduring the nightmares. Ever since she got the news about Jane, she had been dreaming her own death: death by drowning, boats sunk, planes exploding, cars crashing—your basic suburban five-year-old's typical fantasy day.

There had been so many people in the room the night before that it seemed, now that it was empty, that it was an entirely different room. Glass shelves that separated one part of the room from the other held Piggy's wife's shell collection. The furniture was lavender and blue. Enormous, hazy paintings of the sky hung on opposite walls. The richer people became the more they felt comfortable with abstraction. Nowhere in Piggy's house was there a picture of the sky with the sun, or of a vase with flowers, or a scene out of real life; it was all art that relied on blotters instead of brushes. Some paintings that seemed pointillist grew clearer as you came closer. Lucy wandered around Piggy's big house like a person with glaucoma wandering through a gallery.

Letters and telegrams had overflowed the big white wicker basket on the table. A couple had fallen on the rug. Lucy picked those up and carefully put them back in the basket as if they were alive—like birds that had fallen out of a nest, that must be frightened to be alone. She hadn't been able to bring herself to look at any of them, and this morning she was still unable to do it. She stood there awhile, and finally reached into the basket like someone in a contest, drawing a card. Mixed in with all the messages of condolence was a telegram to Piggy's wife saying that *Your lucky day may come soon, Mrs. Proctor. You are now one of ten finalists in Sacramento Bread's fly away to France deluxe vacation.* There were instructions about what Mrs. Proctor should do next. Well, Lucy thought, what would important days be without irony: the blizzard on election eve, enemy troops storming the village as a woman was giving birth, the child hiccuping during its confirmation, the new car stalling as it was driven from the showroom.

Lucy's mother hadn't been able to make the trip. Every time she got out of bed she fainted. The family doctor was visiting her every afternoon. She had picked up her mother's diction; he was only her mother's doctor. They hadn't been a family for almost twenty years. Piggy's wife had asked her if someone shouldn't try to locate their father, to send word of Jane's death. Lucy had told her the truth: she wouldn't know where to begin looking. She really doubted if her mother knew where he was, and didn't think she was in any shape to be asked. "Oh dear," Piggy's wife said. She had been saying it for days.

Nicole alternated between stony silence, not even speaking when spoken to, and weeping and clinging to Lucy. Lucy had gotten used to Nicole's slim body and pretty face—she had taken her for granted—so that now it was quite shocking to have a scrawny little girl with a puffy, tear-streaked face curled against her, with her face buried against her body. Of course she was going to raise Nicole. The thought of giving her to her mother or to Piggy's wife, who thought she should hire a governess and have her move into their house, was unthinkable. Nicole seemed relieved to know that she wouldn't have to do that. But now there was the question of where to live. Nicole had said that she wanted to live in Los Angeles because of her career, but Lucy wasn't entirely convinced that that wasn't just bravado. She had even told Nicole that just because she had a career she was not required to continue doing what she had done—or that she might still have a career, but a different one. Nicole cried and said that she wanted to go back to *Passionate Intensity.* Piggy seconded this notion, emphatically, but Piggy was hardly objective. When Nicole said things like, "I'm a professional," it sounded more programmed than sincere. No; Lucy wasn't sure of that. She was so tired herself that she couldn't think straight. Maybe she was just projecting.

The day before, walking to the parking lot after the funeral, the P.R. man had said to Piggy that he was disturbed because the Nicole Nelson doll was flat-chested: it was going to make the doll look too young, and they would be losing part of their market. Piggy had called the lawyer when he got home, raving about "getting some chest action." Lucy had not known most of the people at the funeral. She had met Pauline once before, and although she did not know Bobby Blue or his mother, she felt as if she did because he had so often been talked about this summer. She had stood across from him as the casket was lowered, thinking how inappropriate it was that she could not get men's testicles out of her mind as her sister's coffin was lowered into the ground.

After the funeral the minister, whom only Piggy's wife had met before (she did not attend church: she had met him playing golf), had come back to the house for lunch. A caterer had set up bowls of fruit salad, bread, and cold seafood while they were gone. Piggy's secretary was there in person to explain that an extremely unfortunate, entirely regrettable accident had happened. She had explained to the caterer, she would stake her life on this, that the cake was to be a dessert for a luncheon after a funeral, and that the baker might do "something meaningful." She had meant, perhaps, a cross or a bunch of icing forget-me-nots or whatever to decorate the cake, but when she came to inspect things in the kitchen, she found that he had baked a large cake in the shape of a submarine. The caterer apologized, saying that his assistant had misread his handwriting, and seen *something meaningful* as *submarine*. Piggy stalked out to the kitchen, took a look, ordered the blue excelsior pulled away from around the submarine, took a knife and cut off the tail, cursed, and told them to bring the cake out when it was time for dessert. The secretary dispensed Valium in the kitchen. Piggy's wife took so many that she fell asleep as the minister was talking to her about the condition of the grass on the back nine. When she woke up ten hours later, only Lucy was still awake, in the living room. She had had too many drinks to try to sleep, and not enough to have the nerve to awaken Piggy to talk to him. After a couple of drinks she had called her mother. Her mother had decided to wallow in her misery, and had taken down the baby album—they had been photographed so much as children that the album contained almost as many pictures as the *O.E.D.* had words—and she wanted to talk to Lucy about the past, rather than hear about the funeral. Lucy was trying to decide whether she should go through with her plans to return to Vermont with Nicole, or whether they should fly to Philadelphia to see her mother. There was no way to tell if seeing them would make things better or worse for her mother. She had asked Piggy's wife, the night before, what she should do, but Piggy's wife was as passive as he was aggressive. When she got nervous, she blew dust off her shells—imaginary dust, because the maid dusted them every day. Lucy had made her puff until she almost passed out. Jane had always been very amused by Piggy's wife. It was part of the reason why she was so fond of her. Jane would have liked it that in her rush to get ready for the funeral, Piggy's wife had not noticed that there was a nametag still stuck to her Chanel jacket. In script, at the top of the piece of paper, it said: HI, I'M, and below that was printed MRS. "PIG" PROCTOR.

Caterers and Chanel suits and swimming pools and Mercedes were all things Jane made fun of, but for years Lucy had noticed that she found it necessary to be around them—they weren't something she could dismiss or just laugh at from afar. "Methinks the lady doth protest too much," which her mother had so often said about Jane, might have been true: that she was more attracted to such things than she let on. It was easier for girls than boys to pretend, Lucy thought: from childhood, the girls were the ones who wore costumes and who acted out their dreams; when they got older they could move more gracefully into what they imagined than men. If people were going to be judged quickly all their lives—judged, even, the minute they walked into a room—it would be more helpful to have thought of yourself as a dancer than a firefighter.

She wondered how happy Jane had been. In spite of her fierce independence, it could be argued that she just turned her back on one world whose stereotypes she disliked for another, whose stereotypes she embraced. Jane had lived close to the limelight most of her life, but she had never been a star. If there was life in the galaxy, it was probably true that Pluto loathed the sun. This life must have made her feel unimportant a lot of the time. Nicole's mother. The daughter Piggy never had. She wondered if Jane might have gotten married as a deliberate act of self-destruction. She had said to Lucy the last time she saw her that she was amazed by all the Hollywood people who were their own best groupies. She saw it as a sign of old age—of being from a different generation—that she was comfortable with being adored, or with adoring someone, but that she couldn't just stand there and adore herself.

Lucy couldn't stand the thought of going to Jane's house and disposing of her things. Jane's husband's relatives had called and expressed their sympathy. He was in a coma and not expected to come out of it. They had said to Piggy that they didn't want anything in the house touched. Lawyers had been called in on both sides. Lucy had overheard one phone call, during which Piggy had shouted, "Do you realize that there's not one possession of your son's in the house, unless he's a drag queen? There's a Harley in the garage. Period."

Piggy came downstairs, in his satin robe. "How's everybody doing?" he said. And just as quickly, "Spare me." He went into the kitchen, yawning. He did not look any more rested than he had been before he went to bed.

"Piggy hates the morning so," his wife said.

The telephone rang. As soon as Piggy got up, he turned the phones back on. The call was nothing that interested him; he was speaking in a normal tone of voice, so Lucy and his wife couldn't hear what he was saying.

"It's better if he gets a stimulating call right off," his wife said. "He does better when he's catapulted into things. Piggy needs a little prodding to seize the day."

Piggy came out of the kitchen. He was holding a bowl with a bunch of grapes in it, which he did not offer to anyone. He sat down, letting his wife get the next phone call. It was Hildon, wanting to talk to Lucy. She realized when she stood how little energy she had, how tired she was. Hildon was taking care of St. Francis. There was no Cindi Coeur column this week. Hildon acted as if just talking to Lucy, she might crack. He lied and told Lucy that everything was fine. He told the truth, that he missed her. St. Francis was holding his own. What he did not tell her was that his wife had left him and that she had decided to sue for divorce and name Lucy as corespondent. If he had ever had the ability to talk her out of this, he didn't now; she had come back to the house, not knowing that St. Francis was there, and he had bitten her on the leg. She had found out that St. Francis was Lucy's dog. This had delighted her lawyer. As Hildon rattled on nervously, she realized, suddenly, that she had inherited St. Francis.

"Piggy making everything worse for everybody?" he said.

"Not really," she said.

"You get some sleep?"

"I've had about five hours sleep in the last three days," she said.

"Still coming in at the same time?"

"Yeah," she said.

Hildon was picking her up at the airport. She decided that she and Nicole should go to Vermont rather than Philadelphia. When she was better able to deal with it, she would see her mother. It really did not seem possible that she would never see Jane again. It had taken Jane awhile, but finally she had figured out what she could do that was too dangerous, and she had done it. None of that silly hot-potato game they had played when they were children, both of them so fearful that it became fun, scalding their hands tossing a hot Idaho back and forth in the kitchen. Early on, Jane had convinced Lucy of the rewards of acting-up: everybody turned their attention to them, their mother doubted her ability to raise children, chaos resulted in later bedtimes and in rewards being proffered if they would only calm down. Maybe, Lucy thought, if Jane was in Heaven, she was enjoying looking down and seeing Piggy Proctor slumped over his bowl of grapes, his wife nervously blowing on seashells, Lucy in a state of shock. Dealing with hot potatoes was much easier than taking the torch when it was passed: now she was a mother; now she was Jane.

Lucy realized what a coincidence it was that nobody in the family had a father. Or not for long, anyway. They were women who raised women. It might explain why they were all half crazy.

No it didn't. Everybody was half crazy. She was being as self-indulgent as Noonan, who pretended to understand the world in terms of heterosexuals' ideas of the way things should be. She had to fight this: it was not going to be the case that Jane, even in death, could still manipulate her so that she seemed to be an arch conservative.

It was far from true. She was only conservative in comparison with Jane. Conservative wasn't exactly it, either; she had always had an advantage. She had always known something that Jane didn't know. When they were teenagers, she had not told her because she wanted to protect her. As they got older, there seemed no way to capture the moment again, to explain.

When she and Jane were little girls, they had played in a backyard smaller than, but almost as congested as, Disneyland. They had been watched over by a woman named Miss Maybel. Miss Maybel was round and smooth, with skin the color of cocoa. She was from Jamaica. In retrospect, she must have been their father's mistress. On Lucy's sixteenth birthday she had been taken into New York alone for a grown-up dinner with her father. The dinner was so grown up that not only did he order a bottle of champagne, but after she had drunk half of it, one of the waitresses joined them at the table. "I wanted you to meet some real women—women who don't act like your mother and all your mother's friends," he had said to her.

"Hey," the waitress had said. "I'm meeting your kid. It wasn't part of the deal that I had to hear about your wife."

"You're used to a bad deal," Lucy's father had said. "Isn't that what you always say?"

Lucy had understood it all in a flash, and for some reason she had been terrified—terrified of both her father and the waitress. It was a rotten thing to have done to her—more punishment in the guise of pleasure—but if he hadn't been so outspoken, and so harsh, what happened next might not have happened. Her father had started to order Beefeater martinis made ten to one. She must have looked miserable enough to have softened the waitress' heart. She no longer remembered how they got from the table to the bathroom, or why she would have gone, but she did remember the waitress drying off the formica counter at the side of the sink, and the two of them sitting there moments later, swinging their legs like schoolgirls. "Nobody is any one way," the waitress had said to her. "I've got a lot of talent. Don't look at me and just think I'm some waitress. Your father has a good heart. He's also got a mean streak. You're not just sixteen years old, right? You're full of energy, like a kid, but another part of you can sit still in a restaurant and sip champagne with the best of them, right?"

Lucy nodded. She had gone into the bathroom afraid of the waitress—she supposed she went because getting away from her father seemed more important than avoiding the woman—but suddenly something about the way the waitress smoked her cigarette and slouched as she talked made her feel sorry for her, sorrier than she felt for herself. She had asked what the waitress did when she wasn't a waitress. The waitress had hopped down from the counter to tap and twirl, and as she did, Lucy had felt happy and then almost elated. The waitress had freed her with the kick of her foot, in a way: if people weren't any one thing, then of course situations weren't. No one ever again changed quite so abruptly in her presence, but that was irrelevant: Lucy believed that the potential was there, and from then on she became the Lucy who was involved in something, and the Lucy who watched herself and the situation from afar. She felt sorry for all the people who didn't realize that their world could change in a second.

It was Jane's beauty and her craziness that made her attractive to men, but it was Lucy's personality that attracted them. Ever since that night when she understood everything differently, she didn't judge people in the same way. When they put on a performance to impress her, she was pleased that they had made the effort, if she liked them. Pleased but restrained, because it was likely that the opposite was also true. And when men she did not care about put on a show, she was dismissive but polite, assuming that, of course, they were also men who were potentially interesting and attractive. Simply because she would not pass judgment, men became more and more fascinated.

This approach took its toll, of course. When doors were left open, it could get drafty at night. Endless opportunities were extended merely because she did not rule out possibilities. And since there were no particular ground rules, even those who were malicious couldn't zip the rug out from under and topple her, because she had made no firm assumptions about where she stood to begin with. Sometimes, like today, what she was most sure of was fatigue. She could see the attraction of winding a turban around her hair, putting on a white robe, and marching off to meet her fate in crumbling Earth Shoes. As Nigel, at the magazine, was fond of saying, "Set the camera on infinity and you're bound to get the long view."

She went back to the living room. Piggy's wife was no longer there, and Piggy stood with his back to her, reading letters and telegrams, head bent. PP was embroidered in elaborate letters on the back of his robe. He was as much of a father as any of them had. She might have thought of him as old, standing with his head bent, but instead of an old man's scuffs, he had on blue Nikes, black knee-high executive socks, and two-pound ankle weights. That took care of that.

JANE and Lucy's mother, Rita, sitting at her desk in her house in Philadelphia, looked out at the park across the street and reflected on the fact that she thought of herself in terms of her connection to them: she was Jane and Lucy's mother. Even though Jane was dead, she was still Jane's mother—to another mother, at least, she would never have to explain that. She did not really feel that she had to explain anything anymore. She could not remember the last time anyone had asked her for an explanation.

In spite of the fact that she was under no obligation to explain anything, she was sitting at her desk because she had gotten up that morning wanting to write Lucy a letter. Lucy felt as bad about Jane's death as she did. If she called to talk to her about it, though, Lucy would be brave. Lucy would not have to be brave reading a letter.

She was not sure what she wanted to say to Lucy. This, for certain: that from the first, the children had had the greatest interest in anything dangerous. They preferred to stand at the top of the landing, barefoot, toes overhanging the top step as if they were standing on a diving board, rather than to sit in a chair in the living room. They were as comfortable with height as the angels. Also, if anything was slightly precarious, they were drawn to it. They would have walked like the Wallendas on the clothesline stretched from the porch roof to the maple tree if she or her husband hadn't grabbed them and lifted them down. They shimmied up the side of the tree like mountain climbers, and later in the day they'd be filthy from spelunking in the crawl space under the porch. There was always a reason:

the neighbor's cat had been down there for an entire afternoon, meowing, and it might be hurt; the bird's nest had to be brought down right away, before Daddy got home, because there was going to be a storm. They always thought of themselves as people on a rescue mission. As though it mattered that the balloon string had gotten tangled around the clothesline. As if the birds didn't build nests strong enough to survive storms. The way they thought about it, inanimate objects were to be cared for just as if they were alive, and the whole world was there for the saving. They loved little things. Seedlings in the garden. Lucy probably remembered going out after a rain and trying to remove the little clumps of mud that weighted the new plants down. She certainly remembered the gardens. She could recite the names, still, of every flower.

Lucy probably did not know—but perhaps it would not interest her—that one time Jane cried all afternoon when a boy in the neighborhood poured boiling water on an anthill. It was as if she'd turned the corner and seen the river Styx.

They developed their own systems for things. That was admirable, of course. Why should mothers be so disturbed by inventiveness? Lucy had had such a terrible time learning the Palmer Method. "Fluid motion," her teacher had said. "It is necessary to feel these curves in the hand," moving her own hand like a metronome. When she wasn't looking, Lucy would copy a page from the book, as she was supposed to. Then she would go back and add swishes to the letters—a combination of writing and painting, it looked like. "Ladies," their dance instructor, Miss Jersild, would say, "spine straight, feel no weight. Head high, body dangling from the sky." They were supposed to think of themselves as marionettes, erect but relaxed, waiting to be put into motion.

One day, in the basement, Lucy had stood on her father's workbench, with torn nylons she had found in the wastebasket tied together, looking for all the world as if she were about to drop a noose over Jane's head. Lucy couldn't possibly have been about to hang her, because she worshiped Jane, always. They were just pretending—wanting to really feel the pull from above. It was one of the few times they ever took an abstraction and tried to be literal-minded about it. They spent their lives doing quite the opposite.

Rita thought that that sort of imaginative ability could help a person. A pleasant notion, to think of dirty clothes piled high in the laundry basket as Monet's haystack. To see the melting ice cream as a cloud.

Dear Lucy—How you two loved bubbles! I'd try to do the dishes and you two would reach around me and dip your blowers into the sink and lift them out and blow and blow. I had to put so much detergent in the water that the dishes almost slipped out of my hands. It took forever to rinse them. To think that I ever thought of all that fun as frustrating. There we'd be, bubbles all around us, a storm of them mirroring everything in the kitchen—all those mundane things, stepstools and canisters, become for a second mere flashes of color that popped and collided.

They were endlessly fascinated with lightning bugs. They would beg to sleep with a jar of them in their room, air holes punched with the ice pick in the metal top. They'd put it by the night-light because they thought they blinked more when there was some source of light. It had its equivalent in Christian thinking—all the little children prospering under God's radiance.

Rita felt sure that their religious training had been neglected. They had memorized the recipe for chocolate chip cookies before they knew the Ten Commandments. They were so worshipful of each other that it was hard to make Mary take on any real character. The apostles paled by comparison with the lives of their stuffed animals. She should have sent the girls to church regularly. Eventually, the minister might have prevailed.

He would not have prevailed. It got to the point where no man could persuade them of anything. Jane didn't even take men seriously enough to bother finding one who was better than the rest. Except that there was a similarity in the men she chose. She liked childish men. Not because she felt threatened by men or because she wanted to have power over them, but because it became increasingly difficult as she got older to find women who were childlike, and Jane always enjoyed childhood so. She would have been perfectly happy to remain a child.

With Lucy, it was another matter. Her father influenced her much more. They weren't close, but he never begrudged giving her time. Jane seemed to bore him. He and Lucy did seem to have some relationship. It upset her very much when he left. She latched on to Hildon, and stayed attached to him.

They were once so naïve that they thought the paisley sheets would make them pregnant. There they were on the floor in the morning, because they wouldn't lie on the sheets. It was one of those mysterious tableaux of childhood that didn't get explained until years later.

They were so busy when they were children that Rita could still not believe that they had grown up and done whatever they could to avoid work. They liked doing things of all sorts. Their days were so scheduled, they barely had time for school. They lived for summer. Night, and summer. At night they turned their bedroom into the Old Vic. Jane's bedroom. Lucy was always in Jane's room. One time she had a cap gun. Rita could remember taking it away and wrapping it in newspaper as if it were a fish. Then she threw it away. Real guns or toy guns too often led to tragedy. She had read, recently, that some man had picked up his son's water pistol, when the paper boy was being adamant about the money he was owed. The paper boy came back with a revolver and aimed it through the window and shot the man in the back of the head. She believed in gun control, no matter what the hunters said. The paper boy with the gun had no more trouble getting it than a person would have going out to buy a candy bar. He was thirteen years old.

She understood that she was not to think about what went on in the world. That the New York *Times* no more reflected the problems of the day than a statement made by the Queen of Hearts. She was not supposed to embarrass people by reading the paper and telling them what she had read.

Dear Lucy—I try not to think of Jane as dead. Frankly, this means, lately, that I try not to think about Jane.

Jane probably got too much attention. People would say,

Oh, it must be wonderful not to have the children fighting all the time, jealous of each other, but the two of them together—they were almost always united in everything—were an ebb tide to a person's reasoning. Insist, and you'd feel like a bully.

Rita believed that little things did get remembered. The small things in her house were quite lovely. One lovely thing made a more perfect statement than half a dozen objects put out on a tabletop.

What were Jane's last thoughts? She hoped that they were peaceful. Jane must have been scared to death even before she died. Or perhaps it made her angry, because she hated predictable things that she couldn't control. Friday night traffic, backed up on the road to the beach.

Vincent van Gogh's "Starry Night" came to mind. It was her favorite painting, for purely sentimental reasons.

It must be very difficult for Lucy. In some ways, she acted as if she were much older than Jane: placating her, indulging her. She was good at distracting her. She could invent a game right on the spot. They loved to scare each other. They would take any excuse to jump out of a closet. Even if one knew the other was in there, she would be frightened enough to jump or scream. They would play Ghosts. Or Africa. What did jumping out of a closet have to do with Africa? She remembered the time Lucy knocked down the clothes bar and all the clothes fell on the floor of the closet. Henry had said, "What game is this? Niagara?"

Henry. Henry Nolan Spenser.

She thought: the aspen is the most beautiful tree, followed by the birch.

She found herself thinking that Mozart was born in 1756, Blake one year later. What an age that must have been. Contemporary poetry was all about young fathers' perceptions of their sons. Speculative poetry, about rocks talking and planets humming.

They loved music. The carrousel. Music boxes. *Dear Lucy—Do you remember that I would sing you to sleep when you were restless? Those songs always seemed sad, sung at night—songs such as "I Love You Truly" and "You Are My*

Sunshine." The sadder the song, the later the hour, the prettier my voice. That really was true. Until I had children I was inhibited about singing. I still would not sing in a room filled with people. Not even a Christmas carol. Two years ago I found myself in such a situation and lip-synched "Jingle Bells."

Most people simply stopped seeing her when Henry left. A common reaction—people felt awkward, as if they themselves had deserted the person. This resulted in their deserting the person.

It was written somewhere that Joseph P. Kennedy agreed with his father that there were only two great things about the modern age. One was that there were window screens. The other thing . . . there was another thing. There were actually many things to like. Digital clocks, although they were not functionally an improvement over regular clocks. The kinds of teas that were readily available were amazing. In almost any small grocery store, you could find camomile, rose hip, mint. Women's shoes were now often quite stunning, though there seemed to be no standardization of the M width. A skate blade would not fit in some M width shoes. In others, the span was adequate.

Dear Lucy—One of the advantages of being old is that you do not have to endlessly explain things. People are afraid to ask you questions—partly because they become deferential and partly because they are afraid that the answer will be too lengthy and boring. They will ask you how you feel instead of what you did on a particular day. This makes it easier to do strange things, because it is unlikely that anyone will question you about what you did. Also, since most people have no way of checking, you can say what is convenient. For example, there is a sepia-toned baby picture on my upstairs table. I have been asked, once or twice, who it is. I have shrugged and said, "Some relative." Actually, it is the baby picture of the first man I loved. His mother, who thought we would marry, gave it to me the Christmas before he died of the flu. The look in the baby's eyes is the same as his look when he was a twenty-year-

old man and I knew him. I don't think I would remember that without having the picture set out. I remember taking a walk on a snowy day and running into his brother, and hearing that he had been taken to the hospital. I was supposed to be home, but I cut across the park with the boy—a younger brother, perhaps fourteen, though he seems in my mind to have been a mere baby compared to Nicole—and I went to see him. He recognized me, but the next day he recognized no one, and the following day he was dead. It was still snowing when he was buried, and they had to delay the funeral until they could dig again in the cemetery. Imagine: the flu, which was so contagious, and I sat at his bedside for an hour.

Or, she could write: People are reluctant to believe that a parent doesn't prefer one child, however slightly, to another. Sometimes there would be a period when one of you seemed sweeter than the other, but then the situation would be reversed. It evened out.

Or, that when she went to the hospital, it was the first time that she saw a hospital room that was not painted white. It was painted green.

Or, that Henry had just come right out and said that he was going to leave. For years he had struggled, with little subtlety, to keep himself rooted. He had held on to the wheel of the station wagon, and before that to the handle of the baby carriage, as though all day, everywhere, he was hearing the voices of the Sirens. He was always grabbing onto things. Grabbing the phone, instead of holding it. All that tension was apparent to everyone. Why not admit that it made Jane and Lucy stay childish longer than they might have. They had had better luck with him when they were young, so they thought that being sprites would please Daddy. They always looked at him full face, with their large, lovely eyes. They always had their arms around his neck. They wore long white cotton nightgowns with punchwork and embroidery at the neckline. It seemed that he would carry them, and they would stay plastered against him, until they were so tall that they would have to be dragged. There were nights when he wouldn't come home.

They would cry and cry. Lucy would make up a story to tell Jane. Lucy hated him a little in the end, and Jane became a dreamer.

Lucy: when Henry left, I no longer rolled toward the center of the bed at night. The mattress wasn't weighted down, and I stayed where I was. I was always astonished to wake up and find myself on one side of the big bed. For a while I doubted that I had slept.

Homonyms. The trouble you had with those, Lucy—you would have thought that you had been raised in a foreign land. Some people seize on some one thing about someone else and then blow it out of proportion, overestimating its symbolic potential. With you, Lucy, it would be homonyms. Once you heard a word and attached it to a particular thing, you couldn't admit that there was an alternate reality. The struggle we had with pair and pare. How you wept over there and their.

My memory of the end of day: Reading you *Pride and Prejudice.* That was like singing "La Marseillaise" to a Frenchman. I would sit at the foot of the bed and read while you were propped against your pillows, the covers pulled high, arms underneath, only head and shoulders visible, toys all around you. Dobbin the donkey. Jeepers the monkey, with that mouth that Henry painted on, not very well, when its felt mouth dropped off. Can't you still see Silly the goose clearly? It was left at a playmate's house, and the family moved to Denver and never did mail it back the way they promised. If I had known, I would have driven back to get it. I hadn't doubted that it would arrive. As time went on, I was as upset as you were, but I knew it would be unwise to show it.

The image of little children in bed asleep is always one that pulls on the heartstrings. Like every parent, I was fascinated: all that commotion, all the shouting and running, it was hard to believe the calm. One advantage of all the dolls and animals was that they kept the covers weighted down. When you stopped wearing your sleep-suits with feet, I always put white anklets on you. It is important to keep children warm at night. Not as important as other things, like nourishing food and vaccinations, but still, something I worried about. Perhaps inordinately.

You both liked the window cracked a bit. Was it because in the cold weather, it made you think of summer? I'd pile on covers, then sometimes put on more as an afterthought, tuck another blanket on top, tapping it down around the menagerie. It was rather like fitting piecrust over the top of a pie. Then, leaving, I would take a final look. Just saying good-night and turning and walking away would be as unusual as glancing only once at a Christmas tree. It seemed so perfect: Jane and Lucy, and Jane and Lucy's mother standing and smiling. The room wasn't entirely dark because a streetlight in front of the next house shone in. You didn't want the shade drawn, of course. I left the door open a crack, as well. That was more for my benefit than yours. You had no fear. Because the door was ajar when I left, I still felt connected. There were always those few seconds in which the house seemed so lonely and quiet; it was as though everything had a sound when you were present, and when you went away, silence fell. I believe that in Oriental rugs, there is often an irregularity in the pattern—a key, it is called—woven that way deliberately, to allow the spirit to escape.

27

Of course Lucy never thought that she wouldn't see Les Whitehall again. From the minute Myra DeVane told her he had written (eventually, she had forced herself to look at the letter), she had to acknowledge that it figured that he'd get in touch when a million things were happening, and she was least ready to deal with him.

The night before he called to say he was coming, she tried to think of good things about Les and the good times they had had. If she could be calm, she would not give in to temptation and ask him what he thought "Love Always" meant. She knew that even if she asked, she would not get the answer she wanted. He would be insincere, he would equivocate, he would lie. He would try to make her look needy and silly for asking. He would pretend—or maybe it would be true—that "Love Always" was a variation of "Yours truly." The few times she had ever faced him down and won, he had pushed a self-destruct button: he never admitted that she was right; he began smoking or drinking—anything that didn't require words—or turned and walked away.

It depressed her, sometimes, that since Les she had not had a new relationship with anyone. It had taken about fifteen years for Hildon to really seduce her, in spite of the fact that she had slept with him from the beginning, and now she did count on him, now she did share his philosophy that since you could get away with anything, it was necessary to start your own fun. They knew how to seduce each other so well, knew how to add to the other's fantasies like children piling one hand on top of the other, over and over, bottom hand pulled out and slapped on top, until it became again the top hand. There was a lot of repetition in what they did. At first her shock had been genuine about Hildon's redneck slumming, but then she had passed through that, and through amusement, into acceptance. It was just a routine: some people liked to shower after sex; some smoked a cigarette; some people liked music; some people liked the lights on; some people did it in boots with spurs. It seemed incestuous; they were so close and had known each other so long that Lucy couldn't believe they weren't related, but they were also attuned to each other's fantasies in a way no family member would be; they knew not only the person, but the dreams and nightmares as well. They cared about each other so much that they knew to be careful. They knew what would hurt. They were too careful. It was too precise; a shrug, instead of passion. Anything goes, because even that won't suffice.

Les said that he would be passing through Vermont and wanted to stop—that he had been calling her for days without success. He knew nothing about Jane's death. He had never met Nicole, and didn't know, of course, that she was at Lucy's. Lucy liked the idea of letting him walk into a sad, complicated situation. Only when someone else observed it and said something did she pity herself, and that feeling was a relief. Let him walk into real life and not be able to do anything about it. Let him deal with some situation that wasn't one he orchestrated in a classroom or took charge of by manipulating her. Of course there was nothing helpful he could say, and no way he could feel comfortable. As Piggy said—more often on the East Coast than on the West Coast, actually—"Welcome to L.A."

That morning Lucy and Nicole had visited Nata Ballard, who would be Nicole's ninth grade teacher in the fall. Piggy had arranged for a tutor for the time Nicole would spend in Los Angeles. In September, Nicole would be picked up by the school bus and driven two miles to school, where she would be a student with farmers' kids and hippies' oldest sons and daughters. The farmers' kids would be named Mark and John and the hippies' kids would be named Ezekiel and Beatrice (four-syllable version). Nicole thought all this was wonderful—"a rip," as she said—and had returned to her reading of *Main Street.* Lucy tossed around the idea of telling her that Nata Ballard had spent a year in the convent and another year strung out on dope before she saw the light and moved to Vermont when she decided it rose over the Green Mountains, but decided against it; it would just be another story that made things tenuous and a bit ironic. She didn't think Nicole needed more of that.

St. Francis had escaped the night before, but they found him before he got into trouble, Lucy driving with her leg shaking so hard it was difficult to apply even pressure to the accelerator, and Nicole screaming, "St. Francis! Here, baby!" out the window, as perplexed people in fields or sitting in lawn chairs looked up and stared at the car. Lucy had been too embarrassed to stop and ask if they had seen the dog. He was in a swamp, not far from the house, and Lucy was so glad to see him muddy instead of bloody that she didn't even care about the damage to the back seat. Today they had gone to the hardware store and bought a lead, stakes, chains, and a wider, sturdier collar. St. Francis looked manacled. It was the sort of thing, Lucy realized, that she was going to have to explain to visitors.

Life was back to normal. That meant, for example, that in the afternoon, the Federal Express man, with whom Nicole had struck up quite a friendship, had brought a package of drawings of preliminary plans for the Stephanie Sykes doll. They looked like blueprints for the Taj Mahal, filled with numbers and incomprehensible notations—what might have been a transcription of a gorilla's best thoughts, on acid, of how to navigate through a Skinner box. The figure on the top page looked more like a cross section of one of Piggy's wife's chambered shells than a human being. Piggy had gotten a duplicate package, and had called to say that under no circumstances was Nicole to sign the release form—it was obviously a deliberate ruse, to disguise the fact that Stephanie Sykes did not have tits. "What the hell does this mean?" Piggy screamed at Lucy, as if she were responsible. "Under the head . . ." She told him that she couldn't make out a head. "At the top, at the goddamn top," Piggy said. "What does this mean: 8 x 3—what are they doing, grafting Wilt Chamberlain's cock onto her throat?"

Lucy wrote this week's Cindi Coeur column:

Dear Cindi Coeur,

I am writing to ask advice about my double life. By day I am a management analyst. I wear silk blouses with floppy bows, gray skirts with a kick pleat, and tiny pearl earrings to suggest conventional femininity. I have taken care to be sure that my hair is shiny and that the leather of my briefcase is not. All day, I go to meetings, talk on the phone, and make graphs. My boyfriend does not know that I work. I have told him that because of all the drugs I take, I sleep all day. At night, Cindi, I am a waitress at his nightclub, Slash. The pearl earrings are replaced by Tampax that dangle from my ears, and my clothes suggest that I have just escaped being torn apart by wild animals. My problem is that while I want to stay with my boyfriend and get deeper into that world, he has been saying that he should sell the business, get married to me, and that we should move to the suburbs and have kids. Should I tell him that I am a more conventional person, already, than he thinks? Can honesty hurt the relationship? How would I get my kicks if we lived in suburbia?

Double Identity Dorothy

Dear Dot,

The child your boyfriend wants may go a long way toward reconciling your two personas. You may still wear many items from your workaday-world wardrobe, which the child will naturally pull, rip, and stain. Give in to your boyfriend. If things go wrong you can, like all mothers, blame both him and the child. Later, if you decide to resume either your business identity or to immerse yourself in punk, your husband will certainly understand why you were driven into such a retreat. Who is not driven into conventionality or total chaos by a child? By capitulating, you can't lose. It is a short distance, really, from blouses with bows tied under your chin, which are the business world's equivalent of the cowbell, to the self-congratulatory support group you will find with the ladies of La Leche. Good Luck!

In the backyard, while she had been in California, Don Severs had planted a willow tree. The limbs swooped low, the delicate green leaves blowing in the breeze; a dozen Mylar balloons in the shape of hearts were attached mid-branch, bobbing as the limbs swept from side to side.

She remembered two of her father's gestures—things he had done to communicate through action rather than words. When Lucy and Jane had told him something he didn't believe, he had looked them straight in the eye and tipped his head, making a cross over his heart with his first finger. When they did something particularly charming, he tapped his chest, over his heart, with his fingertip, then made a fist with that hand and slapped it into the palm of the other. It was like a catcher slapping a ball into his mitt. Maybe their father had even thought of that, subconsciously; that love was just another game, like baseball. A national sport.

Lucy had thought, from time to time, of trying to get in touch with him, but she always stopped herself: he had betrayed them, withdrawn, disappeared. Jane had kept in contact a little longer than she had. He and his new wife had at least two children, and a house in Maine and a house somewhere outside Boston. A girl Lucy once knew had sent her a picture from the Boston *Globe* a couple of summers ago, of Lucy's father standing by a cart in Faneuil Hall, eating some new kind of gourmet hot dog. It was the first picture she had seen of him since he left: the daddy planting the garden, or carrying his daughters on each shoulder, or standing stiffly next to Mommy in evening attire was now a middle-aged man, smiling with a mouth full of food. The college classmate who sent the picture had circled his name and put a question mark in the margin. There could be no question; even if his name was common, he looked very much like Jane and Lucy. Because men's fashions changed so little, it looked like he was wearing a pinstripe shirt that he had worn when he was their father. He was still her father, but Lucy did not know where he was. What would she tell him if she got in touch? That his daugher Jane, whom he had not known all of her adult life, was dead? She felt tears welling up. That was what always happened—only when she connected Jane's death with something else that she was angry about did she feel herself about to cry.

Jane's husband of a little more than a week was the real villain to all of them. He was still in a coma and there had been extensive brain damage, but the family refused to let the doctors take him off the respirator. Piggy, in one of the calls he had gotten from the man's father, had offered not only to pull the plug, but then to wrap it around the man's neck, tie it to his fender, and take him for a memorial ride along the same steep road he had plunged off of with Jane. The autopsy revealed that Jane had been two months pregnant. Piggy had told Lucy, but no one else. Lucy wouldn't give her mother, who had said Jane was self-destructive, the satisfaction of knowing that. She had not told Nicole or anyone else. She preferred to think of it, herself, not as carelessness but as a sign of Jane's faith in life. Lucy had not shown Jane's letter to anyone, either. She read it every day, thinking bitterly that if Jane had not wanted to grow old, she had certainly gotten her way. In homage to Jane, Piggy had flown to Virginia to ride the Cyclone. After the funeral, Piggy had said to Lucy that he didn't see how he'd get over it; every time the breeze blew, he thought of Jane. She liked the wind whether it was on the Cyclone or on a motorcycle—when it wasn't there, she'd find some way to generate wind. She would not have liked the still, sunny day on which her funeral was held. The stiffly arranged floral displays that so many people sent, instead of the wild flowers that grew in the canyons, rustling in the breeze. Lucy remembered Nicole as an infant, sitting on her mother's thigh, while Jane said to her, "How does the rain fall?," tapping her fingertips lightly on Nicole's head. Saying, "How does the wind go?," as she puckered her lips and blew a slow stream of air at Nicole's hairline, sending the wisps of baby hair away from her forehead.

They had learned to take their cues from Nicole. If she fell, they did not react until she reacted. Most of the time, if they didn't rush forward, she would just pick herself up and go on. The baby took her cues from the adults; if they weren't upset, she wasn't upset. She would look, and with fear or dismay that they projected as a pleasant smile, they would say "Baby go boom!" or something to indicate that what had just happened was of slight importance and rather amusing.

Lucy went to the screen door and looked out. Nicole was on

a beach towel, stretching left and right and left and right, listening to an exercise tape on her cassette player. They had talked a lot in California about Jane, and Jane's death, but since they returned, Nicole didn't want to talk about it. She wondered if she shouldn't say things anyway; whether what she was doing now wasn't just another version, and a potentially harmful one, of what the adults had all done by smiling when Nicole went boom as a baby. Then, of course, they could tell by the surface she fell on, or where she banged herself, or how long she stayed spread-eagled, how great the hurt might be. There didn't seem any accurate way to predict now what Nicole was feeling. Obviously, when she exhibited bravado, she was only doing it to cover the hurt. Earlier in the day, on the phone, talking to Piggy, she had overheard Nicole saying, "Yeah, well, I don't think she should have taken chances while I'm still a kid." Piggy had bought postcards of the Cyclone; he took them out of his pocket and examined them as though they were a family snapshot. He put one in a frame on his desk—his equivalent of a splinter of the True Cross, sunk in a Lucite cube.

It was not until Les Whitehall's car pulled into the drive that Lucy realized how many preconceived notions she had had about this visit. She thought that he would be driving the same car he had left in. But the big Pontiac was gone, replaced by a smaller, newer car. When he opened his door and closed it, it didn't hurt her ears. She stood in the doorway, looking deliberately at the car instead of at Les. She had thought that the passenger door would swing open and a girl would step out. Les's notion of being an adult was to do something slightly challenging, which would put anyone who commented in the position of seeming gauche or childish. Lucy had assumed that he would bring a woman with him for protection and dare her to say that it wasn't perfectly adult behavior, which would be difficult because there was no ostensible reason why they couldn't all be blandly sociable. No one cared about anyone else anymore, right? No woman. Les was walking toward the house. He caught sight of Nicole, who didn't interrupt her stretching routine. He waved. She waved back. St. Francis barked wildly, but it was a hot day and he stopped after a minute, settling back into his deep gully beside the rhododendrons. Silver balloons that had been tied to Lucy's willow tree by Don Severs bobbed on the tree. It must have seemed like an unusual scene to Les—it couldn't have been what he expected, either. His first words, as he gestured behind him, were, "What's all this?" She could tell, because he tried to appear casual, that he was scared. Something about the way he walked that she couldn't explain let her know that he was nervous. He looked the same. She had expected him to change: gain weight, lose weight, grow a beard, longer hair, more of a tan—she had no exact image in mind, except that she had been sure he would come across the lawn with a woman at his side, and now there was no woman. It was painful to see him looking the same, as though he had just left briefly, to do an errand.

"Vermont," she said. "Come in."

"Who's the kid?" he said.

"Oh, darling," Lucy said, "Don't you think she looks just like you?"

It didn't get even half a smile. His mouth moved slightly. He looked past Lucy, as if he expected someone else to be present.

"Sit down," she said. "You remember where the furniture is."

She walked past him into the living room. Though she sat in the chairs every day, today she realized how low to the ground they were, forcing you to extend your legs if you wanted to sit without gazing over your kneecaps. The chairs had once been in her mother's house. She had sat in one of them the day Nicole was christened and tumbled into her arms. Today Lucy had on shorts and a white shirt. She had given a lot of thought to what she wore, and had finally decided that what she chose would inevitably make the other woman uncomfortable: it was so casual that anyone else would appear overdressed. Now that there was no one else, she wished that she had put on something prettier so that Les would remember whom he had left.

Les was standing by the mantel, where the sketches of the Stephanie Sykes doll were propped up. St. Francis' old collar was there. A glass vase—Waterford crystal, another hand-me-down from Rita—filled with black-eyed Susans. Lucy noticed that the stems were no longer in water.

"Lucy," he said, "do you really hate me? There's no point in my saying anything if all you feel toward me is hatred."

"Did you think I'd be happy to see you?" Lucy said.

"You're so unforgiving," he said.

She could see the conversation that she was going to get bogged down in. She thought that even if what Les said was true, she was entitled to her feelings. She had not left him. She had not written Love Always, Lucy.

"We didn't have a relationship," he said. "I was a psychological study for you. You thought everything I did was duplicitous. That would drive anybody crazy. You couldn't see that I was sincere."

"You disappointed yourself, Les. That was your problem. Not that you disappointed me."

"How did I disappoint myself?" he said. Before she could answer, he said, "Is it asking too much to try to find out whether we can have a reasonable discussion?"

"You wouldn't be here if you didn't think we could. You never put yourself anywhere—or stay anywhere—where you're not on top. When you weren't voted most popular teacher, you exiled yourself to Vermont. When I tried to deal with you as a real person instead of idolizing you, you left."

"You're the one who thinks of everything in terms of power plays. I was trying to have a saner life, living in the country. I realize that I'm too exacting a teacher to please all the students who want to float through. I know why that turned out the way it did. I just underestimated how sick you were and how tied to Hildon you've always been. I brought that on myself by moving here and putting you under the influence of the person you've always wanted to have overwhelm you. I thought that you loved me, and it wouldn't happen. You never cared about me the way you cared about him."

"Les—it wasn't my feeling about Hildon that made us move to Vermont. You insisted that we move to Vermont."

"How many things did you ever do that I insisted on?"

"See? You're talking about things in terms of who has the most power again."

"You can really be awful," he said. "Are you being awful because I left you and you still care about me?"

He walked across the room and settled himself into the sofa, crossed his legs, and smiled. "Got a new BMW. Handles great," he said. "New girl. New car. New apartment. Just your all-American guy, the one you've always loved."

She reached for the nearest thing and threw it. He caught her sunglasses before they hit him in the face. He looked at them. Then he put them on, and jutted out his chin the way Lucy did when she was angry. "So you've got a new car, Les," he said. "Big deal. At least you're doing what's so important to you by appearing to be prosperous. And the women are a notion pretty much like cars to you, aren't they? Turn one in, get another one. When you do these things, aren't you embarrassed? Or can you really pretend, pretend so well that you convince yourself?"

Next, she threw a glass bowl. It hit the wall in back of him, missing him by at least three feet. The pansy that had been floating in it fell onto the sofa. Water streaked the wall. She started to cry.

"Just because I don't get off on pessimism the way you and Hildon do doesn't mean I'm Pollyanna. My optimism reassured you plenty of times. When you had the flu that first winter and you thought you were going to die. I was the one who told you you could work things out with your mother. Talk about *me* being in exile in Vermont. You couldn't be near her. You barely knew how to talk to her on the phone before you met me. I told you you could get the job teaching art at the school. It wasn't the great Hildon who . . ."

Lucy had stopped listening. She was biting her bottom lip, looking past him to the doorway, where Nicole was standing.

"It's something awful," Nicole said.

Les looked over his shoulder. "Hey," he said, shrugging. "Sorry I was yelling."

Nicole looked at him, tears welling up in her eyes.

"People have got to care about each other to bother to yell, right?" he said.

"No," Nicole said. "I never noticed that." She walked toward Lucy. By the time she got to the chair, she was crying. "St. Francis ran down the road after a tractor," she said. "I just had him off his lead for a minute, and he ran down the road and wouldn't come back when I called him. You've got to drive me. Get the car, Lucy. Come on—we've got to get him."

Lucy stood and looked around the room for the car keys. Nicole had put her hands over her mouth. It was what she had done when Lucy had to tell her that Piggy had called and that Jane was dead. She saw the keys on the corner of the mantel and ran out the door without saying anything to Les.

"What do you want to take crap from that guy for?" Nicole said through her tears as Lucy pushed the key into the ignition. She had left the windows down and the car was full of flies. They flew forward and sideways and Lucy and Nicole had to bat them away from their faces so they could see.

"You know, I'm in this with you now," Nicole said, "and I don't want you to sit around and take crap off some guy."

"It's complicated," Lucy said. She was driving slowly, looking right and left for St. Francis. She hoped that Nicole would call for him, because she thought if she spoke, she would cry harder.

Nicole had already stopped crying. "St. Francis!" she called.

Only a little farther down the road, he heard her and shot up. He had been wriggling on his back, rolling in carrion. He gave a last mighty shake and ran toward the car.

To her surprise, Les was still at the house. He was sitting on the hood of his car, looking down the road, when they returned.

Nicole got out of the car and walked past him with St. Francis at her side without saying anything, like a princess and her consort cutting through a crowd. St. Francis stank and seemed a most ignoble escort. Nicole put him on his lead and began to talk to him earnestly.

"Who is she?" Les said.

"Jane's daugher, Nicole," Lucy said. "Jane is dead."

He cocked his head. "What do you mean?" he said.

"She lives here now. Jane died. She married some jerk who put her on the back of his motorcycle and drove it off a cliff."

"A car must have forced them off the road," he said. His voice was very quiet. "Oh my God," he said. "Jane's dead?"

"I was in L.A. for the funeral when you were calling me."

"She was on a motorcycle?" Les said.

Lucy nodded. Les was doing what she sometimes did herself. The incredulity was real, but the theory was silly: that if you could just repeat facts, stall for time, you might not have to hear the same ending to the story.

28

LUCY was in Hildon's car, parked at a scenic overlook. A baby was sweeping the grass with a broom—a child about three years old, whose hands choked up on the handle as if he held a baseball bat. He tapped the broom against the ground, looked straight forward, then decided to sweep instead of bunt. All the while, the child was singing a song. The mother and father and an obese cocker spaniel were sitting on a tablecloth spread out near a willow tree.

Les Whitehall's visit had made it possible for Lucy and Nicole to have the talk both had been avoiding. Maybe, Lucy thought, it was because Nicole had seen her vulnerability that she was willing to talk about her own. She wanted to star on *Passionate Intensity*. She would stay with Piggy Proctor and his wife, but she wanted Lucy to fly to L.A. and visit whenever she could. When the filming was over, Nicole would come back to Vermont.

So Les's visit had been for the best, but of course he couldn't have known that, and it wasn't why he had come. He had come assuming that Lucy knew that Hildon was resigning as editor of *Country Daze*. The day of Les's visit, Hildon had been in New York talking to an agent about a book he might write. The agent was also Les Whitehall's agent. Les had found out about Hildon's plans by coincidence—and, actually, Lucy had too. Les had come to ask her if she would put in a good word for him with Matt Smith, the publisher, and if she would also ask Hildon not to let his bad feelings for him get in the way of his possibly getting the job.

"When did you intend to tell me?" Lucy said to Hildon.

Hildon had driven to her house, after getting her message, and had found Lucy going up the walk with a bag of groceries. She was resolute: whatever happened, she was going to proceed. None of them was going to hurt her so much that she stopped in her tracks. As though to strengthen her resolve, she had gone out and bought food. Now, the bag was wedged between them, unpacked. She had gotten into Hildon's car still carrying the bag. That was like Hildon: to do things in his own way, in his own time, and then to expect that she'd stop the clock when he felt like talking. Lucy doubted whether he even felt like talking—whether he wasn't discussing this purely because she had forced him to.

"I thought you'd make fun of me," Hildon said. "You're always talking about how the whole world wants to write. Look at what a fraud Les Whitehall was. I didn't want you to think of me as another Les Whitehall."

"You're changing the subject," Lucy said.

"I wasn't going to quit unless my agent thought the proposal would work," he said. "It all happened in a hurry. How could I know that my agent was also Les Whitehall's agent, and that she was going to run off at the mouth?"

"That isn't what I asked," Lucy said.

Hildon was holding the wheel at the bottom, tightly, as if he were driving fast. Lucy had thrown her door open to let what breeze there was circulate through the car. His door was shut, as if they were in motion.

Lucy had had so many bad times in cars. Her father had played games with her—turned off the headlights, said "Whoa!," as though a simple horse had galloped out of control, and accelerated through seconds of danger before he pulled the headlight switch back on. He had also teased her when she was a child by driving and closing the eye closest to her, squinting at the road through the other, saying, "Daddy's gone blind! Daddy's blind! Is the light ahead green or red?" She would describe everything nervously and thoroughly, begging him all the while to open his eyes, afraid to pull his arm or jump in her seat because it might cause him to veer off the road. It was not until years later, when she was telling the story to a school friend in front of him, that he closed his eye closest to where she and her friend sat and then turned his head, revealing the open eye that had been watching the road all along.

"I didn't know how to tell you," he said. "It wasn't a sure thing, and you were going through so much in California. I wasn't going to pack a suitcase and leave town before sunrise, you know."

"I don't know what I know," Lucy said.

"Well," Hildon said. "I wasn't."

The child was sweeping its father's back. The mother was rubbing the dog's stomach. From where Lucy sat, she couldn't see the trickle of muddy river below. The farmhouse with the blue roof she had always loved was visible on the hillside, and people hardly larger than dots were moving around it—people and cows—more of those mysterious people who thought something and felt some way Lucy couldn't fathom. People who lived in a house in the valley.

"I would have told you from the first if it had seemed real to me," Hildon said.

She started to calm down. She was being a little irrational. Of course he wouldn't have just disappeared without saying anything. He had every right to quit as editor of *Country Daze* and do something—as he had said on the ride to the overlook—"serious." It was just a big change, another unexpected adjustment.

"It's okay," she said.

"I'm going to Boston for a while," he said.

She turned and looked at him, startled.

"Lucy," he said. "I need a change. I'm sick of the work I've been doing. I'm under a lot of pressure from Maureen's lawyers. I can't take any more phone calls from Matt Smith."

"What do you mean you're going to Boston?" she said.

"For a while," he said. He chewed his bottom lip. She was still looking at him. "I'm going to move there for a while," he said. She still stared. "Get out of the house," he said, lamely.

It was such an off-the-wall explanation that it made her laugh. "Hildon," she said, "if you ever decide you want to explain all this to me, come over or give me a call. I've got to get back to Nicole."

"Don't be self-righteous," he said softly, and bit his lip.

"Hildon," she said, "I don't understand anything you're saying today, including that last remark. Would you mind driving me home? I have things to do."

He stared straight ahead. The child and the dog walked through his line of vision. He looked at the sun, which had just come out strong, shining on the blue roof that Lucy loved. "I've never been closer to anyone than I am to you," he said, "yet I'm able to just leave."

"I seem to be quite an inspiration to people in that way," Lucy said. "Think of me as Tintern Abbey."

"Don't turn it against yourself," he said. "I hate it when you do that."

"Take me home," she said. "I'm really upset."

"I know you are," he said. He touched the key in the ignition but didn't turn it on. "You're going to get mad at me for saying it," he said, "but shit kickers don't go through stuff like this. They don't introspect."

"I didn't realize we were being introspective. I'd say that what I am is baffled."

"Cindi Coeur?" Hildon said.

"I'm not Cindi Coeur."

"I know," he said. "So it was such a peculiar thing for us both to arrive at. That everything was such a joke."

"You don't think that most of the time and neither do I. We never have."

"Hey, Lucy!" a man hollered.

There was one other car at the overlook. Andrew Steinborn and Lillian were there, still trying to decide what to do about their marriage plans. She wanted time to think. He wanted them to get a blood test and get married immediately. So far, the only compromise that had been agreed upon was that however the afternoon turned out, they would go out that night to a fancy restaurant, for an expensive dinner with wine. Andrew Steinborn leaned out of his window, waving madly.

"Who's that?" Hildon said.

"It's a man who's writing a book, actually."

Andrew continued to wave, shouting something Lucy couldn't hear.

"Shit," she said. "Just a second."

She opened the door and began to walk across the gravel. Cars passed on the highway. Hildon could tell, watching her walk, that she was depressed. There was no spring in her step, no toss of the long hair. He opened his own door to go with her. The grocery bag tipped over and several potatoes rolled across the seat. In a hurry to catch up, he threw two back in the bag and leaned in to straighten it, saw another potato on the pavement and picked it up and put it in the pocket of his denim jacket. When he caught up with Lucy, she had already greeted the people in the car.

"We're getting married," Andrew said. "Isn't it the perfect day to decide that? We knew it before, actually, but sitting here, looking out . . ."

"We're thinking about it," the woman sitting next to Andrew said, leaning across his lap. Lucy smiled and nodded. She introduced Hildon.

"A fellow writer," Andrew said. "I am very, very glad to meet you. Lillian and I were reading your wonderful magazine out on the lawn at the inn the other evening. A very good, very unique piece of work."

"Thank you," Hildon said.

"He just quit," Lucy said.

"You're leaving?" Andrew said.

"He's moving to Boston," Lucy said. "He wants to get out of the house."

Lillian straightened up and sat waiting for the conversation to end. A big, shiny convertible careened around the half-circle, radio blaring James Taylor and Carly Simon singing "Mockingbird." Hildon put his arm around Lucy's shoulder instinctively as the car made the turn. Kids, out having a joy ride.

"Good luck with your wedding," Hildon said.

"I'm going to need it if my fiancée keeps these cold feet," Andrew said nervously.

"You'll get a sign," Hildon said. "I'm a great believer in mystical revelations."

"What do you mean?" Andrew said.

"A signal. A bolt of lightning will flash. Something will tell you."

"Oh," Andrew said. He looked uncomfortable. Hildon leaned forward. "Stay posted," he said to Lillian. He raised a hand to say goodbye. Lucy smiled. As they turned away, Lucy could see Andrew stiffening. Hildon took his hand out of his pocket and dropped the car keys. As he bent to pick them up, he took out the potato and jammed it into Andrew's tail pipe.

"What in the name of God are you doing?" Lucy whispered.

"Come on," he said, his hand on her back, steering her toward his car. "There's going to be a major explosion when that guy drives off."

In the car, with Lucy laughing into her hands, he said, as he turned on his own ignition, "You don't know that trick? You a goddamn stupid *girl* or something?"

As they pulled out, she looked happier. It had passed—for the moment, the tension between them eased up. He hadn't had to bog down in all the details he didn't have the desire, or the heart, to go into today.

For the next minute, as the clouds rolled in front of the sun, she was still smiling: Hildon could sniff a jackass a mile away. She liked his nerve. She liked his sense of humor. She depended on him for that—if nothing more tangible; she could not imagine what her life would be like if he went to Boston, and because she knew he knew this, she didn't think he would really do it. He meant to, though. What he had not had to come right out and say to her was that he was a coward—that it was not only in being a prankster that he was still a schoolboy.

He dropped her off, and she went in carrying the groceries. The Mylar balloons had begun to deflate; if she looked quickly, the tree now looked like a Claes Oldenburg soft sculpture. Nicole, whom she said she had to get back to, was nowhere in sight. She was always gone—jogging into town when she didn't have Lucy drop her off after they did errands. It worried Lucy that she was overly concerned with physical fitness. She thought that Nicole was grieving; she had no way of imagining what way Nicole had found to deal with her mother's death. Lucy began to unpack the grocery bag, on the verge of tears: things to be wrapped, washed, put away—it was so ordinary, life's continuation, so banal it was painful. She heard Nicole suddenly. She had not gone off after all; she was upstairs, bathing.

A few minutes after she heard the water begin to drain, Lucy walked upstairs. Nicole was in her robe—Piggy's robe, embroidered PP, that she had always coveted and that he had given her in L.A. She was sitting in front of the desk that she had fashioned into a dressing table, a three-paneled glass mirror hung above it, with photographs of herself scotch-taped to the border. It was much like the desk that had metamorphosed into an all-purpose treasure trove for Jane, years ago, when she lived in the tiny apartment in New York City.

"Hi," Nicole said, as Lucy walked into the room. The robe was huge; she looked anorectic inside it, a little child lost in a satin tent.

"Let me do that," Lucy said, taking the brush from Nicole and beginning to slowly brush her hair, from the very front to the very back, sensing where the hairline began instead of looking in the mirror to see, gently pulling the brush, over and over.

"Thanks," Nicole said, relaxing in spite of herself. She was remembering the day St. Francis ran away, the day of Les's visit, when Lucy told her that things were complicated. She wanted to sit and have Lucy brush her hair, but she was late already. Harry Woods had the afternoon off, and if she didn't get to his apartment in time, he would go off with one of his friends instead of waiting around to go to bed with her. If she didn't blow it—if she let Lucy feel helpful, and if she herself enjoyed the hair-brushing—it would all work out. She was glad that she had better survival skills than her mother. That she understood how to be patient. Her mouth turned up in a smile, as if the slight tug of the brush through her hair moved her mouth as well as her neck, which was now tipped back, hair spilling over the back of the chair.

Lucy had brushed Jane's hair—brushed it so often that their mother complained that it made it oily and that then Jane had to wash it too often. In truth, Lucy loved to brush more than Jane liked the feel of it. She had always hoped to hypnotize Jane, mesmerize her. She remembered how frustrating it was when Jane abruptly struggled to sit up and get on with other things. "Sit still," she could remember saying, half pleading with her sister. "Let me brush your hair. Stay still." Whispering urgently, "Stay still, Jane. Just stay still."

29

THE boy wondered if, after he finished this assignment, Hildon would call him again. When he had videotaped three things for someone, he considered him a steady customer. He stood in one spot in Hildon's office for the most part, taping Hildon as he took the pictures off the wall and stacked them in a carton. The boy's father and mother were crazy about *Country Daze.* He had never read it, but he thought that Hildon was probably a very good editor. In his experience, crazy people who fixated on something accomplished a lot. If he had thought it was any of his business, he would have asked Hildon why he was leaving. For most of the summer he had taped weddings—recording drunken relatives and red-eyed brides and hovering grooms in large tents or on green rolling lawns, moving through crowds while infants had their diapers changed behind bushes and panting dogs stuck their snouts in fat ladies' crotches. Everyone always got drunk and clowned for the camera, or made fools of themselves by accident, trying to straighten up and act proper, but managing only to lurch around like passengers on the deck of a ship in a storm. The boy insisted on two-thirds payment up front, because there had been some tense times when people didn't like what they saw. It was as if they thought they'd hired Renoir but gotten footage from the Maysles'.

The boy would not have to edit the tape. Hildon didn't want it edited. He let almost everything be filmed the way the boy thought best, except for telling him about the few things he wanted him to come in on close, such as the contents of his top drawer, a pan of the desk top . . . Though Hildon wasn't very talkative, he had said that he loved video because it allowed people to make their own time capsule.

He stepped closer. Through the lens, he saw the clutter of the top drawer: the bright red of a Swiss Army knife, some wrinkled dollar bills, new ones, quite green, like uncurling Jack-in-the-Pulpits that pushed out of the ground in the spring. Loose change, a checkbook, some SX 70s, a wooden letter opener. Junk.

Hildon took a break from packing and stood looking out the window. The boy filmed his back until that got boring, then moved the camera to the coffee table, littered with more things: a pile of magazines, a bottle of vitamins, a stone statue of what looked like an Eskimo woman with a glass ashtray balanced on top. The boy moved in on it. For a second his hand was a blur in front of the lens, while he figured out how the ashtray was balanced. It was glued. There were matchbooks thrown on the table, a squeeze bottle of Cutter, an extension cord, and pens pointing every which way, like pick-up sticks. He moved the camera back to Hildon as he pulled the telephone out of the jack and put it in the carton with the pictures. He filmed him taking the books out of the bookcase and stacking them on the desk, then looking around for something to put them in. Through the lens, everything on the desk top took on a sameness: the brass box looked very much like the silver compass, which in turn looked very much like the paperweight. What the boy took to be a picture of Hildon's wife was Lucy Spenser—a picture taken the summer before at a town fair. He focused on that for a while, because he was sure that it had more sentimental value than, say, the metal ruler, or the dictionary.

He photographed Hildon from the top of the stairs, holding the camera on him as he walked gingerly down, carrying the first of many cartons.

Later, when the videotape was delivered to Hildon, he looked for a long time at his back and his shoulders. Then he fast-forwarded through the long descent and ascent of the stairs. He went back to regular speed and found the sweat on his top lip of some interest. He looked at himself closely. He was definitely more handsome than Les Whitehall. He was surprised now, as he watched the pictures come off the walls and saw the pillows removed from the long sofa, how quickly the office seemed anonymous, that it seemed never to have been his at all. The letters and telegrams might have been sent to anybody; the pictures were almost generic, the maps also a quite ordinary form of decoration. The view through the window wasn't special. You could see a blur of trees. The rooftop of another building. The metal file cabinets were ordinary, the Perrier bottle with dried flowers quite typical (somebody on the staff had put it there). Everything might have been anyone's. Looking at the videotape, he was convinced, long before it was over, that he had never been there at all, in spite of all the things he saw himself lugging away. It was interesting that the boy had decided to hold the camera so long on Lucy's photograph. The way a real card shark knows by instinct, by touch, what card is going to turn up, the boy had turned the camera with an unerring sense to Lucy's pretty face. It was where Hildon would have freeze-framed it, anyway, and the boy had the same impulse.

It was cruel, of course; the cross in front of the vampire as far as Myra DeVane was concerned. But she had gotten bored with the videotape, and with Hildon's game, long before Lucy's image came on the screen. They were at his friends' house, and she was drunk on champagne, lying underneath Hildon, still wearing a camisole and her socks, eyes shut, smile flickering on her lips as he made love to her. Last week with Edward, the Plaza. Today, the floor of the Hadley-Cooper's video room.

Myra had written Hildon a letter—a frank letter, trying to get to know him. He assumed that she was flirting and took her up on it. He agreed that their interview had not scratched the surface of what was meaningful about what they did. About their profession. Why didn't they get together, now that her piece was published, and have a drink? He didn't hate himself for picking up her cue, or because she wasn't his type. She was the one who happened to be there when he realized, finally, that nobody was his type: this routine was his type of routine. The woman didn't matter. He had done this with different women at least half a dozen times when Maureen left and Lucy went to California for Jane's funeral. He was now having a life apart from the person with whom he had shared a secret life.

He looked at the screen. In the clutter of his desk drawer, along with pens and postcards, scissors and a bandanna, was a small blue velvet box. The videotape did not show the pink-pearl-and-diamond ring inside—his great-great-grandmother's engagement ring. He had taken it out of his safe deposit box on the day of the annual staff party at his house, thinking about asking Lucy to marry him. But then he had left it in the drawer, deliberately. If he had the prop, he was sure to go through with the action. He wanted to see what he would do without it, whether he would ask her anyway, or find some way to meet her later, at the office.

He had decided against it that night, so at least he didn't feel like a coward for not asking Lucy to marry him once Nicole came to live with her. It wouldn't have been possible for the three of them to be a typical, dreary family anyway. He trusted Lucy, loved the way she could switch gears, the way she would join in when he put on his torn clothes and boots, calling what he engaged in his sexual fast-food fantasies. She was wonderful, but she wasn't right. She could take an imaginative leap, but only in terms of where she'd go or what she'd do. She wasn't an emotional chameleon, and that was what he needed.

Myra, lying below him on the rug, was the sound track of the video that didn't exist. She was telling him that she loved him.

About the Author

ANN BEATTIE was born in Washington, D.C., and was educated at American University and the University of Connecticut. She has taught at the University of Virginia and Harvard. *Love Always* is her third novel and sixth book. She now lives in Charlottesville, Virginia.

Printed in the United States
by Baker & Taylor Publisher Services